Nefarious

Nefarious

Tina D. C. Hayes

Hazy Moon Ink

Book Layout ©2014 BookDesignTemplates.com

ISBN-13: 978-0615970257
ISBN-10: 0615970257

Hazy Moon Ink

Our greatest glory is not in never falling,
but in rising every time we fall.

~ Confucius

Prologue

Sweet Jesus, this is it, Harlie thought. *He's really going to kill me this time.*

Her mind reeled. She didn't yet feel the pain in her busted lip, fractured nose, or her blackening eye, which was already so puffy her eyelid strained to open. Harlie's only concern was getting the hell out of the house alive with her baby, which looked impossible at this point. Zoey lay crying on a blanket in the corner of the room to her left and the door out was through the kitchen to her right. Even if she managed to break free of his grip, there was no way she could pick up the infant and escape, not without this maniac grabbing her again.

He punched her twice in the stomach, still sore from giving birth six short days before, and she frantically searched for a way out. Her gaze landed on the one thing she hadn't packed.

"This is what you get for trying to walk out on me, you fuckin' bitch. You and that baby belong to me." Jack belted her in the face a few more times, his blows aimed at her nose and mouth. "I'll see you dead before I let you go."

It was a miracle she hadn't miscarried during her second trimester when, determined to end the abuse before her due date, she'd asked Jack for a divorce. The beating she took and his promise to kill her if she tried to leave made up Harlie's mind. Rather than risk losing the baby to one of his temper fits, she did whatever it took to keep him from flying into a rage until after their child was born. She'd spent the last four months planning every detail of her getaway.

Her fear changed into unadulterated fury. *How dare he do this to me. He's beat me, cheated on me, kept me away from my friends and family, but I won't let him kill me, not now. What'll happen to Zoey if I die?*

Harlie spit out a mouthful of blood before she could speak.

"Go to hell!" she screamed, dropping her head back as far as it would go against the wall behind her. She rammed her head forward with all her might and butted Jack square in the nose. His hands flew to his face, blood oozing between his fingers, and Harlie was free to run to the kitchen.

Jack lurched after her, moaning in pain. He froze in his tracks as Harlie pivoted around to face him.

Her wild-eyed glare said she'd had all she was going to take, while the steak knives glistening in each of her fists warned him against taking another step in her direction. Harlie shook with rage and determination as she spoke, her steady voice every bit as cold as the steel blades she wielded. "Why don't you hit me now, you asshole. What's wrong, Jack? Afraid to fight a woman when the odds are evened up?"

"Crazy bitch."

She moved a step closer, since he'd backed into a corner.

"Shut the hell up. I'm divorcing you as soon as I can get to a lawyer, and I never want to see you again. Oh, no," she exclaimed, laughing, near hysteria, raising one knife over her head as Jack tried to walk past her. She reveled in this moment, the first time she'd had control over anything for a long, long time. "You're staying right there until the police come. I'm pressing charges this time."

Jack's eye twitched with fury, but he didn't move.

Her brother pulled up in a moving van a few minutes later, as they'd planned, expecting Jack to be at his office across town. Harlie held a knife in each hand, one of which she jabbed at Jack, daring him to hit her again so she could carve him up like the Christmas turkey he'd thrown at her the previous year. One glance at her battered face—already black and blue, one eye swollen shut, with blood dripping off her chin—explained in vivid detail what was going on.

Harlie convinced him to call the police instead of giving her husband the beatdown he deserved. "If this sorry sack of shit takes one step towards me, he won't live to regret it." Those words made the color drain from Louie's face. He clearly believed she'd cut Jack's throat if he so much as sneezed.

Minutes after the 911 call went out, the sheriff arrived to take Jack to the county jail. The laws being as they were, he walked out of the courthouse an hour later.

After a thorough examination at the hospital, where a nurse photographed Harlie's injuries to document the abuse, Louie took her on an impromptu shopping trip. Harlie refused to let him buy her a gun, afraid Zoey might find it and hurt herself one day. They decided on a butterfly knife instead, a slim gold model with engravings of little birds on the handles. Louie spent the next morning teaching Harlie how to use it without cutting off her hands. She quickly got the hang of her new weapon. If she held the handle with the latch attached to it, one flip of her wrist flicked it open, flinging the other handle back into her hand beside its counterpart, razor-sharp blade exposed. The smooth, flowing maneuver looked quite impressive, as if she'd studied some field of the martial arts. She could use her new toy to scare Jack off, should he decide to hurt her again.

Harlie never left the house without the butterfly knife tucked into a pocket or her purse. If the man she married could hurt her this badly, how could she ever trust anyone else?

Chapter One

"Oh well. I guess that's just gonna have to do." Harlie Steele glared at the mirror, made a face, then hurried down the hall to her bedroom. The concert started in two short hours and she still had to get dressed, drop off her daughter, pick up her best friend, and drive forty-five miles to the stadium.

If she hadn't won tickets on the radio, Harlie would've stayed home again tonight. She still couldn't believe it. Front row tickets to see FireStorm!

She put on the new outfit Randi had helped her pick out, then scrutinized her backside to make sure no cellulite showed underneath her black skirt. She believed herself to be plain. Not really ugly, just not somebody a man wanted to spend much time looking at. Her ex-husband was quick to point out and magnify her every flaw, making the few dimples and spider veins on her thighs seem like grotesque deformities. Whenever people complimented her on her big blue eyes or tiny waist, she brushed it off as polite conversation.

With shaking hands, she fastened the last button on her leopard-print blouse and stepped into black stilettos. "Wake up, Zoey, honey. It's time to go." Harlie glanced once more at the mirror, was less than thrilled with her reflection, then left to take her daughter to her parents for the night.

FireStorm's hit song flowed through the car speakers while Harlie drove down the sun-dappled back road. From the backseat, a high-pitched voice squealed, "That Fi stom, Mommy!" They both sang along with the CD until they stopped at a tidy brick house with peonies blooming on the front lawn.

Zoey was her heart and sole reason for living. With her short blond curls and twinkling blue eyes, the two-and-a-half-year-old always looked like an angel, regardless of what she did or said. Last week at the grocery, when Harlie's cart bumped a display and sent an avalanche of chicken noodle cans clattering to the floor, Zoey's loud inflection of "dame et to hell" made the customers around them burst out laughing.

"Now Zoey, you be good for Nana while Mommy and Aunt Randi go to the concert. I'll pick you up in the morning . . . Love you . . . Bye." She kissed her daughter's chubby cheek before backing out her parents' doorway, then headed toward the car. She knew her mom and dad loved to spend time with their only grandchild, but Harlie always felt a little guilty about leaving her. Winning the ugly custody battle Jack put her through made her appreciate every second with Zoey even more.

Miranda 'Randi' Sommers waited under the porch light, tapping her high-heeled foot as Harlie pulled into the driveway. Despite her BFF's jiggling cleavage and the hem that barely covered her ass, the buxom brunette radiated an aura of glamour as she trotted down to the car and hopped in.

"I knew you'd be running late, as usual." An animated conversationalist, Randi talked fast and never ran out of things to say. "You look great tonight. And, no, that skirt is *not* too short. Want to go to Charlie's Bar after the concert, if you don't get picked up there first?"

"Yeah, right," Harlie said. This concert was a big deal to her, the first thing she'd looked forward to in ages, and she obviously had no intention of bar hopping afterward. Randi was the only reason she'd been out at all in the past two years. She'd prodded Harlie into going on a handful of blind dates since the divorce, and occasionally managed to drag her along on ladies night. "I just hope we have a good view of the band."

"No, you want a good view of that singer and his boney little ass. I still don't get your infatuation with him. The band rocks, but that guy just doesn't look like all that to me. The drummer, on the other hand, him I could work with." Randi licked her lips suggestively, letting her imagination run with that thought.

"Stix is too much of a pretty boy. Lex Callatori is sexy as hell, and he *does* have a cute ass. Are you blind?" she asked, shocked her nympho friend hadn't noticed how the singer practically exuded sexuality. When Harlie was fifteen, her bedroom had looked like a FireStorm shrine, with one wall covered floor-to-ceiling with posters of Lex and the band. She'd blasted their music day and night, screeching along with the lyrics until she'd nearly driven her parents crazy. "Just watch the way he moves around on stage."

"But what about his mouth? Looks like he ODed on collagen injections, if you ask me," Randi teased, egging Harlie on.

"It's just the right size for his face. He's a real virtuoso, sort of like a modern day Mozart, and he writes almost all of FireStorm's music himself. Have you ever really listened to the lyrics? He puts so much feeling into every word, it's like his songs reach out and touch my soul. His voice gives me goose bumps . . . . What the hell is so funny?"

" '*He touches my soul and I get goose bumps all over!*'" Randi mimicked. Tears threatened to streak her mascara if she didn't stop laughing so hard. "My God, you sound like you're twelve or something."

"Okay, so I like their music." A blush warmed Harlie's cheeks. "I haven't been to a concert in so long, I hope I don't act like a fool. And I promise I won't be looking over my shoulder all night either. The restraining order should keep the asshole away from me, at least for a while. God, I'm so glad Jack is out of my life."

Images from the past invaded Harlie's mind as she steered her car down the highway. Her throat mottled with finger-shaped bruises. The way Jack had made her feel like a used condom whenever they had sex. Jack screwing his naked secretary in his office chair. His fist pounding her face while she cradled Zoey in her arms.

The lies she'd told her family and best friend to explain away five years' worth of injuries echoed in her ears. They hadn't found out about her secret hell until the day before she left him. Guilt twisted her stomach into a knot again over deceiving them for so long, but she'd had no choice. She was ashamed for letting her own stupidity get her into such a hopeless situation, and afraid Jack would've turned his wrath on her loved ones if they confronted him about it.

Harlie shook her head to clear out the ugly memories, determined to leave them in the past where they belonged.

Packed to the rafters, Ford Center overflowed with excited fans eager to see the sold-out concert. Fire-

Storm had addicted hordes of people to their style of hardcore, metal-edged, bluesy rock 'n' roll during their twenty-year career. From all walks of life they came, teen rebels in ripped jeans rubbing elbows with middle-aged businessmen wearing dress pants and loafers.

Harlie and Randi made their way down the stairs inside the auditorium. An attendant checked their tickets before they entered the coveted main floor and found their seats on the front row.

"This rocks!" Randi said. "I still can't believe you won these tickets for being the tenth caller."

They sat about twenty feet from a barricade which separated the crowd from the stage eight feet beyond their reach. The mosh pit was already filled with people, some wearing brand new FireStorm T-shirts purchased in the lobby. Scattered puffs of ganja floated above the crowd in spite of the 'No Smoking' signs posted throughout the stadium.

The lights went down and everyone grew quiet in anticipation.

Hell's Fury, the opening act, was a new band known for its ear-splitting blend of modern Metal. With their black cloaks billowing behind them, the musicians cavorted around the stage to warm up the crowd. Their identical red and black hairdos, teased and gelled to stand on end, gave the illusion their heads were on fire. Everyone cheered as their last song ended and the guitarists threw picks into the applauding sea of spectators.

A brief intermission ensued. The lights came up to give everyone a chance to use the restroom or visit the concession stand. Harlie and Randi stayed in their seats, afraid to risk missing a minute of the main act's performance.

"Checking your watch every two seconds isn't going to make them start any quicker," Randi teased. "Damn, I haven't seen you this excited since Zoey took her first steps."

Harlie pointed toward some roadies bustling near the stage. "Hey, I think something's about to happen." The lights dimmed and she held her breath.

An explosion shattered the silence as the stage, enveloped in a veil of smoky mist, was suddenly bathed in red light. The four members of FireStorm stood frozen as the fans went wild, screaming and cheering. Lex Callatori posed mid-stage with his back to the crowd, his arms extended over his head in a V-shape, microphone gripped in his left hand. Harlie's eyes locked on the sleeveless black silk shirt that showed off his muscular biceps. Then, as her mouth twisted into a lusty grin, she noticed the red spandex pants that clung to every curve of his apple-shaped rear end. The lighting changed to a yellow haze as Lex pivoted around, leaping into the air as the rest of the band came to life. They opened with one of their earliest hits, "Come to

Me", and the crowd started rocking.

The ravenous mob fed on every note that poured from the mounds of speakers, amplifying the music until it was the only sound to be heard. People stood on chairs cheering, seeming to lose their minds. Midway through the first song, Harlie grabbed Randi by the arm and started dragging her toward the mosh pit. The deafening din made speaking to each other pointless. Harlie smiled, pointed to the barricade, then back at the two of them, and bobbed her head up and down. Randi gave the thumbs up sign and the pair began to push their way through the crowd. Harlie's heart pounded with excitement.

The next song was "Be My Baby." When the second chorus ended, Harlie stood just two yards from the barricade. It then became harder to push their way through since everyone, at this point, had the same goal in mind: getting as close to the band as humanly possible. They advanced a few more feet during the next song. Randi tapped her on the shoulder and shrugged as if to say she guessed they were stuck. With hands extended overhead as she pumped her fists in time to the music, a bouncing Harlie shook her head, then pointed back to the illusive barrier which now loomed mere feet in front of them.

Randi mouthed the words "you go ahead, I'm fine right here" while pointing to the cute behind of the guy in front of her. Harlie winked and began, once again, pushing herself forward. She thought she heard Randi laugh when she elbowed her way to the very front, but she couldn't be sure. Now only one person stood between Harlie, the security line, and an unobstructed view of FireStorm.

The band was jamming to their latest top ten hit when an epiphany struck Harlie right between the eyes. The thick crowd she'd just waded through didn't allow much movement, but she scooted to the right as far as possible. She stretched out her arm and tapped the woman in front of her on the edge of her left shoulder. In the split second it took the plump lady to glance behind her, she twisted her shoulders just enough to let Harlie grab onto the elusive railing. Uncharacteristically not caring in the least if this looked rude, Harlie pulled past her and positioned herself beside the security barrier.

"Yes!" Elated, Harlie pumped one hand in the air as she kept an iron grip on the railing with the other. At last she could see everything and didn't want to miss one single detail.

Despite her throbbing feet, she was having the time of her life. People had stomped all over her new stilettos as she trudged her way through the mob. She glanced down at her shoes and noticed the bottom two buttons of her blouse had popped off during her crusade through the crowd. She tied the shirttails together, not caring if anyone saw her navel exposed between the knotted leopard material and her black skirt.

When the concert reached the halfway point, the lead singer took a short break to grab some water and rest his sultry voice. The other band members took turns playing solos to fill the time.

Tony 'Stix' Franklin went first. The drummer's handsome face, piercing eyes, long blonde hair, and Aussie accent contributed to his heartthrob status. His bodybuilder physique had graced the pages of countless publications over the years, including *Playgirl* and, more recently, *People* magazine. Stix hit the high-hat at the end of his awesome solo. Hundreds of screaming girls pushed the mosh pit forward, squashing Harlie between the crowd and the railing.

Next up was Ray Richards, his trademark bandana tied around his wavy black hair, performing a bluesy piece on the harmonica. Thanks to his New Orleans roots, he added a rich zydeco flavor to the band, playing a variety of instruments including bass guitar, keyboard, banjo, and tambourine. He did something different with each number, grabbing whatever the song called for. The short, wiry dynamo held an unconventional role in the band, due to the strange assortment of things he jammed on to give FireStorm its unique edge: cowbells, a hurdy-gurdy, old washboards, antique brown moonshine jugs, dime store slide whistles, and even an electric coffee grinder. You never knew what to expect from Ray, but it always sounded fantastic.

The break ended with Dylan Malone mesmerizing the crowd with five full minutes of ass-kicking riffs on his vintage Fender Stratocaster. His fingertips swept over the strings, tap-dancing across the frets in a graceful fury. The stocky musician threw back his sandy brown mane as he jiggled the whammy bar, masterfully distorting the last note that shimmied from his guitar. The fans went crazy, chanting "Dylan" over and over.

A wild roar sounded as Lex Callatori sauntered back onstage singing "Secrets." "*I hear whispers in the shadows of the things that I've done wrong. The past just keeps on haunting me, the pain goes on and on.*"

He traipsed his slender five-foot, ten-inch frame across the stage, shaking his ass with each step. Harlie was close enough to see every detail of his handsome visage: his hypnotic brown eyes, his full sensual lips, high Italian cheekbones, and layered dark brown hair that seemed to massage his shoulders. Flawless skin and lascivious moves helped Lex look much younger than his years.

Animated by the music, Harlie swayed to the next song. Like a snake hypnotized by the charmer's flute, she danced to please only herself, eyes dreamfully shut as Lex belted out the rest of "Nefarious."

"My love is a drug I'll use to seal your fate,
Flowing through your veins to intoxicate.
My perverted scheme will feed on your soul.
Addicted to me, you crave to feel whole.
You come crawling to me, begging for a fix.
Worship me now, kiss this crucifix.
Now's your last chance to run and hide.
In just a minute I'll be coming inside.
  Nefarious, nefarious.
Done warned you once, I'm bad to the core.
I'll do what I want and leave you screaming for
more.
  Nefarious, nefarious."

Harlie's heart almost exploded when she opened her eyes. For one brief moment, she thought Lex Callatori grinned at her over his scarf-enshrouded microphone. *No freakin' way,* she told herself, *it's just my imagination playing a cruel trick on me.* The lights were so bright he probably couldn't see past the edge of the stage. Even if he could, she didn't see why he'd look her way, not when he could ogle the three bimbos to the left who kept flashing their tits at the band. Dylan moved forward with his guitar when the blonde one threw her bra onstage.

Lex announced that the next number, "Last Dance", would be the final song of the night. Harlie couldn't believe the concert had gone by so quickly. She could have stood there in her uncomfortable shoes all night long, listening to FireStorm, watching Lex dominate the stage until the sun came up. She tried to burn each movement he made and every note he sang into her memory so she could replay it in her mind forever.

While Dylan soloed through the first chorus, Callatori motioned for one of the security people to approach the edge of the stage. The singer pointed in Harlie's direction and whispered something in the burly bodyguard's ear. Harlie turned around to see what he was pointing at, but didn't spot anything out of the ordinary.

The next instant, the big guy walked straight to where she stood, and, after tinkering with a key for a few seconds, he cracked open a hinged gate in the barrier. He guided Harlie through and motioned for two men sporting blue security shirts to stop an influx of FireStorm devotees from following.

In a state of total disbelief, Harlie walked toward the stage. The security guy who led the way placed a stepladder in front of her. Lex, now directly above her, belted out the second verse. Someone guided her up the makeshift stairway where Lex stood smiling seductively, his hand extended.

Stunned, she took his hand, her eyes locking with his as the beautiful love song poured from his lips. *God, don't let me wake up yet*, thought Harlie, *because I know I'm dreaming.*

The song ended with Lex still holding her trembling hand. He gave her a quick peck on the lips when the last chord rang from Dylan's guitar. The frenzied crowd cheered as the band, Harlie in tow, headed to the rear of the stage.

During their exit, the singer turned to her and asked, "So, what's your name?"

"I'm . . ." Harlie tried to swallow the big lump clogging her throat. *This is only a dream,* she reminded herself, *so I might as well play it right.* Looking into his dark chocolate irises with an air of coolness, she heard words pour from her own nervous lips, "My name is Harlie Steele."

"I'm Lex Callatori," he said, as if she hadn't known, leading her down the rear stage steps, "and it's my pleasure to make your acquaintance."

Chapter Two

Harlie sat on a small sofa in the backstage lounge and wondered why Lex had picked her from a crowd of thousands. Left to wait there while he changed out of his stage clothes, she nibbled on a turkey sandwich from the buffet and took in her surroundings.

About ten other people occupied the room. She figured the four men and two women in business suits were most likely involved in the professional end of the music industry, record producers and promoters, maybe. The nervous teenage girls in the middle of the room clutched backstage passes, saying how they couldn't wait to meet Stix, up close and in person. The bleached blonde in the corner looked like an over-the-hill stripper, in her tight faded jeans and sequined tube top. Security, on a mission to keep out over-zealous fans, stood beside the door that opened into the hall.

A man with a beer gut and a greasy ponytail walked in, scanned the room with his beady little eyes, and then took a seat beside Harlie. The sofa suddenly seemed way too small.

"Cool concert, huh?" His breath smelled like he'd been chewing on old sweat socks. "You a big FireStorm fan?"

"Uh, yeah. Sure am," Harlie answered, nodding her head but barely glancing in his direction. She hoped he would go hit on the blonde floozy in the corner.

"Me too. I've been a roadie for about five years now. Set up most of the equipment myself," he bragged, his eyes glued to her cleavage. "A lot of these fans would do just about anything to meet the guys in the band."

"Really." Harlie frowned and leaned as far away from him as possible.

"How'd you manage to get backstage, anyway? You better let me see your pass. Nobody, but nobody, is allowed back here without one," he stated, trying to sound authoritative.

Oh, great, Harlie thought. *I don't even know why I'm back here myself, and now I'm supposed to explain it to this dickhead.* "Lex Callatori told me to sit right here and wait for him. He and the rest of the band should be back any minute."

"Okay. So, where's your pass then?" he pressed, his grubby hand held out for something he knew she didn't have.

"They didn't give me one, but the security guy standing over there by the door saw me come in with the band. Why don't you go ask him about it." She was tired of this creep and just wanted him to leave her alone so she could enjoy the rest of this otherwise perfect night. "Excuse me, but I'm going to get a drink of water now. From way over there." She crossed the room to the cooler, hoping he got the hint.

Bent over to fill the disposable cup, Harlie felt a hand on the back of her skirt. She spun around, 'accidentally' splashing her water in his face.

"Hey, I like my women spunky." The roadie chuckled as he wiped his dripping chin on his sleeve. "So, here's how it is. You're hot for the band and want to stay to meet 'em. But you don't seem to have a pass. Hmmmm. Maybe I could find it in my heart to let you stay, if you did somethin' nice for me. Lemme think . . . A blow job oughtta do it."

Harlie took a deep breath to quell the rage building inside her. "You can go to hell and let the devil suck your puny little dick." Her eyes blared while she drawled out the insult as only someone born south of the Mason-Dixon Line could. "If your fat ass spontaneously combusted right here, I wouldn't even piss on you to put the fire out."

She tried to brush past him, intending to go stand by the security guard, but he blocked her way. "I've already told you I'm here because Mr. Callatori asked me to wait for him. If you have a problem with that, then too damn bad."

"You better settle down and be nice to me or I'm gonna have to throw you outta here." He backed Harlie into the corner as he spoke. "You wouldn't want that, would you, Red?" His gelatinous body obstructed the view from most of the people in the room.

"You'll get the hell away from me right now, if you know what's good for you," Harlie warned through clenched teeth. The smell of his breath in her face was about to make her gag. Her shaky but determined hand moved toward the neckline of her blouse. "I'm a guest of Mr. Callatori, for God's sake."

"I already told you I like spunky women. You must be tryin' to turn me on." He leaned in even closer. As he reached for her chest, someone grabbed his hand.

"What the hell do you think you're doing?" Lex Callatori spun the roadie around to face him. "I heard the lady tell you she's with me."

"No, man, she got me over in this corner 'cause she said she was gonna show me her boobs." He looked around the room as if trying to find a way out of his predicament. The crew had seen the boss punch out photographers for less than this, and it was obvious that nobody wanted their name added to Callatori's shit list.

"Yeah, in your wettest dreams she did. Get out of here and don't let me see your ugly face again. You're fired." Lex turned to the door and yelled, "Zeke! Come throw this piece of shit out for me, will ya."

In walked Zeke Zapada, a man Harlie recognized as the security guard who'd led her from the mosh pit to the stage. He stood well over six feet tall and reminded her of a macho version of Mr. Clean, with his shaved head and dark brown goatee. After a nod in her direction, Zeke dragged the roadie from the room by the scruff of his neck.

Harlie adjusted the top button of her blouse as Lex turned to face her. "Are you all right? I'm sorry about the way that asshole treated you." Genuine concern resonated through his apology. "Guess I shouldn't have left you here alone."

"Oh, that's okay. Really, I'm fine," Harlie said, glad her voice didn't sound as shaky as she felt.

"Come on." He draped a protective arm around her shoulder and guided her toward the door. "Let's ditch this circus." Reporters and photographers had swarmed in since the four men who made up FireStorm entered the room. Bulbs flashed around them as they walked out.

Lex's private dressing room was about the size of a walk-in closet, but nice all the same. A rack of stage clothes filled the wall to the left, to the right was a small but comfortable looking couch with red velvet upholstery, and a weathered Gibson guitar sat in its stand beside the doorway. A dressing table with an over-sized lighted mirror took up the wall in front of them, loaded down with an assortment of stage makeup, scented candles, scarves, and a silver ink pen on a stack of stationary. The scent of exotic cologne hung in the air.

Harlie gazed at Lex as they sat down, convinced he was the most gorgeous man alive. He wasn't the classic pretty boy type of handsome, but his features made an alluring package. He had high chiseled cheekbones, smoky brown eyes, and carried himself with an egomaniacal cockiness that played up his streetsy good looks.

"Let me get you something to drink." Lex opened the small refrigerator to his left and glanced inside. "Ginger Ale, beer, or I could find you a wine cooler . . ."

How different his speaking voice sounded from the one with which he sang. On stage, it ranged from deep raspy tones to ear-splitting high notes any opera star would envy. She enjoyed listening to him speak, though it surprised her how ordinary he sounded, without a hint of the robust timbre she'd expected.

"A beer would be fine." Harlie thanked him after he opened a bottle of Corona and handed it to her. She felt unexpectedly at ease with this international rock star, but was glad to have something to hold in her unsteady hands.

As Lex took a swig from his beer, Harlie decided to ask the question that had been on her mind since she walked to the stage. "Why did you pick me out of the crowd tonight? I'm really happy to get to meet you and everything, I've been a FireStorm fan for years, but still, why me?" she blurted, hoping she wasn't talking too fast to be coherent. "And should I call you Lex or Mr. Callatori?"

"Well, when I first saw you, I thought you'd be perfect dancing in one of our videos. You looked hot grooving in your libidinous dance, totally oblivious to the erotic image you cast, the epitome of nonchalance." Lex smiled at her. "That was pretty cool, so I knew I had to meet you. And just call me Lex."

Harlie wondered if he had bad eyesight. This was the most flattering thing that had ever happened to her, but she couldn't conceive the notion that someone like Lex Callatori found her attractive. "Oh, thanks . . . Lex," she managed, not exactly sure what to say. She didn't want to sound like a blithering idiot.

"So, you live in Evansville, Indiana? You sound kind of like you're from Tennessee. I like the accent, by the way." He took another sip of beer.

"No, I'm from Lisman, Kentucky, about an hour south of here. A teensy little town I'm sure you never heard of. You live in New York, right?"

"Yep, born and raised there." Lex glanced toward her bare ring finger. "You're not married or anything, are you?"

"God no. My divorce was final two years ago. Zoey,

my little girl, is the only good thing that came out of that mess."

"My daughter turned twenty-one last month. How old is yours?"

"She's two-and-a-half." She hadn't known he had any kids, but was glad to at least be six years older than his daughter. "I didn't bring my purse or I'd show you a picture of her. She's just beautiful."

"Well, if she looks anything like you, she'd have to be." Lex's arm rested on the back of the couch behind her, so now he moved it around her shoulders.

"Thank you," Harlie said, a blush warming her cheeks.

They made small talk for a while. Trivial things like movies they'd seen and books they'd both read surprised her, and showed her they actually shared a few common interests.

Harlie swallowed the last mouthful of her beer, then scanned the room for a trashcan. "Where should I put this?"

"I'll set them over here," Lex said, placing both their empty bottles on top of the compact refrigerator. "Can I get you another one?" He slid his arm around Harlie once again.

"No thanks. I'm fine."

"Yeah, I'd say you look pretty damn fine to me," Lex said, his voice low and sultry as he leaned closer to Harlie.

A gasp escaped her throat a second before their lips met. This first real kiss was a sensual spark that sent shockwaves of electricity surging through her, rippling over her warm flesh before settling into more intimate crevasses.

She ran her fingers through his dark hair. They shifted positions until her head rested on the arm of the couch with Lex lying on top of her, propping himself up on one arm so as not to put too much weight on her petite frame. Though it seemed like mere minutes, they stayed in this position, kissing, hugging their bodies close together, for quite a while.

Lex unbuttoned Harlie's blouse. A few seconds later, something metal fell out of her bra.

"What the hell," he muttered, picking up the object.

"Oh, let me explain about that." Harlie's eyes widened in fear that Lex, used to having bodyguards around the clock, might think she was some kind of lunatic who brought the butterfly knife in here to kill him with it. Relief swept over her when he laughed.

"So," he said, his eyes twinkling with amusement, "this is the reason you kept fiddling with your shirt buttons when that sleaze in the lounge was bothering you." Then he laughed even harder. "I thought I was helping you, but if I'd been a minute later, you would've pulled this on him. He would've pissed his pants."

She smiled, glad he hadn't misinterpreted. "That was a gift from my big brother, and I never go anywhere without it. I usually keep it in my pocket or in my purse, but I didn't have either of those on me tonight. This seemed like the logical place to put it. You never know what's going to happen, right?"

"Yeah, you could say that. Like tonight, I met this innocent looking girl who turns out to be a knife-wielding badass." He took her in his arms again. "But she's a great kisser, though. Wonder what else she's good at."

Harlie moaned when Lex took her left nipple in his mouth, sucking gently, caressing it with his tongue. His hand found her other breast. Through his tight jeans, she could feel him pressing against her thigh. Her heart raced as their bodies lusted for the ecstasy of release.

Someone with incredibly bad timing knocked on the door. They froze, and she felt like they'd been doused by a bucket of ice water.

"Hey, Lex, you in there? Let me in." The whiny voice dripped with the most annoying northern accent Harlie had ever heard. "Lex, you answer me!" whoever it was demanded, banging on the door. The person finally left after the guard posted by the entrance told her Mr. Callatori had gone to his hotel room an hour before. She stomped off down the hall, spewing a trail of profanity.

An expression of disgust had twisted his face as the episode occurred, but Lex never made a move to answer the door. Afterwards, he tried to dismiss the incident by taking up where he left off. Unfortunately, Harlie put his advances on hold.

"Uh, what the hell was that all about?" She wasn't sure she wanted to know the answer, but she sat up to rearrange her clothes and waited for him to explain.

"That," he replied, "was no one important. Her name is Beth Masters and I used to go out with her, but we were never serious or anything. I broke it off three weeks ago, in Detroit, after I found her fucking some guy on the tour bus. Not that I gave a shit. See, she's not important at all." He pulled Harlie toward him and tried to kiss her.

"Then why is she looking for you now?" Harlie turned her head so his lips only grazed her cheek.

"She called me yesterday wanting to get back together. I told her no way in hell, but then she said she had to talk to me." Lex rolled his eyes. "The bitch is trying to say she's pregnant, but I know she's lying. She was always after my money, so I guess this is her big plan to shake down my bank account."

"Oh. Great." Harlie stood up to check her appearance in the mirror, to make sure her important parts were covered up. No way in hell did she intend to get mixed up in a love triangle with some floozy who might be pregnant, and this Beth person could be his live-in girlfriend for all she knew. Being the 'other woman' wasn't an option, not after all the times Jack had cheated on her. "Well, it was nice meeting you, but I guess I'll be going now." She turned toward the door.

"Baby, please don't be like that," Lex pleaded, and gently grabbed her elbow. "She doesn't mean anything to me. I was hoping, maybe, well, that I could start seeing you." The way he looked at her with his burning eyes gave her goose bumps. She did *not* want to leave.

Her heart sank as she remembered all the tabloid stories she'd read about rock stars and the one-night conquests they left behind wherever they went. "Do you even remember my name?"

"How could I forget anything about you," he said. "Harlie Steele, a name as unique as you are. Please don't go. Give me a chance." Seeing that she still wasn't sure what to do, he added, "Or at least give me your phone number."

"By tomorrow morning, you'll have forgotten all about me." Harlie felt like she'd just been slapped in the face with reality. "But, if for some reason you still want to call me, *after* you have proof that woman isn't knocked up, and *after* you've sent her on her merry way for good, then here's my number." She scribbled on the notepad lying on the table, then tore off the page and handed it to him. "I really do need to be going."

"Let me get my hat and I'll walk you to your car.

Okay?" Lex grabbed a Yankees baseball cap from his wardrobe and shoved his hair up underneath it. "Quick disguise. It should keep the paparazzi away from us."

He walked her out of the stadium, through the deserted parking lot to her car. Zeke Zapada—who turned out to be Lex's personal bodyguard and close friend—trailed far enough behind to give them privacy.

A note tucked under the windshield wiper caught Harlie's attention. "Oh, shit! I forgot all about Randi."

As she read the scrap of paper, Lex asked, his voice amused but apprehensive, "I hope this Randy is your dog or something. You don't have a boyfriend you forgot to tell me about, do you?"

"No, Randi with an 'i'. See." She smirked, showing him the signature on the note. "She's my best friend and she rode here with me. At least she didn't sound pissed off. The note says she saw me go backstage and figured I'd be a while, so she caught a ride with somebody. I can't believe I forgot about her! What a bitchy thing to do."

"Yeah, what *could* you have been thinking?" Lex grinned down at Harlie as she climbed into her car, obviously flattered that she'd been too engrossed in him to remember her friend. "Can I kiss you goodnight?"

She nodded. A blush burned across her face as she looked up at him through her eyelashes. His lips met hers, the tender kiss intensifying until their passion threatened to overtake them both. He kissed her again, on the cheek this time, and took a step back.

"Bye," she said, wondering for a moment if she remembered how to drive. Her heart continued to tap dance in her chest as she started the engine and put the car in gear.

In the rearview mirror, Harlie saw Lex watching her taillights while she drove away. The scent of his cologne still clung to her blouse and the taste of his last kiss lingered on her lips, a reminder of how badly she wanted him, but the last thing she needed was to end up as just another notch on a rock star's bedpost. Would she ever see him again, or would she be better off if she didn't?

Chapter Three

The electric screech of his travel alarm woke Lex up at eight o'clock the morning after the Evansville concert, an unthinkable hour for someone is his line of work. He tapped off the alarm, certain he'd feel much better after he put the morning's unpleasant business behind him.

"Wake up, Lazy Bones." He nudged the big lump in the covers beside him. "Come on, it's time to get up and start the day."

A head emerged from underneath the sheets and lavished Lex's face with a barrage of sloppy kisses.

"Oh, man. Enough with the slobbering, already." Lex laughed, enjoying the attention from his companion of the last three years.

The thirty-eight pound bulldog wagged his tail and jumped off the bed. Mugsy's stout body disappeared around the corner, then trudged back to Lex's bedside moments later to drop his empty bowl on his owner's bare foot.

"I know it's chow time. Just give me a minute, buddy, and I'll take care of it."

When Mugsy had trotted past the 'No Pets Allowed' signs in the lobby yesterday, the hotel manager's upturned nose showed his reluctance to make allowances. Lex insisted that none of the band members or their entourage would stay in a place his guard dog wasn't welcome. Sometimes being famous had its advantages.

Lex phoned the front desk for coffee and some breakfast.

"Will that be all, Mr. Callatori?" the ass-kissing voice on the other end of the line asked after he read back Lex's request for ham, scrambled eggs, and OJ.

"Oh yeah, Mugsy needs a fresh pitcher of mineral water, hold the ice, two orders of bacon, and a ham bone. You need to cut the bacon into bite size pieces for him or he might get the squirts and shit all over your nice white carpet." He heard the concierge grit his teeth and visualized steam pouring from his ears. Fuck him, that's what the snooty bastard got for dissing a rock star's dog.

The food was waiting when Lex came out of the shower. Silver lids covered both his meal and Mugsy's, and a carnation in a crystal vase sat in the center of the tray. He dressed in jeans, a hoodie, tennis shoes, and a baseball cap before he sat down to eat.

After breakfast and a long walk around the parking

lot, Lex settled Mugsy back in the suite, then climbed in his rental car and drove down the highway.

With a frown on his face and a bag tucked under his arm, he knocked on Beth Masters' motel room door. She usually slept until noon, so this was the best time to catch her.

"Who the hell is it?" she yelled. A quick glance through the peephole did wonders for her attitude. Her tone became much more cordial. "Oh, Lex, it's you. What a nice surprise. Just a minute."

He heard her fumble around, probably trying to fix her makeup before she let him in.

"I dropped by after the concert last night but they said you were gone. I'm so glad you decided to come up and see me," Beth said, grinding out a really bad Mae West impression. She threw one arm around his neck and groped him a little lower with her other hand.

"I didn't come here for that." Lex pushed her away. "Look, I don't want any hard feelings or anything, but I don't think you got it the last time we talked. We're through." His voice was firm, but not harsh.

"Hey, I told you there's nothing going on between me and that guy from Detroit, not anymore. How can you break it off with me when you know I'm gonna have your baby?" she whined, feigning despondence, and threw herself across the bed.

Lex rolled his eyes. Beth was going to try to milk

him for everything she could get. "You're not pregnant, and even if you were, it wouldn't make any difference. You've slept your way through so many people, you could hold a goddamn lottery to pick the daddy."

"How can you say that to me?" She squeezed out a few crocodile tears. "You know I love you . . . . We can work this out. I know we can, if only you'll try."

"Like I said, it's over. Been there, done that, soaked the T-shirt in Lysol." Lex wanted to get away from the bitch as soon as possible. He tossed her the bag he'd picked up at Walgreens on the way over. "I brought you a consolation gift. Just a little something to make sure we part company on the right terms, with no misunderstandings."

A grimace spread over her face when she peered into the sack. With a mock show of disbelief, Beth pulled out a home pregnancy test. "I don't need this. I've already been to the doctor."

"Then you have nothing to hide. Last chance to prove you're not lying. Either take it or I'm gone. What's it gonna be?"

"Fine! I'll take it after lunch. My stomach is empty right now and-"

"No, you'll take it now," Lex insisted. "I read the instructions in the car. Just piss in this cup and I'll do the rest. Leave the door open so I'll know what's in the cup came out of you."

Beth huffed, muttered "fine", then stomped her way

to the bathroom, and reluctantly left the door ajar. She returned with a full cup. Piss sloshed over the rim when she slammed it down on the nightstand.

"We're gonna sit down and wait. If a pink heart shows up, which it won't, it'll mean you're knocked up." Lex stirred the urine with the test wand. "If the blue square I'm expecting to see shows up, then I've just proved you're a liar. Sure do wish I had some popcorn."

Lex counted the seconds until he could leave. Beth, on the other hand, rocked back and forth chewing on her hot pink fingernails; she paused once to spit out a hunk of polish that chipped off in her teeth. The color drained from her face, making her appear washed out and older than usual. Unattractive red blotches mottled her cheeks as the last seconds ticked away.

When the time was up, Lex sauntered over to check the results. Beth just sat there, defeated.

"I knew it." Lex stuck the negative pregnancy test in her face. "Note the pretty blue square. What a surprise! Guess your doctor fucked up, huh."

There was no sense telling more lies at this point. Since "fuck you" was the wittiest response Beth could come up with, she repeated it a few times.

"I'll show myself out." Lex walked toward the door, then paused with his hand on the knob. "For the record, you understand that we're over, right?"

After adding one last "fuck you" to the conversation, Beth yelled, "Your voice sucks! And your dick is so little, I have more fun putting in a tampon."

Lex slammed the door behind him and smirked as he walked away, glad to be done with the Tuna Queen for good.

That afternoon, he put the finishing touches on a new song. He enjoyed composing lyrics in solitude while listening to guitar tracks through headphones. Lex had a passion for manipulating the English language, poetically fitting each syllable together like intricate pieces of a puzzle. A perfectionist when it came to his music, no song was complete until every word was superlative, each sublime note inscribed on the staff. His music was an addiction worse than any drug, the ultimate adrenaline rush.

Ironically titled "Good Riddance", this song had nothing to do with today's episode. Nodding his head, Lex read over the lyrics he'd just finished.

Satisfied with his work, he thought he deserved a break. He took a scrap of paper from his wallet where he'd put it for safekeeping the previous night, then ran his finger over the ink. Written in neat script, a tiny circle dotting the 'i', he read the phone number and name belonging to the sexy little redhead. She seemed so different from the women he usually met—sweet, intelligent, unaware of how beautiful she was, full of passion yet able to control herself. Even her name,

Harlie Steele, sounded like it should be the title of a love song.

Lex found himself attracted to her in a way he couldn't explain and didn't completely understand. They'd only spent a precious few moments together, yet he ached to be near her again. They shared an animal magnetism for each other, but he felt it went far beyond mere physical lust. He'd sensed a strong, almost spiritual connection since the moment he pulled her onstage. Harlie even had morals; she'd insisted he end everything with Beth before he could call her. And when Lex saw that sleazy roadie come on to her, he'd actually wanted to kill him. He'd grown even more intrigued when he found out she was capable of taking care of herself, with a tongue as sharp as the dainty knife she carried in her bra.

With the digits memorized after staring at the slip of paper for so long, Lex picked up the phone and punched in her number. He hung up during the first ring. What was he going to say to her? Wiping his sweaty palms on his jeans, he laughed out loud at himself. He who sang to crowds of thousands was tongue-tied thinking about this girl.

Lex paced around the room. He thought of ten different topics he could discuss with her, along with three different ways to address Harlie, when and if she answered the phone. She might not even pick up, in which case he'd have to leave a message on her voicemail and wait for her to return his call, which would drive him crazy.

Mugsy cocked his head sideways, curiously watching his master jabber away to himself.

Ten minutes went by before Lex picked up his cell phone again, determined to let the call go through. He hoped Harlie would be glad to hear his voice, but wondered what she could possibly see in him.

Feeling like a nerdy jackass, he pushed redial and held his breath.

Harlie woke up early the morning after the concert, despite all the tossing and turning. She'd spent most of the night gazing at the ceiling, her mind's eye replaying the previous evening's events as if she were watching a movie starring herself and Lex Callatori. When she opened her eyes, it took a few moments to realize these images were real memories, not just a dream.

She paced around her living room for a while before she drove across town. Afraid her friend might still be snoozing the Sunday morning away, she didn't want to show up too early to cram all the lurid details down her throat. Trouble was, she just couldn't wait any longer.

The note on Harlie's windshield last night had made it clear Randi wasn't angry. She'd congratulated her on meeting Lex and let her know she was getting a ride home from a guy she met at the concert. Randi ended the note with 'Way to go! Tell me all about it first thing tomorrow,' then signed it 'Your jealous buddy, Randi.'

Harlie rang the doorbell on Randi's front porch at nine o'clock.

Randi answered the door wearing a red nightie and a sly smile. "Well, this is a surprise. I thought you'd be holed up with the band in some seedy hotel room," she teased, leaning against the doorframe. "With a big stupid grin plastered across your face."

"I brought cappuccino and chocolate donuts for a peace offering," Harlie said, holding out the bag. "I'm so sorry I ditched you last night. You're not mad at me, are you?"

"I'm not pissed at you, so quit with the little puppy dog face." Randi grabbed the bag of donuts. "I'd have done the same thing and you know it. So, did you have fun? Get your ass in here and tell me the whole story." She yanked Harlie into her home by her arm. "And don't leave out any of the sleazy stuff!"

They plopped down in Randi's living room to eat breakfast and fill each other in on what happened after they'd went their separate ways the previous night. Harlie went first. Randi's mouth kept dropping open as she took in the details, interjecting a few "oh my God"s and "you're kidding me"s. She ended her story by asking Randi who drove her home.

"Oh, I met that guy who was standing in front of me. You know, the one whose ass I pointed at," Randi explained. "His name is Jeff Something, and he lifted me up on his shoulders so I could have a better view of the band. Come to think of it, maybe he just liked having my vajayjay wrapped around his head. Anyway, that was right about the time they pushed you onstage. I'll never forget that look on your face!" She made a perfect imitation of Harlie's wide-eyed deer-in-heat-caught-in-the-headlights-of-a-steamroller expression. They laughed until tears made them pass around a box of Kleenex.

"Jeff was really sweet and brought me home after the concert. I knew you'd be occupied for a while." Randi winked and took another bite of donut. "We're going out Tuesday for pizza and a movie."

"I'm glad you enjoyed yourself too." Harlie dabbed her eyes with a tissue.

"Enough about me. What do you think will happen between you and Mr. Rock Star? You gonna call him or what?"

"I gave him my phone number, remember. I really don't know what to expect, but I'd absolutely love to see him again." Harlie's face darkened as she stared into her Styrofoam coffee cup. "But let's face reality here, okay. He's a major celebrity who probably has a girl in every town FireStorm plays in. What in the world would he see in me? I doubt he remembers my name, much less that he'll ever call me." She swallowed the last drop of cappuccino, wishing it was laced with something stronger than cream.

"Why wouldn't he want to get to know you? He picked you out of that crowd, and did you notice the way he leered at you while he sang that song? He looked almost as starstruck as you did."

"You really think so?" Harlie talked faster, hoping Randi was right. "Okay, so suppose he does call me. Then what? We live such different lives, what are we supposed to talk about? Me changing Zoey's diapers or him tuning his guitar? And," she said, still excited but practical, "what if all those stories we've read about him turn out to be true? Like the stuff about him being a drug addict with a bad temper."

"When he calls, and most likely he will or he wouldn't have taken your number," Randi reasoned, "just give him a chance. Most of that stuff in the tabloids is one hundred percent pure bullshit anyway, like those 'I Cheated on Bigfoot with a Space Alien' stories. You said he seemed like a nice guy, so ride it out and see what happens. Who knows, maybe he'll turn out to be your soul mate. And girl, if anybody deserves to have a good man in her life, it's you."

Later that afternoon, Harlie sat in her own living room with Zoey beside her watching *Sesame Street*.

When she'd picked her daughter up at her parents' home, she'd found it difficult to answer her father's simple questions of, "How'd the concert go? Did you girls have a good time?"

"The band was great," she'd answered, afraid of sounding like some teenaged groupie drooling over an idol on an album cover. She had tried to play the incident down, hoping he'd take the hint and change the subject. "I went backstage and met the singer. It was fun, he seemed really nice and everything . . . Oh, and Randi met some cute guy named Jeff who's taking her out next week."

To Harlie's relief, her parents said they were glad she had fun, then filled her in on everything their grandchild had done in the past twenty-four hours. Zoey had colored in her new coloring book, then, when the doting grandparents turned their heads for a second, she drew a big pink happy face on the wall.

"That was just fine," Nana Roxanne said, smiling. "Comet and a dishrag took it right off. Then Zoey helped me make cookies. Oh, did I tell you about her chasing the cat around the dining room saying 'nice key key'?"

Harlie had visited with her family for a while, then thanked them for babysitting when she was leaving. The Garretts told her they were more than happy to watch Zoey any time, and that Harlie should try to get out more often.

Now, as Zoey giggled at Big Bird and Cookie Monster's rendition of the alphabet, Harlie fought the images of Lex that kept creeping inside her head. She blushed about the time she'd spent with him on the velvet love seat, when those sultry lips of his covered the top half of her body with titillating kisses, then her forehead puckered into a frown as she wondered whether she'd ever see him again. In person, not just in FireStorm videos. Harlie had felt much better after her visit with Randi that morning, but now, growing restless, she needed something to occupy her mind.

When Zoey drifted off to sleep, Harlie decided to check her email and waste some time surfing the net. She covered her daughter with an afghan, then went to sit at the kitchen counter with the laptop she used mainly for bookkeeping for her father's business.

Alone and isolated during her marriage, she'd found companionship on the internet. Intrigued when she stumbled across chatrooms, this discovery opened communication with people from around the globe. At first she hid behind a veil of anonymity, lurking more than chatting. Eventually she found the freedom to express herself more boldly online than she could with the real people in her life.

As with most things that gave her happiness, Jack had nearly managed to take cyberspace away from her. One night he found the first chatroom Harlie'd joined, a site set up for expectant mothers a nurse at the gynecologist's office had told her about. She'd used her real name on screen, a mistake she would never make again during their marriage. He slapped Harlie awake and dragged her by the hair to the PC, to a recent chat screen beside the computer's open 'history' box. "Stupid whore, trying to find people to fuck on the goddamn internet." Jack beat the shit out of her because there were two soon-to-be dads using the forum. "Don't you *ever* touch this computer again or you'll really be sorry."

A few days later she'd called her dad and asked if she could charge a laptop to his business account. Pete believed the lie she made up about a thunderstorm frying her hard drive and told her to pick out whatever she liked. Harlie hid the new laptop in the linen closet each day before Jack got home, after she'd cleared out the history archive.

During the months before her divorce, one chatroom in particular had helped her through the toughest time of her life. She'd regained a little self-confidence talking to these faceless characters, people who accepted her based on the comments she posted, not because they expected anything from her, not because she owed them anything, but simply because they liked chatting with her. Harlie didn't have to hide cuts and bruises from eyes that would never actually see her face.

She treasured her online friendship with Barbed*Ivy, a self-described thirty-five-year-old sales clerk from Queens she'd met in the chatroom one month before Zoey was born. While Harlie counted down the hours until she could finally leave her abusive husband, Barbed*Ivy had lifted her spirits with funny stories and jokes, just when Harlie needed it the most.

Zoey snoozed in the next room while Harlie booted up the laptop. Today's email held only standard junk mail and Viagra spam, which she deleted. Nothing new on Facebook either, not surprising since she'd only friended nine people.

A few months earlier, she'd set up a Facebook page for Pete's garage, then decided to open an account for herself. The silly games were addictive, and it was a fun way to keep up with people she knew. Aside from her parents and brother, her list of Facebook friends consisted of Randi, Grandma, her cousin Billy, a girl she'd went to high school with, Barbed*Ivy, and Elizabeth, mother of Zoey's playdate buddy, Bree. Jack spied on her whenever he had the opportunity, so she was afraid to update her status with anything he could use against her, like where she'd be at any given time, or, God forbid, if she had a date. With that lovely thought in mind, she left Facebook and clicked the chatroom book-marked in her favorites file.

The screen turned pale green, the words 'The Chit-

Chat Room' in bold purple lettering across the top. The dialog box at the bottom prompted Harlie to enter her nickname, so she keyed in 'CyberBitch'. On her first visit, she'd reread the entries from the others, trying to think of something original to call herself, something Jack would never recognize and associate with her. At the time, someone named Virtual_slut had been ignoring the advice of others that she should flit over to a porn site where she'd be more appreciated. Harlie christened herself CyberBitch, then used her wit and Southern charm to tell the compu-idiot off. Virtual_Slut soon retreated from the screen with her hot little tail tucked between her cyberlegs, earning Harlie—AKA CyberBitch—accolades from the remaining chatters.

Spaces weren't permitted in the usernames, so any two-word handles included underlined spaces, slashes, asterisks, or whatever characters the individual decided to insert. New people logged on every day, but there were plenty of regulars: LaDeBug, a receptionist in her twenties who came in during her lunch hour, or whenever her job got boring; Studmuffin, sixty-eight, the harmless sweetheart, always full of jokes; and Bitsy_Boop, the sixteen-year-old who logged on every day during her high school computer class and on weekends when she found herself grounded or dateless.

Harlie scrolled through the recent entries to catch herself up on the current topic. ChickenLittle planned to sleep the first two days of her vacation the following week, then maybe spring clean her kitchen cabinets. Happy~Ass suggested ChickenLittle might enjoy going to a club to meet some interesting people, maybe find a little adventure. ChickenLittle said she met all the colorful people she could stand right here, and that she just wanted to relax, putter around in her bathrobe, and not have to bother with anybody except her cat. She wanted to catch up on her soaps too. Just what was Erica Caine up to these days?

Harlie grinned when she reached the bottom of the screen. The last entry was from Barbed*Ivy, breaking the news to ChickenLittle that her favorite soap opera had been cancelled a few years ago.

Harlie keyed in her first message. "Hey everybody, the Bitch is back! Have fun on vacation, ChickenLittle. Barbed*Ivy, what's going down?" She clicked the send button and watched. New messages appeared at the bottom, pushing old captions off the top of the screen, giving everyone a chance to read at their own pace. The page read sort of like a play, with the cybernames in bold followed by a colon.

Harlie typed and read the following correspondence:

~ CyberBitch has entered the room. Welcome ~
CyberBitch: Hey everybody, the Bitch is Back! Have fun on vacation, ChickenLittle. Barbed*Ivy, what's going down?
Happy~Ass: Well, time 2 go. Bye 4 now.

ChickenLittle: Hi, CB. Barb, Cancelled! That sucks. Gotta go. Catch you guys later.

Barbed*Ivy: Later HA & CL. Guess it's just us for now. How was the concert?

CyberBitch: I had the time of my life, it was so cool! You absolutely will NOT believe what happened!

Barbed*Ivy: Of course, I'll believe U. Just try me. What happened? Did U catch one of Stix's drumsticks R something?

CyberBitch: No, but you could say I had a little brush with the band.

Barbed*Ivy: Tell me. Out with it.

CyberBitch: Ok, but I know you won't believe me. I went backstage and that's not even the most exciting part. Do you remember which band member is my favorite? Well, he's the one I met!! AAAAHHH!

Barbed*Ivy: OMG. The singer? Was he an asshole N person?

CyberBitch: No, nice as he could be. I just couldn't believe it! I've never met anyone famous B4, except that local news guy at Kmart.

Barbed*Ivy: What happened? Did U get his autograph and leave?

CyberBitch: I didn't even think to ask for an autograph. We just talked for a while, then he walked me out to my car.

Barbed*Ivy: Shut up! I bet he tried to get in UR pants.

CyberBitch: No, but he kissed me, and he asked

for my number! Can you believe that? There's probably no chance in hell he'll call me, but I'm still thrilled shitless.

Barbed*Ivy: Eew! I can't believe U let him kiss U! Those big lips look gross 2 me. He looks like a bag of old bones a stray dog wouldn't chew on.

CyberBitch: Why am I the only one who appreciates how attractive he is? I like his lips.

~LaDeBug has entered the room. Welcome~

LaDeBug: C-Bitch, I can't believe it!! U got 2 meet FireStorm! They R so hot! Congrats!

Barbed*Ivy: Yes, LaDeBug. Our Bitch must have been shot in the ass with luck.

CyberBitch: Thanks Bug! It was awesome.

Barbed*Ivy: You'd B better off if he doesn't call. I've read all about him N magazines. Sounds like trouble. U looked pretty cute on that card U sent me last Christmas. Way too cute for the likes of him, I might add, but I won't since U think he's all that and a bag of hot shit.

CyberBitch: LOL Thanks, but I'm nothing special. He could have his pick of groupies all day long, so I just don't get what he would see in me.

LaDeBug: Did U get 2 meet Tony Franklin? Sooooo hot!

CyberBitch: Sort of. He said hi to me. But hey, I only had eyes for Lex, so I probably wouldn't have noticed if the rest of the band walked in naked. LOL

An unexpected knock pulled Harlie away from her cyberbuds. She closed the laptop and walked to the door, hoping the loud knocking wouldn't wake Zoey from her nap. She slid the dead bolt back expecting to find her brother on one of his impromptu visits.

The second the door opened, she regretted not looking through the peephole.

Jackson Steele's silhouette darkened her doorway once again.

Chapter Four

"What the hell is the meaning of this?" Jackson Steele shoved the Sunday paper into Harlie's startled face. "Looks like proof you aren't fit to be a mother." His tempestuous green eyes bore down into hers until her blood ran cold.

Harlie pushed the newspaper away and backed up until she bumped into the wall behind her. Jack glared down at her like a bull gearing up to charge a red cape.

Harlie's mind flashed back to a heated argument that took place years earlier. He'd called her a piece of shit, then grabbed her by the hair and plunged her head into the toilet for a sick metaphoric illustration. Luckily, a flush sounded during the struggle and spared her the added humiliation of swallowing the fresh piss in the commode. Harlie had inhaled water through her nose and knew she was going to drown in the porcelain bowl amidst odors of bleach and urine. Jack finally let go of her, but slammed the lid down on her head as she came up gasping for air. Now, the back of her head reverberated with the memory.

"Keep your voice down or you'll wake Zoey. You know you're not supposed to be here, Jack. Leave now or I'll call the sheriff." She stared him dead in the eyes, listening to her own heartbeat thump a warning in her ears. Allowed on her property only to pick up and drop off their daughter on alternate weekends, Jack's presence was in direct violation of the restraining order.

"I'll leave after you explain this to me." Jack thrust the newspaper toward Harlie again. "What kind of people are you exposing my sweet little girl to? Have you lost your mind? It's bad enough that you're a whore, but now you have to make a public spectacle of yourself. What are people going to think when they see this?"

Determined to stand her ground, Harlie placed her shaking hands on her hips. "I do not whore around, Jack, which you know perfectly well, since you like following me everywhere I go. What's wrong with you, barging in here like-" Struck dumb when her eyes landed on the thing that had so enraged her ex, she grabbed the newspaper.

Two pictures from the FireStorm concert topped the front page of the variety section. One showed Lex jumping through the air between the drums and guitarist, the caption underneath reading "FireStorm Attacks the Nefarious Crowd." It was the other photo that was causing Jack to turn purple—a close-up of Lex singing to Harlie, holding her hand, eyeing her as if he wanted to fuck her on the spot. The caption said, "Mystery Woman Sets Bad Boy Lex Callatori's Heart on Fire."

"Oh, sweet Jesus." Her hand felt cool against her burning cheek. She imagined a blush nearly matching the hue of her auburn hair sweep across her face, her eyes threatening to pop out of their sockets. She leaned against the wall to keep from fainting. Still gaping at the picture, she noticed the ardency in Lex's expression. Maybe he did feel something for her, after all.

"You think this is funny, bitch?" Jack's gravelly voice jolted Harlie back to the present. "That's got to be the ugliest piece of shit in the entire music industry, and there you are, big as life, in front of millions of people, making goo-goo eyes at the sleazy bastard! How could you? I hope you at least had the good sense not to fuck him. That's obviously the only thing he wanted from you."

Dazed by the pictures, Harlie searched for the right thing to say. "You need to leave."

Jack misinterpreted the expression on her face as a confession of guilt. "You did, you slut. You slept with that motherfucker!"

He paced up and down the living room shaking his head in mock disbelief, pausing occasionally to glare at her in disgust and roll his eyes toward the ceiling. Fortunately, Zoey was a heavy sleeper, used to napping with the television on, and slept through her father's sanctimonious tirade.

"Great. The damage is done. It's a good thing for you that you'll never hear from that fuckhead again. He's probably on his tour bus right now, snorting dope, laughing it up, telling the band all about screwing you, calling you Ole What's Her Name." A bit calmer, Jack added, his voice like a Baptist preacher giving an adultery sermon, "I hope you're happy. How do you plan to explain this to poor Zoey, when the day comes that her little friends ask about her groupie slut of a mother?"

"This is the last time I'm telling you to leave before I call the sheriff." Watching Jack make an ass out of himself was wearing her patience thin. "Anything that may or may not go on between me and Mr. Callatori is none of your damn business. As for Zoey, unless you've forgotten, she's not even three years old yet. By the time she starts kindergarten, I seriously doubt anybody will remember that picture of me and Lex. Now, if you're all done with your hissy fit, please don't let me keep you. Believe it or not, I *do* have a life that doesn't involve you." She held the door open, hoping like hell he'd go away while she was still in one piece.

"I'm leaving. But I suggest you watch who you choose to socialize with in the future," he said, strutting past her. "I'd hate to put Zoey through another custody fight, but I won't have my daughter associated with a bunch of drug-addicted sex maniacs from some washed up band."

"No, I'm sure we'll have enough problems explaining the slutty bimbos Zoey sees you with. But thanks ever so much for your concern." The door slammed in Jack's condescending face.

Harlie walked to her chair and sat down, then noticed the paper still clutched in her hand. She took another long look at the color photos as she dialed Randi's number, thinking how surreal the whole situation was.

"Hi, Randi, it's me. You're not going to believe this. Have you looked at the *Courier* today? No, of course not or you'd have called me already. Stupid question."

"What's going on?" Randi asked, clueless. "I looked at the sale ads, but that's as far as I got. Macy's is having a big sale on lingerie this week. Is something wrong? You sound kinda shook up."

"Look at the variety section, then you tell me."

"Hang on a minute." Randi returned seconds later, paper rattling in the background. "Okay, I've got it. Here it is, the variety section, right? So what's got you so . . . Holy shit, Harlie! Get a load of this!"

"I take it you see my picture."

"At least they got your good side," Randi said, optimistic as always. "He looks pretty good there beside you, himself. I wish I could see Jack's stupid face when he lays his eyes on this. Boy, will he be pissed. Maybe the son of a bitch will drop dead of a heart attack."

"No such luck. Jack was kind enough to hand deliver a copy. Then he put on a floor show, prancing around, acting a damn fool."

"I hope you called the cops. He knows he's not supposed to be anywhere near you. Are you all right? He didn't hit you again, did he?"

"No, I'm fine. And you know the drill. If he doesn't touch me or break my stuff, the police can't do anything to him, except piss him off." Harlie fidgeted with the phone cord.

"God, I hate that asshole. What did he say?"

"Jack claims I'm a bad influence on Zoey. Then he starts in on how I must have slept with Lex, because I'm such a big nymphomaniac and can't control myself. He said Lex just wanted to get laid and that I'll probably never see him again. That part seemed to make Jack real happy, because he got that smug self-righteous look on his face right before he left."

They talked on the phone for about half an hour, discussing Jack, the photos, and Lex. Despite the serious nature of the conversation, her heart felt a bit lighter after she vented to Randi. The conversation ended when Zoey woke up hungry. She got off the phone to cook supper.

By eight-thirty, Zoey was tucked into her toddler

bed for the night, which gave Harlie a chance to relax. First, she soaked in the bathtub surrounded by a froth of lilac-scented bubbles. Then she slipped into her favorite, most comfortable sleepwear—worn gray sweatpants, a purple T-shirt with a penguin on the front, and an extra large red flannel shirt with the sleeves rolled up to her wrists. She accessorized this ensemble with the big floppy bunny slippers her grandma had given her on her last birthday. A claw clip held her hair up in a careless pile.

She caught a glimpse of herself in her bedroom mirror and laughed at the irony. "Oh, yeah, wouldn't every rock star in the country just fight over me now. So hot," she said, mimicking the blonde socialites she sometimes watched on reality TV.

Harlie reached to flick off the lightswitch. "What the hell?"

The darkened room brought the shrubs outside her window into view, and she could have sworn she saw something move. The wind swayed the tree branches in the yard, she noticed when she took a cautious step closer and pulled the curtain aside. Mrs. Jenkins' calico sauntered along on the fence, her tail held out for balance as she tiptoed across. Harlie guessed her neighbor's cat must have been what she saw moving by the window instead of a Peeping Tom, but one could never be too careful. She double checked the latch, pulled down the shade, and put the incident out of her mind.

Snuggled under a handmade quilt in the living room, she found a horror flick on one of the cable channels. She watched a serial killer decapitate a mailman, place the head in a gift box addressed to the victim's mother, and deliver it to the elderly woman's room at the rest home. The poor old lady, a sweet smile on her face, had just untied the frilly pink bow and was removing the lid from the macabre package. At that exact moment, the telephone on Harlie's end table rang. She jumped off the couch, a scream escaping her throat as she fell to the floor. Imagine, a grown woman nearly pissing herself over a ringing phone. She laughed at how silly she must look.

By the third ring she'd composed herself enough to answer it. Who would call her at nine-thirty on a Sunday night? She'd already spoken to practically everyone she knew today, except her brother Louie. She figured it was probably Jack calling to bitch at her some more.

"Hello?" Harlie braced herself for another tirade.

"Hi. Um, am I speaking with Harlie Steele?"

"Yes, this is she." Her pulse quickened. Could this really be *him*? Although she hoped Lex would call, she hadn't been able to imagine him actually picking up the phone and dialing her number. "Is this who I think is?"

He hummed the intro to "Secrets", banishing any doubt from Harlie's mind as to who was on the other end of the line. No one was talented enough to imitate that sultry voice so perfectly.

"It's Lex. Remember me?"

"Of course I do. It's not every day I get pulled on-stage at a concert." Harlie struggled to keep her voice steady. "It's nice to hear from you."

"I thought I'd never get through. I've been trying your number since this afternoon."

"Sorry about that. I think Zoey must have played with the phone earlier. I found it off the hook on the floor beside a pile of toys right before I put her to bed." Harlie made a mental note to keep the phone out of her daughter's reach from now on. If she'd had the slightest inkling Lex was trying to call, she would have stared at the thing all evening and made herself a nervous wreck.

"I hope I didn't catch you at a bad time," he said, sounding like he wanted to spend some time with her, even if it was only through AT&T.

"No, I'm just sitting here watching a horror movie. Actually, you spooked me when the phone rang." Harlie told him about being startled into falling off the couch.

"I wish I was there," Lex said, his voice soft and sensual. "I'd put my arms around you and make you forget all about it. But," he said, changing to a less perverted tone, "I don't know exactly where you live, just that you're in Lisman, Kentucky. You said that's about an hour away from where I'm staying here in Evansville, right?"

Harlie was surprised Lex remembered that, but then again, what wasn't surprising about the past twenty-four hours of her life. "That's right. I guess you must get tired of being on the road all the time. It must get old." Recalling why their time together had been cut short, she added, trying her best to sound disinterested, "Speaking of old things, have you heard from your girlfriend today?"

"That's why I tried to call you earlier. I paid her a visit first thing this morning." He explained how he'd gotten Beth to take the pregnancy test, the negative results, and that he'd made it crystal clear he wanted nothing more to do with her.

She was relieved to hear this news, and flattered he'd gone to the trouble to ease her mind about the matter. She couldn't help but wonder where this chance meeting might lead. Could Lex possibly want a committed relationship? Her heart raced as she remembered being in his arms the previous night. Or did he just plan to have a tawdry little fling with her? That was something Harlie wasn't prepared to put herself through. She returned her focus to their conversation and asked Lex if he was enjoying his stay.

"The suite is comfortable. A little lonely, but it's okay. I'll be glad to finish this tour, though. Just two more dates and I'm due for some time off. Actually, I have ten free days before I have to be in Los Angeles for a taping. I was sitting here in my empty room, thinking I should find some pretty redhead to keep me company."

Could that be a hint of nervousness she heard in his voice? Harlie dismissed the idea, remembering how cocky and self-assured he always appeared to be.

"If I stick around here," Lex continued, "it would give us a chance to get to know each other. You know, spend some time together, tear up the town a little. What do you think?"

"That would be awesome!" She put her hand over the mouthpiece of the phone so Lex couldn't hear her jumping up and down. To get a grip on herself, she quit bouncing and paced around the room instead. "What did you have in mind?"

"Do you like Chinese food? The place that catered our lunch yesterday has a restaurant downtown. I thought we might go there tomorrow night, if you're free."

"Chinese food sounds great. I'm hungry already," Harlie said. "I just hope you don't get bored around here, though. I'm afraid it's nothing like the exciting places you're used to."

"I could never get bored around you. One minute you're about to pull a blade on some asshole to defend yourself, and the next, you've got me lusting after you on the sofa. During all of that, I could tell you have no idea how damn beautiful you are. You've been on my mind all day," Lex said, his voice husky and sincere. "You've done something to me I can't explain. We just met yesterday, but I feel like you're going to be a very special part of my life." After a short pause, he asked, his voice nearly a whisper, "Do you feel it too, Harlie?"

"Yes, I do." Touched by his words, she felt a tear carve a salty trail down her cheek. "It's like being in a dream, but different than anything I could've imagined. You're this big celebrity, but when I'm with you, or talking to you now, you seem so . . . real. I don't even know your favorite color or when your birthday is, but yes, I feel it too."

"My birthday is March fourteenth and my favorite color is blue, just about the shade of your eyes."

Harlie forgot all about the horror flick on her television. She and Lex talked into the night.

Chapter Five

Garrett's Garage and Custom Paint Shop attracted customers from all over the tri-state area of Kentucky, Indiana, and Illinois, along with some regular customers from Florida and Nevada. Known for his expertise in restoring classic cars, trucks, and, his one true passion in life, vintage motorcycles, Pete Garrett specialized in one-of-a-kind paint jobs and bodywork.

Harlie walked into her dad's shop, Zoey's little hand held in her own. The faint scent of motor oil perfumed the nostalgic atmosphere. Framed Harley Davidson posters dotted the wood paneling. Three large shelves over the red leather couch displayed models her father had built, with hotrods from the fifties and sixties intermingled with Model A's and T's. Centered on the wall nearest the door, a reproduction jukebox filled the room with vintage rock 'n' roll, although it sometimes played contemporary tunes that set Pete's toes a-tapping. The wall opposite the red laminated countertop held Coke and candy machines, two pinball machines, and a video game used by his employees during their breaks.

Pete entered the office from his workshop, a smile splitting his face when he laid eyes on his two favorite girls. At fifty-three, a light sprinkling of gray highlighted his dark auburn hair and the few lines etched on his tan features enhanced his rugged good looks. A Harley Davidson tattoo emphasized the muscular biceps on his right arm, when it wasn't hidden inside the sleeve of his favorite leather jacket. He carried himself in a stalwart manner that gave people the impression he was much taller than his actual height.

"Hey, Daddy. What's up?"

"Not much, but Nana tells me Zoey gets to spend the night with us. Won't that be fun, honey?" He squatted down to give his granddaughter a mini-bear hug. A sparkle danced in his blue eyes when he looked up at his daughter. "So, what do you have planned for this evenin'?"

"I'm sure Mom told you all about it." Harlie grinned, letting Pete know it was obvious he just wanted to wheedle more details out of her. "Lex is taking me out to dinner. Should be fun."

"Lester who?" Pete struggled to keep a straight face. "Is he the guy that works in Henderson?"

"No. I don't even know anybody named Lester." Harlie looked at him like he'd lost his mind. "I said Lex.

You know, he's that singer I met at the FireStorm concert."

"Oh yeah." Pete picked something up from the counter. "This guy."

He handed her a copy of *News Flash*, the pages folded back to a glossy photo of Lex leading Harlie through the crowded backstage lounge, his arm draped across her shoulders.

Her eyes widened in surprise. "I can't believe they didn't cut me out of that shot." Unlike yesterday's local paper, this picture was in a national publication.

"Al brought that in this morning and asked me if it was you. So tell me about this guy. What's he like?"

Pete's curiosity was understandably piqued. He was concerned about how this musician the tabloids referred to as 'The Bad Boy of Rock 'n' Roll' would treat his daughter. Lex Callatori looked different from the handful of men his daughter had dated in the past. That was no big deal for Pete, who drew sidelong glances himself, decked out in leathers riding his bike through town. He didn't judge people on appearances; a good thing considering the long hair, spandex pants, and jewelry that dripped off this FireStorm dude would be enough to make most parents start popping Valiums. It was the lifestyle that worried him, the sex, drugs, and drama synonymous with the music industry.

His ex-son-in-law was the perfect example of how

clothes and outward appearances did *not* make the man. Jack looked like he stepped straight out of the pages of *GQ Magazine*, with his blond hair, square jaw, and the way his designer suits hung from his tall, lean physique. Still irked at himself for not having seen what was going on until too late, Pete shuddered to think how that asshole almost cost Harlie her life. Even now, nearly three years later, he'd like nothing better than to rip Jack's head off and piss down his throat. For Harlie's sake, and for Zoey's, he had to leave the past alone.

Proud of Harlie for learning to take care of herself, Pete felt fairly confident she'd make the right decision about this new guy. He prayed to God that Callatori was as good a man as Jack was evil. He'd be damned before he let Harlie go through that kind of hell again. Not in this lifetime.

"I think you'll like him, Daddy. He's really cool, obviously, but he's really sweet too." Harlie spoke so fast, she reminded Pete of a chirping parakeet. "You'd think a big time rock star would be hard to talk to, but he's not. I just hope his fans don't mob us at the restaurant."

"I do like his music, especially that one song, 'Secrets' or something like that," Pete said, wanting to show his support. Aside from being the apple of his eye, Harlie was the kindest, most adorable sweetheart in the world, and she deserved only the best. He smiled and tried to sound casual. "Just make sure he treats you right. Don't forget, he's the one that's lucky to be going out with my little girl, not the other way around."

Pete Garrett would be leery of anyone Harlie took an interest in. Hell, he'd probably put a tail on the Secret Service if the President himself invited her for afternoon tea at the White House.

Harlie took home a packet of receipts and the deposit bag holding the money she needed to put in the bank that afternoon. She worked at the garage on Mondays, Wednesdays, and Fridays, then took the paperwork home to finish on her computer.

Today, Harlie balanced her father's accounts at her kitchen counter, Zoey happily coloring beside her. Seated in front of her laptop, she hoped to keep her mind off tonight's date with Lex by drowning herself in work. Her plan succeeded for a while as she balanced the books, recorded transactions, figured payroll for the previous week, and wrote out the deposit ticket. This usually took four hours, so when the clock on the wall showed that she'd finished in half the time, she was pleasantly surprised. Now she had time to get her errands out of the way before lunch.

The teller at the bank's drive-thru window gave Zoey a green Dum-Dum sucker, which Harlie hoped wouldn't get stuck to the car seat. After a pit stop at McDonald's, they returned home just past noon, a Happy Meal in Zoey's delighted little hands. Harlie's nervous stomach only let her eat half of her McChicken sandwich.

When Zoey took her afternoon nap, Harlie decided to visit her favorite chatroom for a while. Barb was always there at this time of day, come hell or high water.

Harlie logged on to find Barbed*Ivy chatting with Bitsy_Boop. Somewhere in Florida, Bitsy sat in her fifth period computers class, ignoring her boring teacher by popping into the forum. Harlie entered her nickname and joined the conversation.

~ **CyberBitch has entered the room. Welcome** ~
CyberBitch: Hey, hey. The Bitch is back!
Barbed*Ivy: Hi, Bitch. Was that U in this week's *News Flash*? Page 8, I believe?
Bitsy_Boop: Barb filled me N on UR social life last night. I can't freakin' believe it! Lucky U!! Could U introduce me 2 Stix? That would B so kwl.
CyberBitch: Yes! That's us!! I can't believe another picture got published with me in it. That one was taken in the backstage lounge. Bitsy, LOL, I really don't know the rest of the band, but if I run into Stix again, I'll tell him Hi from you.
Barbed*Ivy: It looked like he's trying to hang all over U. I know U think he's fine and every-

thing, whatever, but U 2 make an odd couple. Like a beauty queen with a homeless bum. Don't get POed again. That's just how it looks to me. I think U would B much better off if U let me fix U up with my cousin Artie. He's cute and isn't a drug addict, unlike some people U know.

Bitsy_Boop: Oh, come on Barb. The FireStorm guy really doesn't look that bad. I think Stix is hotter, but CyberBitch's man seems pretty kwl and he has a great voice. Tell us C-Bitch, what's it like kissing those sensuous lips?

Barbed*Ivy: Oh, PLZ don't. I'm about to puke all over my keyboard just thinking about it. YUCK!!!

CyberBitch: You know, somewhere deep down, maybe, but you have to know that Lex is gorgeous. Your cousin sounds like a nice guy, but Lex got to me first. LOL And Bitsy, I don't like to kiss and tell BUT he's a great kisser! Actually, I came on here to keep my mind off Lex until he picks me up tonight.

Bitsy_Boop: U mean U 2 R gonna have, like, a normal date? That is sooo kwl! Have fun. Gotta go. My dipwad teacher is passing out a test. L8R girlz!

Barbed*Ivy: So, where's he taking U? Better watch out for him. I'm not trying to put a damper on things 4 U, but I'm afraid UR destined 2 get hurt if U keep seeing him. Be careful.

CyberBitch: You're a good friend, trying to look

out for me, but I really don't think you have
anything to worry about. Lex is honestly a nice
guy. I do appreciate the thought, though. Oh,
and he's taking me to a Chinese place. Mr. Foo's
or something.

Barbed*Ivy: Well, have fun. And I do hope everything works out 4 the best 4 U. At least U
know he can afford the most expensive thing
on the menu. Order the duck, and maybe some
stir-fried caviar! LOL

CyberBitch: LOL I have a nervous stomach, but
I'll keep that in mind.

Harlie stayed online for about an hour. She could
always count on Barb to take her mind off things by
joking around. She gave hilarious descriptions of the
shoppers milling around the boutique, certain they
thought she was busy at her work as she sat typing
away on the laptop. They chatted until time for Harlie
to start getting ready.

She passed the next couple of hours fixing herself
up, with forty-five minutes devoted to makeup alone.
She wore a red top with an ankle length floral skirt
that hid her legs and showed off her tiny waist. Her auburn locks were twisted into an elegant up-do that emphasized her sky blue eyes. She inspected herself in the
mirror and nodded at her reflection. Still not deluded
into believing she was beautiful, her self-esteem had
taken a boost since she realized she couldn't look quite
as bad as she thought, not if someone like Lex found

her attractive. The question of whether Lex might be going blind was crossing Harlie's mind when she heard her mother let herself in the front door.

"Well, don't you look pretty tonight." Roxanne beamed at Harlie, obviously glad to see her all dressed up and looking happy.

"Thanks, Mom." Harlie gave her a quick hug. "I'm not exactly sure what the name of the restaurant is or where else we'll be going tonight. I can call and let you know when I find out. You know, in case there's an emergency or something."

Nana's voice brought Zoey running into the living room, jumping up and down in excitement when she saw her grandmother. Beside the couch, her little pink suitcase was packed and ready, with Sassy Susie perched on top. Forgetting that doll would have been a disaster, since Zoey couldn't sleep without it.

"Don't worry about a thing, dear. I do have your cell number, remember? You know we'll be perfectly fine. I put away all the chain saws and razor blades before I left," Roxanne teased, smiling at her little joke. Harlie had always been a bit overprotective of Zoey. "You go and have a nice time on your date."

Too anxious to sit still, Harlie paced around the room for the next hour, occasionally stopping by the window to gaze in the direction of her backyard. If hungry leopards chased wild elephants around the swing set, she wouldn't have noticed. All she could think of was seeing him again.

She almost jumped out of her skin when the doorbell rang a full ten minutes early.

Exhaling the deep breath she'd taken on her way to the door, Harlie tried to calm down as she squinted through the peephole. She ran her sweaty palms over her skirt before she turned the knob.

"Come in," she said, holding the door wide open for him.

Oddly enough, Harlie relaxed the instant Lex said hello. After their phone conversation, she felt almost like she was greeting a friend. This friend just happened to be a gorgeous world-famous Rock icon whose songs were probably playing on radios in five different countries while she stood looking at him, but she tried not to think about that aspect just now.

He strolled in wearing Levi's, a white silk shirt with the top three buttons left open, and a simple gold chain around his neck. His long dark hair flowed past the earrings that dangled from his lobes. As he brushed past her, she found the scent of his leather jacket even more alluring than his cologne.

Lex's eyes never left Harlie while she shut the door. "You look beautiful, exactly the way I remember you," he said. "I've missed you." Unable to go another second without some kind of physical contact, he kissed her on the cheek. "You ready to go?"

Harlie blushed as a tingling heat swept over her face and down the back of her neck. "I've missed you too." She ached for him to kiss her again, the way he had in his dressing room, but knew she had to control herself. Taking a deep breath, she picked up her purse and tried to push those thoughts out of her mind. "I'm ready if you are."

Chapter Six

Lex's stomach growled as his rental car pulled into the parking lot at Mr. Woo's Cantonese Dragon. If the food was half as good as it smelled, they were in for one hell of a meal.

Walking beside him toward the restaurant, Harlie spotted Zeke getting out of his car. The bodyguard looked surprised when she waved to him, but acknowledged her with a grin, a wink, and a nod. Lex glanced from one to the other and smiled. The women he'd dated in the past had never given Zeke the time of day, let alone been cordial to him. He realized it wasn't exactly the appropriate thing for her to do in this particular situation, when Zeke's job required him to be inconspicuous, but Lex knew she'd never dealt with bodyguards before. He'd explain it to her later.

"We have a reservation for two. The name's Callatori," Lex said. The host, an Asian man who very well might have been *the* Mr. Woo, checked a book lying beside the telephone on the counter. He led them to their booth, oblivious to the celebrity status of the man at his side.

The scent of ginger and spices drifting from the kitchen added to the restaurant's atmosphere. Lantern-shaped chandeliers graced the ceiling, a living rainbow of exotic fish swam in the aquarium, and ornately carved dragons seemed to guard the potted plants.

A waiter took their order and left them sipping hot oolong tea from delicate Chinese cups. They'd passed on the soup but decided to share a plate of crab Rangoon, a dish of crabmeat and cream cheese tucked inside won ton wrappers. As the hors d'oeuvres and two small bowls of sauce were placed on the table between them, Lex asked Harlie about her unusual name.

"That's actually a funny story." Harlie dipped an appetizer in sweet and sour sauce and took a bite. "Hey, this is pretty good. Anyway, my dad loves his motorcycle. So much so that I was conceived on the back of his Harley, late one night after he and Mom left some wild party. Hence the name Harlie Dawn. Every time Mom tells this story, she stresses that they'd been married for four years and already had one kid, so I'm not illegitimate." The corner of her mouth turned up as she rolled her eyes. "My brother was named after Dad's favorite song, 'Louie, Louie', so I think I got off pretty easy."

"So you're named after your old man's hog," Lex said, amused.

"They did at least spell it differently, with an 'i-e' instead of 'e-y'. Daddy thought it looked more feminine that way."

"That's pretty cool. It fits you. Bad and beautiful at the same time." Lex had never seen eyes so big and deep and blue, and the demure way she kept looking up at him made him want to leap across the table and make love to her right there. He could imagine the expression on Mr. Woo's face if he caught them doing the nasty in his booth.

"Thank you." Harlie blushed at the compliment. She dipped a piece of crab Rangoon in the hot Chinese mustard and popped the dripping morsel into her mouth.

"You might want to go easy on that stuff. It's kind of potent," Lex warned. The mustard had a touch too much horseradish in it for his taste.

Harlie's eyes began to water as her face contorted. Choking and sputtering, she covered her mouth and nose with the white linen napkin, previously folded in the shape of a lotus flower.

"Here, take a sip of this." Lex passed her a glass of water and tried not to laugh. The scrunchy expression on her face was funny enough, but the snorting, gaspy noises she made behind her napkin were just too much.

"Thanks." Harlie grabbed the glass. Her eyelashes fluttered as she tried to stop the tearing, but the water seemed to help a little. She dabbed under her eyes with the napkin and looked across the table at Lex, his hand over his mouth in a feeble attempt to conceal his amusement. The second their eyes met, they both cracked up until laughter-induced tears glistened on their cheeks. The host, startled to see two customers who appeared to be in deep mourning, rushed over to ask if anything was wrong.

"No." Lex put on the straightest face he could manage. "But the lady would like some more mustard, please. This simply isn't hot enough for her."

To the consternation of everyone else in the establishment—except Zeke, who'd been watching the whole episode from his table—the couple fell into another convulsive fit of laughter. Mr. Woo walked away from the table with a frown on his face, probably assuming these crazy Americans were on drugs.

The waiter brought their meal after they'd composed themselves enough to eat. His Szechwan beef and her Kung Pao chicken were both spicy dishes, but Harlie passed when Lex offered her the hot mustard.

"No thanks, my nose is still tingling. Back to the subject of names, how did you think of FireStorm for the band?"

"Dylan came up with it when we were starting out. I thought it sounded cool, but liked it even better when he showed me the definition in the dictionary. It means a fire fed by inrushing winds on all sides, so I picture myself as the flame and the audience as the wind feeding our energy." He speared a piece of beef with his fork. "The other definition was a strong violent outburst, and that kinda symbolizes the power that explodes from our music."

"Cool, I always wondered about that. It sure fits." Harlie smiled across the table. An expression passed over her face that made him think she'd just remembered something. "Did you see the pictures of us in the newspaper over the weekend? Surprised the heck out of me." She took a bite of chicken.

"No, but I wish I had." Lex explained that with so many bogus stories printed about him in the past, he only read the *New York Times*. FireStorm's staff kept scrapbooks filled with every article and photo ever published about or relating to the group, which Lex looked through occasionally, mainly to laugh off the ridiculous stories. "I'll get a copy faxed to the hotel."

Harlie used the subject to bring up a few questions that had been on her mind. "Just out of curiosity, how much of the stuff in those tabloids is actually true. I mean, I know most of it's one hundred percent pure BS, but I was just wondering which parts were based on truth. I've read that you're a real heartbreaker—two nuns and your high school Geometry teacher included—have violent temper fits, and like to get into bar fights a couple times a week just for the hell of it. And, that you're addicted to all the pharmaceuticals you can get your hands on. Not that I believed all that crap, I was just wondering . . . ."

Lex knew she'd eventually ask about all this stuff, so her questions didn't surprise him. He'd guessed it wouldn't take her long to bring up the drug issue, since she did have a small child to look out for, and he respected her for it.

"I've always been a big fan," she continued, before he had a chance to answer. "When I was a teenager, I bought every magazine with a single printed word about you in it. Don't laugh, but I wallpapered my room with pictures of you and your band."

"I'm flattered that you used to go to sleep looking at my ugly mug. Did it make you have any interesting dreams I should know about?" he asked seductively, then dove into the meatier issues. He wanted to be honest with Harlie without scaring her off. "Back to your questions. Hmmm, my womanizing ways. Well, when I was younger I sowed my share of wild oats, I guess you could say. Hell, I must have planted a couple hundred acres worth, to be honest. But as for the heartbreaker part, I never intentionally hurt anybody, and I've settled down a whole lot. I'm a one woman man now. I hope you know that." He said this last sentence staring deeply into her eyes, hoping she would sense his sincerity. She was the only woman he wanted, not a harem of sexual acrobats.

"I hope so." Harlie looked relieved.

"I think question number two was about my temper," Lex continued. "I do get into the occasional fight, but it's not like I go out looking for somebody's ass to kick. Reporters really piss me off. Photographers have actually followed me into the john and snapped pictures of me taking a dump. Can you believe that?"

Harlie's eyes widened as she shook her head.

"After I wiped my ass, I force fed that son of a bitch a couple rolls of his own film. When I'm pushed into a corner like that, I come out swinging. It makes the paparazzi think twice before they invade my privacy again.

"The down side to being a celebrity is that some people take an instant dislike to me and want to stir shit up. That's why Zeke watches my back. I've had a few run-ins with lunatics who wanted to rid the world of me. One asshole came up and started hitting me in the jaw. Zeke pulled him off and I never even got a chance to punch him back. Two days later, the cocksucker tries to sue me for battery!

"But, I'm not a violent person. I've never been accused of knocking women around, if that had you worried. I could never do anything as fucked up as that."

"Oh . . . I know you couldn't do that." Harlie stared

at her rice and fidgeted with an earring.

Lex wasn't sure how to read the strange, haunted expression that passed over her face. Dismissing it as possible indigestion, he went on to the last issue she'd brought up.

"Okay, so that brings us to the drugs. I've been clean for the past five years. Cocaine was my thing. I used it for a while thinking it helped my creativity, but I got hooked on the shit," he confessed, stirring his oolong tea. "I lost a bunch of weight and started acting messed up during concerts and recording sessions.

"Went into rehab after I saw myself on *The Late Show* with David Letterman. Sitting in that chair by his desk, he couldn't understand the shit I was trying to say. I was bleary eyed, bobbing my head around all over the place. Ole Dave knew what was up so he went to commercial early, then tried to rush me off the set before I made a bigger ass out of myself. Well, that pissed me off so I called him a fuckhead. The cameras came back on and caught me sneering at Letterman, then I stormed off the stage." Lex looked back up at Harlie. He'd been staring at the spoon in his hand, fiddling with it as he talked.

"I didn't even realize what a dick I'd been until I watched it with a room full of friends. I was waiting for my dealer to bring in some blow, so I wasn't very messed up yet. When I saw myself prancing off the set, I just couldn't believe it was really me. I didn't even remember getting pissed at Letterman. Of course, all the druggies in my living room thought it was funny as hell. 'Cool, man. You should've decked the bastard. Ha, ha, ha'.

"That was it for me. I got high for the last time that night, mainly to cover my embarrassment. Checked myself into detox the next afternoon. After a week of hell getting the stuff out of my system, I called Letterman up and apologized. I explained why I'd acted so bad, and he was cool about it." Lex's expression made it clear that this was a painful subject for him.

"That must have been a difficult thing to go through." Harlie put her hand on his. "Thanks for being so open and honest with me."

"No problem. I want to be up front with you about every aspect of my life, now that you're in it." Lex gazed hopefully into Harlie's baby blues. He paused for a few seconds before continuing. "The press ran with the story, making bad enough into awful. They said I was on crack and heroin, that I had a fifth of Jack Daniel's with my Post Toasties every morning. Total bullshit. I want you to know I've never shot up in my life. I'm this rock 'n' roll badass who's scared to death of needles." He flashed a big grin to take the serious edge off. "I had to get shots last year before the European tour and I fainted. Got up from the table and just passed out cold. The doctor thought it was pretty goddamn funny."

"I'm the same way," Harlie admitted. "Show me needles or blood and out I go."

"To bring this tale to an end, let me tell you I'm completely clean now. I don't even smoke cigarettes anymore. I do have a drink from time to time, which makes the Narcotics Anonymous people bitch, but hey, at least I don't lie about it. I never had a problem with alcohol, just dope. . . . I hope I haven't turned you off or anything."

"No. Like I said, I'm just glad you can be so open with me," Harlie said, her voice sincere. "I didn't mean to pry, I just wanted to make sure there wasn't anything for me to worry about. I could pretty much tell by talking to you that you weren't some raving crackhead or anything. I feel bad about nosing through your past though, so feel free to ask me anything you'd like to know about my boring little life."

Lex pondered this for about ten seconds. "The only thing I want to know is why the ex-Mr. Steele let you get away from him. I don't want to make the same mistake."

Harlie took a big sip of her tea, rattling the Lilliputian size cup when she sat it down on its matching saucer.

Lex noticed the same haunted expression darken her features as he'd seen earlier during their conversation. "Are you all right? I'm sorry. Maybe that's too personal. Never mind, you don't have to-"

Harlie cut him off. "No, that's fine. Let's just say Jack screwed up in every possible way you can imagine. He cheated on me. He tried to manipulate every aspect of my life, didn't want me to have any friends or spend time with my family. A total control freak . . ." Her voice trailed off as she skidded down memory lane.

"He was an idiot to treat you like that," Lex said. "What about your daughter? Did he treat her badly too?"

"No, he actually loves her. To be honest, he never got a chance to mess that up. I filed for divorce the week after Zoey was born, so she'd never have to witness the hell her father put me through." Harlie paused to take a deep breath. "I don't want to sound like some pitiful little fool, but I'm not going to lie to you by omission either. You see, the truth is . . . well, Jack liked to get rough with me, on top of everything else. But I came through it in one piece, and that's all that really matters." Her weak attempt to smile failed to lighten the mood.

Revulsion distorted Lex's face, something he didn't realize until he heard rage darken his own voice. "You mean he hit you?"

Harlie nodded but didn't elaborate.

"I'll kill that bastard if he ever lays another finger on you." Afraid he was going to scare her if he didn't calm down, he willed his face to soften. "I'm so sorry, baby, I had no idea. I will *never, ever* hurt you. I can promise you that. Does he still push you around?"

"He doesn't have the balls to touch me again, not now." Harlie explained the details concerning her divorce. "So, that's why I carry the knife. I'll never be anybody's victim again."

Appalled and astonished by the things he'd just heard, Lex sandwiched her hand between his own. He hated to see the agony of these memories cloud her eyes. "It blows my mind that someone as cute as you can be such a hellcat." He grinned at her, hoping she'd smile again. "You're like a walking contradiction, full of piss and vinegar." He honestly wouldn't be surprised to see Harlie dance naked in the snow, eating an ice cream cone.

"Hey, I'm proud to say I can be a real bitch when I need to be."

"Baby, I'll never let anyone hurt you again," Lex said, his voice husky and passionate.

With eyes full of trust and raw emotion, Harlie's gaze met his. Lex hoped she knew he meant every word.

Later on, Lex cracked open his fortune cookie and unfolded the small paper rectangle he found inside. He signaled to Zeke before he read it to himself: 'Confucius say our greatest glory is not in never falling, but in getting up every time we fall.'

Zeke nodded toward Lex, then paid for his meal before going out to wait in the car.

He was surprised no one had recognized his boss, especially after that laughing outburst, but guessed people in Evansville didn't expect to see many celebrities walking around town. He only noticed one person paying attention to the couple, an average guy in his thirties who sat alone at a table in the corner. He looked disgusted about something, picking at his food as he glared at Lex and Harlie. Maybe he was the conservative type who just didn't like longhaired men in leather. Zeke didn't think the guy was a threat, but he'd kept an eye on him anyway, just in case. You could never tell when some crackpot was going to turn up and cause trouble.

Chapter Seven

Lex and Harlie went for a drive around Evansville after dinner, to take in the sights the city had to offer. Harlie pointed out Willard Library and the Reitz museum, beautiful Victorian mansions that now served the community as historic public buildings. They passed the Tropicana—a riverboat casino with Vegas-style gambling, live entertainment, and four-star dining—as they cruised along the scenic riverfront walkway.

They didn't plan to make any more public appearances, so Lex phoned Zeke on his cell and gave him the rest of the night off. Then he drove over the twin bridges, crossing the Ohio River back into Kentucky, and pointed his rental car toward the countryside. Harlie had lived in this area her entire life but had absolutely no idea where they were headed.

About five miles outside the city limits, Lex turned down a narrow gravel road, then pulled up to a sturdy homemade gate leading into a large pasture. He got out of the car and walked around behind it to take something from the trunk.

When he opened the car door for her, Harlie cast a curious eye at the bag he carried, wondering what could be inside it and why he parked there. Lex draped his arm over her shoulders and led her to the gate. It was tied shut with fencing wire, so climbing over it seemed much easier than trying to untangle the mess. Good thing she'd worn the long flowing skirt—the hem of which she gathered in her hand before she swung her leg over the old wooden gate—instead of the tight minidress Randi tried to talk her into.

"Isn't this like something off a postcard?" Lex sighed as he looked around. "When I was a kid, I used to dream of living in a place like this."

Harlie agreed the scene in front of her was beautiful. Atop a hill in the center of the tranquil meadow, illuminated by the light of a full moon, stood an ancient barn, its walls weathered by time and the elements. The roof had been painted black years ago, with the worn advertisement 'See Rock City' written in large white lettering. Scattered cattle dotted the landscape, reminding Harlie of a picture from one of Zoey's storybooks.

"How in the world did you find this place?" she asked. Honeysuckle perfumed the breeze as they trekked up the steep hill toward the barn.

"Stix drove his car down for the tour, so I came with

him instead of riding our bus. When you're on the road as much as we are, you'll do anything to break the monotony," Lex explained. "Anyway, nature called so we pulled off the road here to take a leak, and the place sort of stuck in my mind. I thought we could look around. Sound like fun?" He pushed open the creaky barn door.

"Yeah, as long as some pissed off farmer doesn't follow us up here with a shotgun to find out what the hell we're doing," Harlie wisecracked.

Lex withdrew a flashlight from the duffel bag and shined it over their rustic surroundings. One of the stalls contained piles of old tractor tires, and there was an antiquated hay wagon in the next, partially obscured by a ragged tarp. Propped against the wall for most of the last century, an obsolete manual plow marked the age of the building. Bags of feed sat stacked in the corner with rusty horseshoes and grooming tools hanging from nails above them.

"Oh, wait. I smell fresh hay." Lex closed his eyes and inhaled the sweet earthy scent. Harlie was a little surprised that a ramshackle old barn could fascinate a man who'd traveled the world over and visited places like the Taj Mahal and the Eiffel Tower. She thought it was cute, in a Huckleberry Finn sort of way, when he insisted, his eyes dancing, "We have to see the hayloft. I've always wanted to be in a hayloft."

He grabbed Harlie's hand and up they climbed. Lex led the way, clearing dusty cobwebs that enshrouded the wooden ladder.

The loft was indeed full of fresh hay. They sat down on stacked bales near a large window-like opening Harlie guessed was the hay chute. He put his arm around her shoulders, hugging her as they took in the bucolic ambiance. Lightning bugs twinkled like lost fairies over the rolling meadow as the deep voice of a bullfrog accompanied the crickets' serenade.

"You're right. This place is beautiful. Thanks for sharing it with me." Harlie turned her head to gaze up at him, his features even more handsome bathed in moonlight.

Lex peered into her eyes. He kissed her, gently at first, then deeper. Harlie shifted her body closer to his, her arms around his neck, pressing herself against him. Her movement caused them to fall backward, unconcerned about the bits of hay that stuck in their hair and clung to their clothing as they rolled around, a tangle of arms and legs.

"Harlie, I want you so bad." Lex ran his hands over her body. While his fingers unbuttoned her blouse, he spoke softly into her ear. "Not just now, but forever. I feel like we're this perfect yin-yang, two souls that need each other to really exist. The perfect cosmic fit. It's like we've spent our whole lives waiting to come together so we could finally start to live."

"I feel the same way," Harlie responded, breathless. She took his face in the palms of her hands and kissed him, her tongue relishing the taste of passion.

"Just a minute, I almost forgot." Lex pulled a chilled bottle of Dom Perignon and two fluted glasses from his duffle bag. He popped open the champagne, let the cork fly through the hay chute, and poured them each a glass. "Just a little something I picked up to make this night even more special. Here's to us and our future together."

Wrapped around each other, they clinked their glasses in a toast before sipping the bubbly. Harlie shivered when some of the champagne splashed down her front.

"Allow me." Lex bent his head to lick up the spill. Harlie moaned as he sucked the liquid from her belly button. He slowly worked his way up to her breast, his long dark hair tickling a trail on either side of his tongue.

She had never wanted anything as badly as she wanted him right now.

They quickly undressed each other, popping un-yielding buttons without a second thought. Lex dipped into his duffel bag one last time to grab a Trojan. Harlie took the package from his hands and put the condom in place, a little taken aback by the generous size of his penis.

Lex laid her on his leather jacket to protect her delicate skin from the coarse hay. He paused with the tip of his ample manhood on her threshold and whispered in her ear, "Baby, I'm falling in love with you."

He kissed her before she had a chance to answer. Harlie knew without a doubt she was in love with him, but feared she might jinx everything if she said those three little words too soon. She couldn't shake the awful feeling that some dark force was going to come along and steal her happiness. How she could bear it if that happened?

She didn't want to think about that now. Her voice little more than a whisper, she looked up at him. "Make love to me . . . please."

Lex granted her wish. With each slow, deep stroke Harlie moaned, her body spasming in delight. They panted in unison as Lex, speeding his gait, pulsed himself vigorously in and out, in and out, until they simultaneously burst into orgasmic delirium.

Harlie felt as if she were floating on a cloud of ecstasy, a magical sensation such as she'd never before experienced.

Lex walked Harlie into her house hours later, knowing he should be heading back to his lonely hotel suite. Ethically it would be the right thing to do, but he couldn't bear the thought of being away from her. It was obvious she felt the same way, so when she asked if he could stay the night, it was an invitation he couldn't refuse.

Tonight Harlie had looked like a goddess to him, with moonbeams reflecting in her eyes and playing on her auburn hair. He'd never felt this kind of all-consuming, overwhelming love for anyone else in his whole life, like an ache and an orgasm at the same time.

They went straight to bed, but neither slept a wink on Harlie's silky sheets that night. They spent the twilight hours in a sexual marathon, unable to satiate their need for one another. Bathed in the pink glow of dawn that poured through her lace curtains, they finally drifted off to sleep, spooned together, their faces wanton masks of contentment.

Chapter Eight

Harlie slept until nine o'clock the next morning, still wrapped in the comfort of Lex's arms when she opened her eyes. She'd only gotten a few short hours of sleep, but felt rejuvenated and full of life. Her mouth curled into a naughty smile. Lurid details of the previous night flashed through her mind like a romantic trip through the pages of the Kama Sutra.

Oh my God, she thought, trying to finger comb her curly locks turned bedhead nightmare. *I bet I look like shit!* She snuck out of bed and dashed to the bathroom, hoping to get to her cosmetics and hairbrush before Lex saw the mascara smeared across her face or her messy auburn tangles. She quickly jumped in and out of the shower, fixed her hair, put on fresh makeup, and wiggled into her favorite pair of jeans.

Last night's love marathon had left her with a voracious appetite. She could eat a whole side of beef, judging by all the growls from her empty stomach. After raiding her refrigerator, she popped some Eggo waffles in the toaster before heating up half a package of brown-and-serve sausage links in the microwave. She turned on the coffee maker, which soon sent the aroma of fresh brewed java wafting through the house.

Harlie filled her great-grandma's crystal wine glasses with orange juice. If ever there was an occasion to break out her best dishes, spending last night with Lex had to be it. It wasn't just the fabulous sex that made her feel special, but also the beautiful things he'd said to her, lyrical sentiment from his soul to hers.

Harlie headed down the hall to call Lex to breakfast, but met him as he walked out of her bedroom. Weak-kneed at the sight of him, she thought he'd never looked sexier, with his rumpled hair and bare chest.

"Morning, baby." He took her in his arms and planted a long lascivious kiss on her lips. "Is that hot food I smell?" Harlie led him to the dining table where his eyes lit up like he'd hit the jackpot.

"Everything came from boxes in the freezer, so it's not exactly home cooking." Harlie hoped it tasted better than the room service he usually ate. "Are you hungry?"

"Starving. You didn't have to go to all this trouble," he said through a mouthful of sausage, "but thanks. It's delicious."

Between bites, his glances sent warm tremors down Harlie's spine, into deeper regions of her anatomy.

"Do you know what time it is?" Lex wiped maple syrup from his chin after wolfing down the last forkful of waffle. "I need to get to the hotel before Mugsy pisses all over the walls. He does that when he feels neglected. Want to come with me?"

"I'd love to, but I need to pick Zoey up pretty soon," Harlie said. "My mom has a dentist appointment this afternoon and I don't want to make her late. Can you come back tonight for supper? I can't wait for Zoey to meet you. I have no idea what she'll think in that little head of hers, or what she'll say, but she's just as cute as a button."

They made plans for the evening. Lex insisted on taking them out for dinner since she'd gone to the trouble of making breakfast, prepackaged or not. He finished dressing, then gave Harlie a lingering kiss at the front door that left her daydreaming long after he was gone.

When Harlie picked Zoey up from her parents' house a little past noon, Louie helped her carry a mountain of his niece's things to her car. He couldn't resist offering a little brotherly advice when their conversation turned to her new relationship.

"Make him treat you right, Sis. You've still got that *present* I gave you, right?" This was how he always referred to the butterfly knife, though Harlie never understood why. Louie had a lot of quirky habits she found oddly endearing. "Just in case things ever get out of hand."

"I keep it with me all the time." Harlie patted the lump in the back pocket of her jeans. "I won't need it around Lex, though. He treats me like I'm special, and a bodyguard follows him around all the time. So you see, big brother, I'm in absolutely no danger of anything. Unless you count getting shot with cameras. Did you like my pictures? I know Mom must have showed 'em to you by now."

"How'd you know?" A grin spread over Louie's face. "Yep, she called yesterday and told me every detail she could remember about your new social life. And the pictures were . . . interesting, I guess." He went on to explain how Roxanne had stuck them in his face the moment he walked in the door, insisting that he not make a big fuss over it since that might embarrass Harlie.

Backing out of the driveway, Harlie put in a Fire-Storm CD that filled the car with Lex's sultry voice. When "Nefarious" ended, Harlie tried to explain things to the toddler.

"I've got a surprise for you. Guess what we're going to do tonight?"

"Yay! Supwise," Zoey squealed as her face lit up. "Tell me, tell me!"

"Remember when I told you about Mommy's new friend? The FireStorm man?" Harlie saw Zoey nodding in the rearview mirror. "Well, he's going to take us out for pizza. I think you're really going to like him. He's so nice, and when I showed him your picture, he said you looked like a little doll."

The only thing Zoey seemed to get from the conversation was the part about pizza, something she loved to eat but couldn't quite pronounce yet. Clapping her doll's hands together, she chanted, "pia, pia, pia."

Harlie, Lex, and Zoey arrived at Spumoni's Pizzeria later that evening, followed closely by Zeke. Dolled up in a pretty pink and yellow dress and Mary Janes, her blonde curls held back in a frilly bow, Zoey scrutinized her mom's new friend with leery eyes.

Harlie knew that in the small town restaurant in Lisman, Kentucky, they'd draw more attention if Zeke sat off by himself. By the time they parked, she'd convinced Lex to let the bodyguard sit at their table. He got out and motioned for the big guy to join them, explaining the new plans as Harlie lifted her daughter from her car seat.

Lex introduced the goateed giant to "little Miss Zoey", who surprised everyone by lunging toward Zeke, holding her arms out for him to take her. With a sheepish smile, he carried the child into the restaurant. Harlie apologized when the little girl refused to sit an-

ywhere other than on his lap, though Zeke obviously
didn't mind the attention. The pair made quite an odd
sight, coloring the cartoon placemat while they waited
for the waitress to take their order.

Before the pizza arrived, Zoey noticed the jukebox
situated by the restrooms. She asked her mom for
coins, then nodded her head up and down with excitement. "'eke go with 'oey! Make moosic!" She couldn't
pronounce her Z's or L's yet, though people usually
managed to understand her anyway.

Envious of the attention Zeke was getting, Lex tried
to get in the child's good graces. He dug a handful of
quarters out of his pockets and slid them over to her
rainbow-colored placemat. He thought Zoey was adorable, with her curly hair and her mother's big blue
eyes.

Zoey said "thanks, Wex", then grabbed Zeke's hand
and yanked him across the room. Harlie called after
them, asking him not to let her put the coins in her
mouth. The bodyguard held the little girl up to push
the lighted buttons.

When they dug into their delicious pizza pie a little
later, "Nefarious" played on the jukebox. Lex smiled at
Zoey. "Hey, you've got great taste in music. Did you
know that's my voice on that song?" He sang along for
a couple of bars to prove it, trying his damnedest to
make a good impression.

Zoey stopped chewing and stared incredulously at

the man sitting across from her in the wooden booth. "Fi stom man. On Mommy's CD?" she asked, frowning.

"Yes, honey, that's right. That song's on the CD we listen to all the time in our car," Harlie explained. "FireStorm is Lex's band. Isn't that nice?"

Zoey's horrified screams shattered the serene atmosphere at Spumoni's Pizzeria. Lex was amazed so much noise could come out of one tiny kid. She slid off Zeke's lap and hid under the table, shrieking at the top of her lungs.

"I guess that's what I get for tooting my own horn, huh." Lex felt like an idiot. "I didn't mean to scare the hell out of her. Does she just hate my vocals or is it personal?"

"I'm sure it doesn't have anything to do with you, but I have no idea what's wrong with her. She *never* acts like this. Come here, baby. What's the matter?" Harlie climbed under the table after the hysterical toddler, leaving the men to shrug at each other in confusion.

The little girl, still sobbing, reappeared moments later, hiding her face against her mother's shirt. Harlie grinned and took her seat next to Lex.

"I think I figured out what the problem is." She turned her attention back to Zoey, giving her a quick kiss on the cheek. "Go ahead, honey, look at his eyes. It's okay."

Sniffling, Zoey wiped her tears on a napkin before doing as her mother asked.

"That's why she's been looking at you so funny," Harlie said. "See, Zoey, his eyes look just like yours and mine and Zeke's. It was just a costume, like the pumpkin outfit you wore last Halloween. Remember that?"

Zoey studied Lex's brown eyes, her face softening a bit as she leaned in closer for a better look.

"It's that 'Nefarious' bit that's got her so terrified. You know, the one where you have those glowing cat eyes and that spooky expression. She always liked the video, though. It never seemed to bother her before now. When she figured out who you were, she was afraid you were about to turn into some kind of monster." Harlie shrugged, then she and Zeke both laughed. "What's a kid to think?"

"So she thinks I'm the goddamn boogeyman," Lex muttered under his breath. "Great."

"No key cat eyes?" Zoey squeezed Lex's cheeks between her pudgy hands. "Wex, you not gone have key cat eyes *noooo* more."

"No, Zoey girl, I won't dress up like that again. I promise," Lex reassured her. "I want to be your buddy. What do ya say? No more scary outfits if you'll be my little friend." Lex extended his hand. "Can we shake on it?"

Zoey put some serious consideration into Lex's peace offering before taking his outstretched hand.

First she looked at her mother, who nodded her head in encouragement. Then she turned to Zeke, as if telepathically asking for his opinion.

"Ah, Lex is pretty cool," Zeke said, forcing a straight face. "I'd shake on it if I were you, give him a chance. Bet you could get him to throw in a trip to the zoo, since he thinks you're so cute."

That seemed to convince her. Jabbering about the zoo, she took Lex's hand in her tiny palm and shook it from side to side.

"The zoo it is, then, tomorrow afternoon," he said, smiling. "Hey, you gonna eat your pizza before it gets cold? I'm awful hungry and might have to eat your piece if you don't finish it."

Zoey giggled and hopped back on Zeke's lap. Convinced that Lex wouldn't mutate into a horrifying monster in front of her little eyes, she warmed up to him.

"I wike you funny talk," Zoey complimented Lex, then popped a cheesy pepperoni into her mouth.

"I think she means your New York accent. I sort of like it myself." Harlie leaned over to whisper in his ear. "Especially when you're saying those personal things to me, like last night. Remember?"

Zoey shifted her gaze from her plate to her mom and Lex. "Why you face turn pink, Wex?" Zeke choked on his pizza.

After dinner, Lex gave Zeke the key to his suite and asked him to check on Mugsy. The couple turned in early, going to bed as soon as Zoey was down for the evening. It was fortunate she was such a sound sleeper, since all the moaning and heavy breathing coming from the bedroom would have been hard to explain.

The next morning, Harlie finished her bookkeeping while Lex made a trip to the hotel to change his clothes. Musgy met him at the door and plopped his food bowl down on top of Lex's foot.

"I'll make it up to you, Mugsy, ole boy." Lex bent to pet the dog. He might score some brownie points with Zoey if he brought the pooch along for the afternoon. Plus, Mugsy would enjoy the fresh air and sunshine after spending so much time in the suite.

He grabbed a canvas tote with 'Doggie Bag' embroidered on the front. Inside were some of Mugsy's chew toys, a box of treats, a pooper scooper, cans of the only brand of dog food he would eat, and his leash. After the dog finished his lunch, Lex washed out the dish and added it to the rest of his stuff.

Zoey was ready and waiting, jumping up and down, jabbering a mile a minute when Lex arrived. He hoped her excitement had something to do with seeing him, but figured it had more to do with the zoo trip and the dog wagging its tail at the end of the leash.

"She's been sitting here by the door waiting for you for the past forty-five minutes. She's so excited." Harlie slid her arms around his neck. "I missed you," she whispered before their lips met. With the little girl beside them, they pulled themselves apart sooner than they would have liked. Zoey, lavishing her attention on the dog, wouldn't have noticed if the couple danced around the room stark naked.

"So this must be Mugsy." Harlie stooped to pet the dog's head. "Does he usually like kids?" She frowned at the indignant glare the dog seemed to be shooting at her daughter.

Lex assured Harlie that Mugsy was harmless. Zoey planted a big kiss between his bulging bulldog eyes, then nuzzled his nose with hers. Harlie moved in their direction but stopped when the dog seemed to warm to all the affection, wagging his tail and licking the toddler's cheek.

"Looks like our babies are gonna be pals." A smile spread across Lex's face as he watched the cute scene at his feet.

The fun afternoon at the zoo left Zoey exhausted when bedtime rolled around. Lex sang her a lullaby as she fell asleep, a happy song about ice cream mountains and cotton candy clouds he wrote for his own daughter, Tasha, when she was about Zoey's age.

That evening, they decided Lex would spend the rest of his stay at Harlie's house instead of the hotel. Since neither could bear the thought of separation,

they avoided the topic of his upcoming trip to Los Angeles as much as possible. The hotel delivered his lug-
gage the next morning.

Lex and Harlie made the most of the next five days,
with Zeke's mammoth shadow looming close behind
whenever they ventured out in public. Randi and Louie
joined the couple for supper at the Garrett's home
Thursday evening to give Harlie's family and Lex a
chance to get acquainted. Her parents were a little surprised to learn their daughter's new beau was only ten
years their junior and fifteen years older than Harlie,
but everyone seemed to hit it off pretty well.

Pete pulled his daughter aside after dinner, to have
a word with her in private.

"I know it's Jack's weekend for visitation, so why
don't you let me drop Zoey off at her dad's tomorrow
afternoon? That way you won't have to bother with
seeing the son of a bitch."

"I'd hate for you to go to any trouble, Daddy."

"No trouble at all. I'd be happy to," Pete insisted.
"The last thing I want is for Jack to come around stirring things up for you."

"Thank you." Harlie gave her dad a big hug, grateful he was looking out for her. "I've been dreading it."

"We better head back to the living room before your
mom sends out a search party," Pete said. "Lex seems

like a nice guy. Just remember, he's the one that's lucky to have you."

With Lex dressed in jeans and his ball cap, he and Harlie made a trip to the grocery Friday night. They waited until after midnight to avoid running into any fans who might spot him. Lex put his arm around Harlie's waist in the dairy section, whispering lewd suggestions in her ear about the things they could do with a couple cans of ReddiWhip. With a grin on her blushing face, Harlie grabbed four cans before pushing their cart up to the register to check out.

Lex handed the sales clerk his MasterCard. Harlie giggled in his ear, amused because the girl waiting on them wore a FireStorm T-shirt. In the past week, Harlie had nearly forgotten his celebrity status, until the shirt with Lex's face plastered across it reminded her just how famous he was.

The sales girl, identified by her nametag as Tori, overheard part of the conversation. She read the name on the credit card in her hand, looked Lex up and down, then proceeded to ricochet around her station, screaming in an earsplitting monotone, "Oh my God! Oh my God! It's really you! I'm FireStorm's biggest fan and you're the lead singer! I can't believe it. Please, can I have your autograph? Oh my God!"

The outburst stunned Harlie at first. Then she realized that had she been behind the counter in Tori's place, she would most likely have acted a fool herself.

Lex seemed unruffled about the whole thing. "Calm down, and then I'll give you an autograph, okay. You have to quit yelling first."

Tori searched under the counter for a Sharpie and a piece of cardboard. After Lex signed it, she yelled at her friend stocking shelves. "Come over here and meet Lex Callatori, the guy from FireStorm!"

Within fifteen seconds, everyone in the store gathered around them, begging for autographs. Two teenage girls left the group to search for Stix.

Harlie gripped Lex's left arm to keep from being pushed aside by the swarm of FireStorm aficionados. She wished Zeke had been with them, but they hadn't thought security was necessary in the middle of the night while they shopped for whipped cream and dog food. Ten minutes into this mayhem, the manager came out to see what all the commotion was about. He apologized for the clerk's unprofessional behavior and refused to accept payment for their purchase. Lex signed the last autograph before store security escorted them to their car. Now Harlie understood the need for bodyguards.

"Hello." Silence poured from the receiver. "Hello, who is this?" Harlie repeated, a bit annoyed. The person on the other end of the line didn't say a word, but then music, a FireStorm song, sounded in the background. "If you can't say anything, please don't call anymore."

She hung up the phone and slid back into bed. "That was our shy caller again."

"Whoever it is sure has bad timing," Lex said as Harlie snuggled next to him. "That damn phone either rings in the middle of the night to wake us up, or as soon as the bedroom light goes out."

"I think it's one of your fans. This time they cranked up one of your songs." Harlie kissed his neck. "You must have an admirer."

Apprehension clouded Lex's face. "This couldn't be your ex, could it?"

"Jack, make anonymous calls? No way. He's more the type to call ten times in a row, cussing me at the top of his lungs." She trailed kisses down the other side of his neck. "Anyway, the Caller ID said it was an unknown cell. Probably some kid with a crush who tracked you down."

Harlie and Lex, occupied with each other, soon put the strange calls out of their minds. The person who made the calls, however, did not forget about them.

Chapter Nine

All was fine in Harlie's world until Sunday rolled around. Jack was supposed to drop Zoey off at the Garrett's house, then Pete and Roxanne would take her out for ice cream before they brought her home. That being the plan, Lex and Harlie were taking advantage of their privacy that afternoon—all over the living room floor, shades pulled and candles flickering—when the doorbell rang.

"Come back here, baby." Lex groaned as Harlie jumped off him and threw on her T-shirt and shorts. "Maybe they'll go away."

"I have to see who it is. Keep that spot warm for me, though," she said, shooting him a wicked grin. Headed toward the door, she paused to look back at him. "Uh, are you just gonna sit there, naked, while I open the door? What if it's a pack of door-to-door holy rollers?"

Lex stood up and kissed her cheek. "I'll stand in the hall while you get rid of 'em, but please, baby, make it quick. And if it is somebody who wants to know if you've found Jesus, tell 'em he's in the backyard between a goat and some snake handlers who got here first. Then I'll jump out and do a naked hootchie dance. That should scare 'em off."

"That would explain the candles, I guess." She laughed as Lex, jeans slung across his arm, disappeared around the corner, his stiff penis wobbling from side to side as he strutted across the room.

Harlie squinted through the peephole to see who to blame for interrupting their love romp on the rug.

"Oh shit." Her ex-husband stood on the other side of the door. Pretending no one was home seemed like a good idea, until she saw Zoey standing beside him. *Damn it!* Now she had no choice.

After a deep calming breath, Harlie opened the door and stood in the foot-wide crack so Jack couldn't barge his way in. "Hi, Zoey. Did you have a good time with Daddy this weekend?" she asked, her tone loud and happy as she forced a smile for the child's benefit. Then she turned to face Jack. "Why are you here? You know my folks expect you to bring Zoey to their house, or did that slip your mind?"

"I think we need to talk. Zoey's been telling me all kinds of interesting things I think you need to elaborate on." Jack's smug face loomed inches from hers. "Stuff about that asswipe FireStorm singer staying here all the time, and something about a bald giant with a mutt. Let me in. I don't want the neighbors to hear all the lurid details." He took a step toward the threshold.

Harlie blocked him by stepping out onto the porch. "Go on in, Zoey. We'll go to Nana's house later. They're gonna take you out for ice cream. Won't that be fun! Okay, you go play for a while." She said this loud enough for her house guest to hear, pretty sure he'd had plenty of time to put his pants on.

She willed her voice not to shake as she turned back to face Jack. "We'll talk out here. You know you're not welcome in my home. And the neighbors couldn't care less about anything you have to say. So? What the hell do you want to know?" Hands on her hips, she stood in front of the door, nervously tapping her foot.

"Out with it, Harlie. Are you screwing that Fire-Storm prick or not? And what about all that shit Zoey's been saying?"

"I've started a *relationship* with Lex, if that's what you mean. We've been seeing a lot of each other lately." Harlie's voice echoed both defiance and caution. "The giant she mentioned would be one of his bodyguards, and Lex has a dog named Mugsy that Zoey just loves to play with. Is that it?"

"You fucking slut! I don't want my daughter near a bunch of longhaired dope addicts. You're not screwing that motherfucker anymore, do you hear me? Go call your little boyfriend and break it off right this second or you'll be sorry, you damn whore!" Jack had been yelling up to this point, but now he spoke in a lethal whisper. "To start with, I'll take the kid away from you."

"I hate to break this to you, Jack, but we are divorced. That means you have no control over my life, whatsoever. I will see Lex as much as I want, any time I want, and there's not a damn thing you can do about it. I have custody because you're a violent bastard and I'm a good mother. As for my 'little boyfriend' as you called him, he's a much bigger man than you could ever dream of being, and you can take that comment anyway you want." Harlie quivered with outrage as well as fear. Her eyes blared as she added, forcing her calmest go-to-hell voice, "You're not God, I'm not your property, and this was a free country the last time I checked, so you can kiss my sweet Southern ass."

Jack looked like he'd swallowed a golf ball. His eyes bulged out of his head, his face turned a deep shade of purple, and the veins in his neck stood out like snakes burrowed beneath his skin.

"You stupid bitch!" he growled through gritted teeth as he swung a punch at her face. She saw it coming and ducked. His fist bounced off the wooden door. Crouched down with her arms covering her head in anticipation of the next blow, Harlie hoped he'd broken his hand.

She felt hands on her shoulders lifting her to her feet. *Why did I have to be such a smartass? I'm so stupid.* Harlie lowered her arms and turned her head to the side, eyes tightly closed. If she was about to have the living shit beaten out of her again, she was prepared to take it without giving Jack the satisfaction of seeing the terror in her eyes. A few seconds passed without any blows, so she cautiously opened her eyes. Surprised to see Lex holding her, she hugged him in gratitude and relief.

"You're okay, baby, I'm here. Go in the house and call the law." His gaze shifted to Jack, who stood to the side rubbing his bloody knuckles. Lex looked the man up and down, then straight in the eyes. "You better call an ambulance, too."

Harlie disappeared into the house but watched them through the open door.

"You like to hit girls, pretty boy?" Lex snarled. "Try to take a piece of me, you fuckin' bastard." Lex landed a punch on Jack's jaw.

Jack retaliated with a wild blow aimed at the rock star's head. Lex blocked it with his left arm, then used his right to jab Jack's nose, remembering it was his weak spot. He fell to the porch in pain, his bleeding face covered with both hands as he tried unsuccessfully to regain some composure and stand up. Lex had been in plenty of street fights growing up in New York and knew how to handle himself. Jack, on the other hand, was only good for using women as punching bags.

"If you *ever* hurt Harlie again, in any way, I will fucking kill you." An ominous shadow enveloped Jack as Lex bent over him. Lex slowly and clearly articulated every syllable so there would be no room for misinterpretation. "Hit her again, push her, step on her big toe, you'll be a dead man. I'm not blowing smoke up your ass, either. I fucking mean it. Do you understand me?"

Lex would not move until Jack looked him in the face and said yes.

A siren's screech from down the street announced the police car headed toward Harlie's brick house. Sheriff Maxwell Roberts found Jackson Steele squatting in the middle of the porch, covered in his own blood, cradling his nose.

"You all right, Harlie?" Relief flickered in Roberts's eyes when he saw that she was shaken but unharmed. "What's going on here?"

"Is *she* alright? Look what that cocksucker did to my nose," Jack complained, pointing to his own face.

"You had it coming. Not another word out of you." The sheriff read him his rights, then listened to Harlie and Lex explain what happened.

"It's nice to see that you're taking care of this girl. She sure deserves some good in her life after putting up with him. Nice to meet you." Sheriff Roberts extended his hand to Lex. "Are you going to press charges, Harlie? You can get him for breaking the restraining order and assault, since he swung at you."

"You bet I'm pressing charges. I appreciate that you got here so quickly. Thanks." This was the same officer who took Jack to jail the day he'd beaten her so badly for leaving him. She hoped his stay behind bars would be longer this time.

Handcuffed in the back of the police car, Jack glared back at the couple on the porch, hatred burning in his eyes. Lex, his arm draped around Harlie, flipped him the bird as the car pulled out of the driveway.

The sheriff seemed to think the gesture was pretty damn funny. He laughed even harder when Jack said, "I'll show them one of these days. That big-lipped son of a bitch."

"Yeah, son, you go ahead," Roberts said. "Then he can kick your punk ass again. You deserved everything he gave you, and then some."

Back inside the house, Harlie's first concern was Zoey, hoping she hadn't witnessed any of the violence. Lex had handled things perfectly, taking charge of the situation as soon as he learned Harlie's ex was at the door. He told Zoey Mugsy missed her and was waiting to have a tea party in the playroom. When she ran to see the dog, Lex switched on the television—turning up the volume to drown out the racket from outside—

then went to Harlie's defense. He'd opened the door right after she dodged Jack's fist.

Lex peeped into the playroom, then returned to the worried mother seated on the couch. "Zoey's fine."

"What would I do without you?" Harlie melted into him and broke down sobbing on his shoulder. "You took care of Zoey, you saved my ass, and you slugged Jack while I just stood there like a big stupid fool. I shouldn't have been so mouthy. It's all my fault. I'm *so* sorry you had to get involved in that." She was more worried that Jack could have hurt Lex than the fact she'd almost had her head knocked off.

"Hey, you didn't do anything wrong so please, *please* stop apologizing to me." Lex took Harlie's chin in his hands, turning her head so she would have to look at him. "I'm just glad I was here to help. Remember what I said that night at Mr. Woo's? Well, I meant every word of it. I will *never* let anyone hurt you again, baby. I love you, and Zoey, and I'm here for you. Everything is going to be okay."

"He didn't hurt you, did he?" Harlie took his hands in her own, inspecting them to make sure he hadn't bruised his knuckles on Jack's face. She covered his fingers with loving kisses before looking back up at him. "I haven't even thanked you yet for rescuing me out there. Thank you," she whispered in gratitude.

"You don't need to thank me. It broke my heart when I saw that expression on your face. You were braced for a beating, but you never even screamed for help." Lex's voice shook with emotion. "My soul ached for you, realizing this was your conditioned response to all the abuse you went through over the years with that sadistic asshole. None of that was your fault, and I'll never let it happen again. Not while I'm still breathing."

Lex held her in his arms while he phoned her parents to explain what happened. Harlie knew they'd be worried since Zoey hadn't shown up on time. Pete handed the phone to his wife and headed straight for his shotgun before Lex could explain that Jack was in the county jail. Luckily, Roxanne managed to stop him before he reached the front door.

The Garretts rushed over. They needed to see their daughter with their own eyes to make sure she was okay.

"I couldn't get the image of how you looked after your last showdown with Jack out of my mind," Roxanne said through tears. Harlie broke down again, embarrassed and humiliated, blaming herself for Jack's violence.

"How can I ever thank you for what you did today? My blood runs cold thinking about what would have happened to my girl if you hadn't been here." Still beside himself with rage, Pete shook Lex's hand, then hugged him. "I wish I'd killed that son of a bitch years ago."

Pete and Roxanne took Zoey home with them for the night so Harlie could collect herself.

Harlie's nerves were a shaken mess, but Lex's arms felt like a safe haven to her. Cuddled next to him, she reflected on how much things had changed for the better over the past two weeks. With Lex beside her, she felt loved, protected, and safe. She desperately hoped nothing else would come along to rip the joy from her life.

Chapter Ten

Three days later, Harlie watched a plane taxi down the runway carrying Lex, Mugsy, and Zeke to Los Angeles. The other three members of FireStorm had flown ahead to California for a few days of fun in the sun before their live television appearance. Lex was a perfectionist when it came to music, so the band most likely wanted to enjoy their vacation before he arrived cracking the proverbial whip.

One of FireStorm's songs played on the radio while Harlie drove home. Lex had taken off just twenty minutes before, but she already missed him like crazy. She hadn't felt this degree of separation anxiety, like a gaping hole had been ripped into her heart and filled with crushed ice, since Zoey's first visitation with Jack. At least she could still hear Lex's sultry voice over the airwaves, even if the rest of his body was flying through the clouds hundreds of miles away.

Harlie's fingers touched the gift Lex had given her

the previous night, and she daydreamed about their future. After the Nefarious Tour ended, they planned to move in together. They decided to spend three weeks a month at his penthouse in New York, with the remaining time spent at Harlie's home in Kentucky so she and Zoey wouldn't get homesick.

The only problem Harlie saw with the impending move centered around her daughter. Her lawyer would need to modify the custody arrangement, but with Jack's upcoming trial date, he was in no position to argue and wouldn't pose much of an obstacle. Harlie's main concern involved babysitters and the fact that she never left Zoey with anyone besides her family and Randi. She didn't know anyone in New York City and the prospect of leaving Zoey with a paid stranger scared Harlie to death.

Lex had eased her mind by telling her about his Italian housekeeper of the past twenty years. "Luisa used to help me take care of my daughter, so she's always been like a grandmother to Tasha. She's a sweet lady, plus she can whip up the best zabaglione you ever tasted. Don't worry about anything until you've met her. If for any reason you're not comfortable with Luisa babysitting, I'll get Tasha to come over and watch Zoey whenever we need her to."

That complication sort of out of the way, Lex surprised her by pulling a small gift box from his pocket. "Here, baby. Just a little something to remember me by while I'm away."

Harlie ripped into the lemon yellow paper, wondering when Lex had had the time to go shopping. Inside the box was a dainty silver necklace with a small yin-yang dangling from its joining.

"Thank you! It's beautiful." She lifted it carefully, afraid of breaking the delicate links.

"When I think about us, our relationship and everything, the image of a yin-yang comes to mind. It symbolizes the way we belong together, our perfect fit. With us, everything balances out, like your beautiful face and my beastly looks." Lex grinned, caressing her cheek. "The good cancels out the bad. Know what I mean? Like you have no idea how beautiful you are, inside and out, while the only thing bigger than my ego is my dick. Did you see the inscription?"

Harlie was surprised so many words could fit on such a tiny pendant. The inscription read, *'Harlie, you're the other half of my soul, the yin to my yang. I love you, now and forever, Lex'.*

"I love it." Deeply touched by the sentiment, Harlie lifted her hair up so he could fasten the necklace around her neck. "Almost as much as I love you."

Lex adjusted the clasp, then showed her the matching charm hanging from a thicker chain around his own neck. Minus the inscription, of course.

Now, driving down the highway by herself, she listened to the low zipper-like hum the friction made as she slid the yin-yang slowly back and forth on the chain at her throat. She sang along with his voice on the radio.

That night, she found it impossible to fall asleep in her empty bed. The scent of Lex's cologne still clung to her sheets, a reminder of his absence. She didn't know how she would make it through the next week without him.

At two o'clock in the morning, Harlie gave up and tiptoed into Zoey's room to snuggle up beside her. With the words to Lex's lullaby playing softly in her head, she finally dozed off. Ice cream mountains and cotton candy clouds filled her dreams that night, along with a handsome man dressed in black leather who sang to her through the most luscious lips she'd ever seen.

Determined not to spend the week pining away for Lex, Harlie made a list of all the odd jobs that needed to be done around her house. If she organized the clutter now, it would make packing for the New York move easier when the time came.

With three loads of laundry folded and every nook and cranny in her kitchen spring-cleaned, Harlie decided to take a break when Zoey went down for a nap. The power button brought her laptop to life as Harlie realized she hadn't checked in with her computer friends during Lex's stay. She hoped Barb wasn't too upset about her absence, then laughed at Barb's message on her Facebook wall: 'Alone again, whoop-te-doo. I'll check in every so often, in the off chance you may stop by. Something you haven't taken the time for in the last 2 weeks. :('

A quick glance under Facebook's friends online section showed a little green dot beside Barbed*Ivy's icon, which featured a Jimmy Choo pump wrapped in, what else, pink barbed wire. Barb used the same screen name on everything, but Harlie's Facebook page was under Harlie Dawn Steele. Happy to find her online, Harlie opened up the private chat/message feature and typed in 'Well, I'm here now. Sorry!'

Barbed*Ivy pulled herself away from FarmVille to respond a few minutes later. The two clacked away at their keyboards for a while, and Barb wanted to know what she'd been up to. Harlie summarized the highlights, glossing over the incident with Jack but making sure Barb knew how Lex had gallantly stepped in to protect her.

A delivery boy rang the doorbell while Harlie stood cooking Sloppy Joes for supper later that evening. She signed for the shoebox-sized package and guessed that Lex must have sent her another gift, as if the necklace she hadn't taken off since he fastened the clasp wasn't enough.

She opened the parcel and carefully sliced the brown packing tape with her butterfly knife. A puzzled frown replaced Harlie's excited expression when she pulled back the layers of tissue paper. Inside was a black rose, sharp thorns still intact, she noticed as she pricked her finger. Underneath the flower were a red-headed Barbie and a Ken doll, long dark hair glued on top of its head, Nefarious written on its shirt with white puff paint. She tried to lift the two figures but discovered they were somehow attached to the box. The reason became clear when she turned the container on its end. Stapled to the top of the box, a double-ended noose connected the two tiny throats. Red paint trickled from the corners of their mouths. Chill bumps dotted Harlie's flesh as she stared at the diorama, stunned at the sight of herself and Lex hanged in effigy.

Trembling fingers ripped open the card she found beneath the dangling doll feet. Harlie read the typed note aloud, "Sometimes dreams really do come true. You have your fantasy. Soon, I'll have mine. Watch out."

What the hell was that supposed to mean? Who could be warped enough to send such a thing to her home?

One name popped into Harlie's head.

"Jack, you son of a bitch!" Even after getting his ass

kicked and spending the night in jail, it looked like he still hadn't learned his lesson. Angry and shaken, she wondered why he couldn't just leave her alone. Jack had gone too far with this stunt, even for him.

Harlie jerked the receiver to her ear and dialed Jack's number, intent on giving him the cussing of a lifetime. Before it had a chance to ring, she hit the disconnect button, her promise to her lawyer resonant in her memory: no contact of any kind, for any reason, under any circumstances, or it could invalidate the restraining order.

She dialed Lex's cell instead, left a short message on his voicemail, then paced around the room waiting for him to return her call.

FireStorm was in the middle of rehearsal, but Lex cut the session short to phone Harlie. The instant he felt his cell—always set on vibrate mode while he jammed with the band—he knew something was wrong. Intuition twisted his gut as he rushed to the dressing room, Zeke close on his heels.

Every nerve in Lex's body tensed while he listened to Harlie describe the care package, livid that Jack could do something like this. As she read the card to him, her voice betrayed the anxiety she tried to hide. "'Sometimes dreams really do come true. You have your fantasy. Soon, I'll have mine. Watch out.' Lex, what do you think he means? I can't make any sense out of this."

"I don't know what the sick fuck meant, but he's the one who'd better watch out. I'll shove his goddamn Barbie dolls down his throat," Lex vowed, shaking with rage. It appeared that Mr. Steele was begging to get his ass kicked again. His tone softened. "Don't worry about it, baby. I won't let anything happen to you."

His first impulse was to jump on a plane, fly to Kentucky, and guard Harlie himself, holding her in his arms all night long to make sure nothing happened to her. But then he remembered his live television appearance scheduled for the following evening, and the last leg of the Nefarious Tour; both were impossible to cancel without landing FireStorm in a lawsuit. He knew Harlie wasn't able to come out to California, since she had to meet with her lawyer to discuss both the custody matter involved in her upcoming move and the assault charges against Jack. If Lex couldn't personally be there to watch out for her, he would do the next best thing.

"Hold on a minute, baby." Lex turned to face the only man he trusted with the job. "Zeke, *paisan*, how soon can you pack?"

Harlie kept her promise to Lex by calling the police to document the threat and have the package taken for evidence. Someone knocked on her door soon after.

"Hi Sheriff Roberts." Harlie held the door open for him. "Come in."

"Just call me Max." He took a close look at the macabre package and note, an expression of disgust crossing his usually pleasant features. "Well, we can add terroristic threatening to Jack's list of charges after this doll mutilation, so long as we can prove he did it. I'll haul his butt in for questioning first thing in the morning." He paused on his way out. "I'll be happy to send a patrol car by to check on you later, if that would make you feel any safer."

She politely declined, and explained that Lex was sending someone.

Zeke arrived shortly after midnight. With fresh sheets on the sofa bed, Harlie heated up the leftover Sloppy Joes for him. He might be on FireStorm's payroll, but Harlie considered Zeke to be a friend doing her a favor. She planned to treat him like a guest in her home, especially since he'd had to fly all this way because of her. While she watched him chow down on the sandwiches and chips, she called Lex to let him know the bodyguard arrived safely.

The next morning, Zoey was delighted to find Zeke in the living room. The two kept each other entertained for the duration of his stay. They made quite an unusual pair playing Zoey's favorite games and watching cartoons.

Mrs. Jenkins sat on her porch across the street. She couldn't figure out who the very large bald man was who gave Zoey piggyback rides around the yard.

"Oh well," the elderly lady said to the cat curled up on her lap. "First rock stars, now professional wrestlers, I guess. Maybe next week we'll wake up to see Barnum and Bailey's three-ring circus across the street, complete with acrobats and a freak show. Nothing would shock me anymore. And that Harlie seemed like such a quiet, sensible young lady too."

Chapter Eleven

Friday evening, everyone gathered around the TV in the Garretts' living room. Louie, Harlie, Zoey, and Zeke—who said he was beginning to feel like part of the family, due to all the Southern hospitality Harlie had heaped on him the past couple of days—had been invited over for dinner. After dessert, everyone sat and waited for the main attraction to commence.

The television special *Let's Hear It for the Hits* came on, a tribute to music from the past with contemporary bands paying homage to their favorite oldies. Before he cut to commercial break, host Jammin' Johnny Sunset gave a rundown of all the guests slated to appear on the live broadcast.

"This is so exciting!" Roxanne sat on the edge of her chair when a shot of Lex crooning into his mic flashed across the screen. "To think we're seeing someone on television who actually had his feet under my supper table!"

After the first three acts, Jammin' Johnny announced, "Up next, FireStorm. Front man Lex Callatori just informed me of an impromptu song change, but first, a message from our sponsors."

Everyone fidgeted through a McDonald's commercial, a woman testifying to the cleansing power of Clorox, and an embarrassing endorsement for tampons before the program resumed. Zoey clapped her hands and bounced on her grandpa's knee, exclaiming, "Wex on TV! Wex on TV!"

A close-up of Lex's handsome face filled the television screen. He addressed the audience after introducing the band. "We were originally supposed to perform Elvis Presley's 'Jailhouse Rock', but decided to go a different route. Tonight we're going to demystify one of the greatest songs in rock 'n' roll history, the only classic hit where everyone recognizes the tune, but nobody knows the lyrics. This number goes out to my new friend, Pete Garrett, who just happens to have the most beautiful daughter in the world. This is his favorite song, made famous by the Kingsmen in 1963. 'Louie, Louie' . . . Come on, boys! A one, a two. A one, two, three, four . . . ."

Harlie, reeling from the nationally broadcast compliment, turned to catch her father's reaction. His face was split from ear to ear with the biggest, silliest grin she'd ever seen. "Well, I'll be," was the only thing Pete managed to spit out, but his foot tapped in time to the beat.

To say Dylan Malone's opening guitar licks did justice to the song was an understatement. Utilizing the whammy bar to glorify the bluesy spin he put on it, the tune kept the intrinsic quality that made it a hit over forty years ago, at the same time rejuvenating it with a modern edge that only FireStorm could pull off.

Lex's phenomenal voice articulated each syllable in raunchy perfection. The only deviations he made from Richard Berry's original lyrics were to substitute 'I's for the 'me's, and alluding to the blue moon of Kentucky rather than the original Jamaican one.

The last chorus ended and the crowd went crazy. In his flamboyant stage persona, Lex asked, "What do ya say? You want to hear it one more time?"

When the mob roared, Jammin' Johnny gave the thumbs up for FireStorm's encore. Lex danced around the stage with even more vim and vigor the second time, putting on a floor show of acrobatics that ended with the splits during Stix's drum solo. Since the segment ran long, they had to cut to commercial during the second verse.

Harlie knew beyond doubt that Lex had earned himself a place in her father's heart. First by rescuing her from Jack's attack, now by honoring Pete on the show with intelligible lyrics to his favorite song—the one he'd named his son after.

"The next time Lex is in town," Pete said, still awestruck, "tell him he can use my bike. So he won't have to rent a car."

No one, not even Harlie or Louie, had ever been given permission to drive Pete's Harley Davidson, his cherry prized possession. The only higher honor Pete could have bestowed on Lex would have been to adopt him.

FireStorm's concert in Anaheim the next evening went just as well. They rocked the auditorium, called back by the cheering crowd to perform two encores. Critics penned rave reviews even before the band left the stage.

Although Zeke was hundreds of miles away with Harlie, there was no shortage of FireStorm security backstage. Before he walked out to his rental car, Lex told the two bodyguards accompanying him to take the rest of the night off. The concert ended well over an hour before, so everybody had pretty much cleared out of the stadium while he showered, changed into street clothes, and ate a huge meal of catered ham, mashed potatoes, corn, biscuits, and three different kinds of pie. Food was always written into the contract, depending on whatever the manager had a craving for when he arranged the gig.

He passed a man in drab green coveralls with the

stadium logo printed on the back. "How's it going, man." The janitor, busy sweeping the private parking garage with an industrial-sized broom, responded with a shrug as he continued his job.

Lex smiled to himself as his ringed hand reached to open the car door. He thought of Harlie, her red hair illuminated by moonlight, walking beside him through the meadow. That night they'd first made love in the old barn seemed magical to him. He could almost smell the sweet aroma of hay when, suddenly, everything went black around him.

Caught up in his memories, Lex hadn't seen the man in the janitor's uniform sneak up behind him. The thick wooden handle had been unscrewed from the broom, then used to club the singer in the back of his head. Dressed in the uniform he'd stolen that afternoon, he struck Lex twice more to make certain he wouldn't come to any time soon. With strength unusual for a man his size, the assailant placed Lex in the passenger seat and propped his head against the window.

They left unnoticed, en route to carry out a madman's twisted plot.

One hour later, at approximately 1:32 in the morning, the manager of a 7-Eleven in Anaheim went out to the parking lot to investigate what his last customer had told him. Apparently, some junkie pulled off the highway and passed out behind the wheel. If that were true, he'd have to call the cops and fill out a load of bullshit paperwork before he could go home. He approached the vehicle thinking how bad his job sucked.

"Hey, buddy. You all right?" The clerk used his index finger to poke the guy slumped in the seat. He thought the unconscious man looked familiar, but he couldn't quite place the face. Since his prodding got no response, he returned to the store to phone 911.

When the police and ambulance arrived, Lex Callatori was still out cold. Authorities on the scene found a vodka bottle in his right hand and fresh track marks on his left arm. The two vials of heroin in the pocket of his leather jacket suggested an overdose. No syringe was found but a black rose lay on the dash. One officer swore under his breath when he pricked his finger on a thorn.

An officer opened Lex's wallet and took out his driver's license. His eyes widened when he read the name of the strung-out mess in the red sedan. Probably hoping to get his picture in the morning paper, he gave the ambulance a police escort all the way to the hospital.

Chapter Twelve

A little past five o'clock Sunday morning, noise ripped Harlie from a sound sleep. She reached for the phone on her nightstand but plopped her head back down on the pillow when she heard Zeke's deep "Hello" come from the living room down the hall.

Minutes later, he knocked on Harlie's bedroom door.

"Yeah, Zeke, come in." She propped herself up on one elbow, ran a hand through her tousled hair, and tried to focus her sleepy eyes.

Zeke stuck his head in the room and nervously stroked his goatee. "Um, sorry to have to bother you so early but your dad's on the phone."

"Do you know what he wants?" She pulled her robe on over her shorts and cotton T-shirt. A frown scrunched her forehead when she noticed the time on the bedside clock. "Is something wrong?"

Harlie knew her parents woke up at the crack of dawn every day, but they never called her or anyone else before eight o'clock. It just wasn't polite.

"Pete just needs to talk with you about somethin'," Zeke said, his gaze aimed at his size fifteen shoes.

More worried with each passing second, Harlie followed him down the hall to the living room and the phone sitting on the end table. Zeke handed her the remote control, which seemed a bit strange. If he wanted to watch television, why didn't he turn it on himself?

"Morning Daddy. What's going on?" she asked, clutching the receiver.

"Harlie, I'm afraid I've got some bad news." Pete spoke calmly, but she could tell the gravity of the situation from his tone.

"Is Mom all right? How's Grandma?"

"They're fine. Me and Roxanne were sitting here a minute ago, drinking our coffee when the anchorman on *Wake Up America* said the next story was about Lex. Is your TV on?"

Harlie fumbled with the remote in her hands, changing her set to the news broadcast. "What happened? Please, just spit it out."

"The story's up next." Pete sighed into the receiver. "All we know so far is that he's in the hospital from a drug overdose. I'm sorry, Harlie."

"Well, there has to be some mistake. That just can't be true," Harlie insisted, confused but now fully awake. They both fell silent as the program resumed.

Harlie sat on the floor and turned up the volume. A

FireStorm video played on the monitor beside the anchorman's head as he reported the story.

"In Anaheim, California, early this morning, Lex Callatori, lead singer for the rock band FireStorm, was found unconscious in a car parked in a convenience store parking lot. An open container of alcohol was in his hand and numerous vials of heroin were found in the vehicle."

The monitor switched to a still picture of Lex, obviously snapped during one of his live performances. His long hair stood out like a lion's mane around his head, his face frozen in a bizarre expression that made him look psychotic.

"Callatori was transported to an Anaheim hospital where his condition has been upgraded from critical to stable. It is yet unclear as to whether the heroin overdose was accidental," the newsman paused for dramatic emphasis, "or an attempt to take his own life . . . . In other news this morning-"

Harlie clicked the television off and tried to make sense of the words she'd just heard. Not sure what to believe, her queasy stomach twisted itself into knots.

"They said heroin." Harlie spoke out loud to no one in particular.

She picked up her phone conversation with her father. "Don't you have to use needles to shoot up with that?" Her shoulders relaxed when Pete said yes. "No way. Lex hates needles. He told me so. I don't have any idea what happened out there, but no way am I going to believe he got drunk and shot himself up with drugs in some parking lot. Not without proof."

Harlie turned to the bodyguard seated on his make-shift bed. "Zeke, have you ever known him to use hero-in? What do you think went down last night?"

"You're right about Lex being afraid of needles. And he hasn't touched drugs in years." Zeke shook his head, noticeably worried about his boss. "He drinks, but I've never seen him get drunk and drive a car. Nev-er. I think somebody set him up."

"Oh my God." Harlie raked her fingers through her hair, then held a handful in a lopsided ponytail at the crown of her head. "I have to go to him."

She couldn't stand the thought of Lex, hurt and alone, lying in some cold hospital room. The possibility of his not making it was too upsetting to contemplate. She couldn't imagine her life without him.

She asked her father to come get Zoey, then hung up so Zeke could make some calls to find out more about the situation. Harlie changed clothes and tossed some things into her suitcase, unsure of what she should take and too upset to give it much thought.

Zeke hung up the phone as she returned to the liv-ing room. He'd gotten through to FireStorm's manag-er, Stan Fredrick, who also thought things sounded suspicious. Fredrick was concerned that Lex still hadn't regained consciousness.

"I booked two tickets to California but the flight takes off in a few hours. Is that okay?"

"That's fine. Thanks, I appreciate you taking care of the details." Harlie had never flown before and wasn't sure how to go about getting tickets. "You want some breakfast before we go?"

"No thanks, we can get a bite on the plane. Hey, Harlie." A grin spread over Zeke's worried features. "You might want to leave that pocket knife of yours at home. We have to go through metal detectors at the airport and it might be a little embarrassing if they arrested you for carrying a concealed weapon."

The flight to California was an experience Harlie, who'd never felt the desire to venture into the wild blue yonder, didn't exactly find thrilling. The concept of a vehicle that weighed thousands of pounds, was bigger than a football field, and had no feathers yet soared high above the earth at breakneck speed was completely illogical to her mind. She kept thinking the plane should, by all the rules of gravity she'd learned in elementary school, drop out of the sky like a rock at any minute.

The flight attendant brought her a nice stiff drink when she saw Harlie sitting there, wide-eyed and silent, clutching the arms of her seat in a white-knuckled death grip. To Zeke's amusement, Harlie knocked back the booze, then downed two more just like it. For a while, the tasty concoctions helped ease her fear of flying. She even relaxed enough to swap raunchy jokes with her traveling companion.

Zeke raised an eyebrow when the flight attendant offered to bring Harlie another round. "You sure you need that?"

"Oh yes, thank you, sure do." Harlie punctuated the sentence with a hiccup. "This stuff is helping my nerves." She didn't realize the fruit-flavored cocktails contained a large amount of vodka, a substance that never agreed with Harlie's delicate digestive system.

Her stomach flip-flopped out of control when the plane approached the airport. She spent the last half hour of her first flight in the john, puking her guts up.

The stewardess must have heard her heaving in the restroom. She smiled sympathetically and handed Harlie a cold can of ginger ale as Zeke led her off the plane.

Later, standing in the hospital elevator, Harlie's stomach had settled but her heart beat like hummingbird wings. Although she hoped to find Lex's condition improved, she prepared herself for the worst. She could see the concern in Zeke's face and squeezed his hand as the doors parted on the third floor.

En route to Room 342, they spotted Stix in the lounge. He explained that Ray and Dylan had just left to grab a bite to eat, then filled them in on Lex's condition. Evidence of three blows to his head pretty much proved somebody attacked him. The doctors expected him to pull through, but weren't sure how much permanent damage, if any, his body had sustained. They couldn't tell if Lex's unconsciousness was due more to the concussion, the heroin, or a combination of the two.

"I'm sure your pretty face will be the first he'll want to see when he comes to." Stix flashed Harlie his Aussie smile. "Lex has done nothing but yammer on about you since he arrived in California. I can certainly see why."

Harlie tried to twist her mouth into a smile when Stix patted her arm in an attempt to comfort her. "Is it all right for me to see him now?"

Stix led them down the hallway to Lex's room.

"If Tasha rings again, you can take the call, mate." Stix directed this comment to Zeke. "When she heard her old man was on drugs again, she hit the bloody roof. Said I was a fuckhead to let him fall off the wagon, then proceeded to bless me out good. Lex better hope the doc can prove it wasn't his fault, if he doesn't want his daughter to rip him a new one."

Harlie got her first peek at him through the observation window beside the door, then went in alone. Pale and weak-kneed from the sight of his injured friend, Zeke headed to Lex's hotel to feed Mugsy and clean up the mess he'd probably made after being left unattended for so long.

He looked horrible, lying there with tubes and wires

connecting him to all sorts of medical contraptions. An IV dripped medication into one arm, an oxygen tube was up his nose, and the monitor beside the bed beeped with the rhythm of his heartbeat. This was the only time she'd seen his age show on his handsome face, now swollen and pale.

Seated in a bedside chair, Harlie took Lex's hand in her own. "I'm here, Lex. I love you." Her lip trembled as she lost the battle against tears she'd struggled so hard to hold back. "Please wake up."

Chapter Thirteen

She stayed glued by his side throughout the night, con-
stantly touching his hand or his cheek so he'd know she
was there next to him. After remembering an article
about comatose patients being able to hear everything
that went on around them, Harlie talked incessantly.
She reminisced about all the romantic interludes they'd
shared, daydreamed over how nice it was going to be to
wake up beside him every morning, chirped about how
cute Zoey and Mugsy looked playing in the yard, and
joked about the awful plane ride she took with Zeke.

When a nurse came in to change Lex's intravenous
bag early the next morning, Harlie was already awake.
She freshened her smudged makeup with cosmetics
she'd crammed in her purse during her packing frenzy
the day before. With her auburn curls twisted into a
ponytail, she decided to brush Lex's dark hair. By the
flattened state it was in, she knew nobody'd touched it
since he'd been admitted.

Brush in hand, she found the three goose eggs Stix had told her about near the crown and back of his head. Careful not to cause Lex any more pain, Harlie rearranged his hair. At least now he looked more like himself.

Deep in thought, Harlie jumped when someone tapped her shoulder.

"I hope this suits you." Stix handed her a box of Dunkin' Donuts and a Styrofoam cup of cappuccino. "I couldn't find any of that cocktail Zeke tells me you were so fond of on the plane."

"Damn." Harlie grinned at his joke. "Guess this'll just have to do for now. And I was so looking forward to barfing again. But thanks."

"Has there been any change?"

"Not really." Harlie's gaze darted back to Lex. The rise and fall of his chest reassured her that he was still breathing. "I've noticed some eye movement under his closed lids, but he's basically still the same."

"Let me tell you a story about our band's lone problem, to keep you from feeling sorry for Sleeping Beauty over there." Stix flashed his famous smile.

Harlie was grateful for any distraction he could offer. "Let me guess. Too many naked groupies?"

"Never a shortage of those, but you're close." Stix gave her a wink. "FireStorm's only complication was an ego problem, your boyfriend. He expected the spotlight to showcase him, in all his glory, ninety-eight percent of the time. Can you imagine?"

"Nah, shut up! Not my shy, quiet, insecure wallflower."

"Ah, your dancing eyes say you know him well," Stix said. "The problem came to a head onstage in a crowded nightclub one night. Lex noticed a pretty blonde flirting with me instead of him during the first set, and he was both jealous and insulted. After a double shot of bourbon between songs, he vented his anger at me. He got all flamboyant, clapped out the tempo he wanted, and then the bastard says, 'I could keep better time if I put drumsticks between my toes and kicked a fuckin' garbage can. If you can't keep up, I'll piss on your bass drum. Come on, pick up the beat.'"

"Ha!" Harlie's cappuccino had almost spewed out through her nose during Stix's impersonation. "That sounded just like him."

"Thanks darlin'. Anyway, Lex shook his head at the audience when the next song reached the chorus. He grimaced toward me, opened his fly, and stepped up to my drum set." Stix pantomimed that part. "He even let the microphone amplify the sound of his zipper for comedic effect. 'Can't say I didn't warn him,' he says, and the room erupted in laughter."

He glanced at his friend, now unconscious in the hospital bed, and grinned in spite of everything. "Lex was reaching for his, to hear him tell it, gargantuan penis when I jumped over the snare drum and tackled him to the ground. We tossed each other around the stage while Ray and Dylan raced to protect their gear from the brawl. The crowd cheered us on, thinking it was part of the act. Not to brag, but when he realized I was about to kick his ass in front of everyone, Lex apologized. Can't imagine anything would humiliate him more than getting knocked down a peg in front of his fans. Made him promise to spit shine the bass before I let him up. We shook hands, finished the show, and haven't exchanged a cross word to each other since. Whenever his ego climbs out of control, I remind him of that. 'Plan to take a piss, mate?' That's all I have to say to get him to tone it down a notch."

A nurse came in to check her patient's vitals. They watched her take his pulse and scribble in his chart before she left.

"Don't worry. I'm sure he'll come through all this just fine." Stix patted her hand. "He's too cocky and conceited to expect anything less." He gave her his cell number and asked her to call the minute Lex's condition changed.

Fortified by the donuts and coffee, Harlie walked around the room reading the cards on the flowers people had sent. When she came to a beautiful bouquet of lilacs from her parents, she took one of the fragrant purple blooms from the vase. On Lex's bed, she fanned the blossoms under his nose and wondered if he could smell their sweet perfume. She laid it on the pillow beside him, then leaned over to place a gentle kiss on his full lips. He twitched.

"I'm here, sweetheart." Movement under his closed lids made her think he was dreaming, but she hoped it was a response to the things going on around him instead. She lifted his pale hand to her lips and kissed it, then rubbed it against her own cheek, remembering all the times he'd caressed her face.

The first time Lex's eyes fluttered, Harlie feared it was only her imagination. As she sat watching him, a groan came from deep within his throat.

"That's it, Lex! Come on. Please wake up."

His eyelashes slowly parted, unveiling the chocolate brown irises hidden for so many hours. He cleared his throat, then his mouth moved in a laborious effort to speak. All that came out was a moan. He extended his unsteady arm and mumbled incoherently, "Mmmm angels, ss fa ss izz."

All the movie death scenes she'd ever seen flashed through Harlie's head. Her mind zeroed in on the black-and-white image of Shirley Temple lying in a large canopy bed, dressed in a beautiful nightgown, surrounded by her loved ones. Harlie remembered the way the small girl stretched her arms to the ceiling, saying the angels were calling her to heaven before she fell back on the bed, dead as a curly-haired doornail.

"No, Lex!" Harlie frantically pushed the button to summon the nurses. They ran to the room and found Harlie crying and shaking their patient by his shoulders. "Hang on. Don't you even think about dying on me! To hell with the damn angels! Come back to me. I love you so much, and you still have your whole life ahead of you-"

One of the nurses interrupted. "Miss, I need you to wait out in the hall."

"Like hell I will." Harlie had no intention of leaving what she believed to be Lex's deathbed.

The nurse grabbed her by the arms and gently pulled her backwards in an attempt to end her hysterics. Fueled by raw adrenaline coursing through her veins, Harlie broke loose and shoved the woman away from her, which sent the nurse sprawling across the tile floor.

"Move *away* from the light, Lex." Harlie knelt on the hospital bed, straddling the previously comatose patient. "Don't you die on me!"

An orderly asked her to stand aside, then grabbed Harlie's arm as the nurse got up from the floor and headed to assist.

"Why don't you just do your job? Save him and leave me alone," Harlie shouted, yanking her arm free. Her head hurt, her nerves were frazzled from the stress she'd been under, and she wasn't thinking straight. The only thing on her mind was Lex, and she refused to let herself be separated from him. Harlie drew back her hand, fully intent on coldcocking the nurse heading toward her if she had to.

Everyone on the floor who wasn't stone deaf heard the commotion in Room 342, including the members of FireStorm seated in the lounge and Zeke on duty outside the door. Afraid Lex may have taken a turn for the worst, they all stampeded into the room about the same time the nurse had hit the ground.

Luckily, Zeke got to Harlie in time and caught her fist mid-swing in the palm of his hand. He convinced her to stand at the foot of the bed while the medical team saw to Lex. Zeke stood beside her, holding her hand for moral support as the doctor examined his patient.

With Harlie under control, Dr. Cravitz stepped in to size up the situation. He shined a small light into Lex's eyes, took his pulse, and checked the monitors set up on both sides of the bed. "Nurse, what's that he's trying to say?"

The RN who'd skidded across the floor positioned her left ear in front of Lex's mouth. She listened, then focused her sarcastic gaze in Harlie's direction.

"I believe he said, 'My Angel, you're a sight for sore eyes.'"

It took these words a few seconds to sink in. Harlie locked her eyes on Lex for the duration of the doctor's examination, too relieved by his consciousness to think very hard about what a dumbass she must have looked like to the staff.

Dr. Cravitz announced his findings to the over-crowded room. "Mr. Callatori came through his ordeal as well as can be expected. He's out of the danger zone but I won't be able to tell you more until I get the test results back from the lab. The best thing for him right now is to stay quiet and sleep."

Injecting medication into the IV, Dr. Cravitz explained that he was giving Lex a mild painkiller to make him more comfortable. He instructed Harlie to give Lex sips of water to soothe his dry throat, but no solid foods or soda for the next twelve hours, until they got his system back on track.

When the medical personnel cleared out, Lex's friends gathered around him. They only stayed a few minutes, since he could barely keep his eyes open and his speech was still incoherent from the medication that coursed through his bloodstream. On their way out of the room, Stix, Dylan, and Ray teased Harlie about her transgression with the nurses. Stix called her a red-hot little vixen, Ray invited her to join them for a bar fight down the street, and Dylan asked if she'd ever considered taking up nude mud wrestling. Harlie, though embarrassed, was glad they found humor in the situation instead of thinking she was crazy. The good-natured ribbing even made Lex laugh, which triggered a coughing fit. She gave him a sip of water from a Dixie cup.

Alone in the room, Harlie snuggled up on the narrow hospital mattress beside him. Lex tried to speak, but she shushed him by tapping her index finger on his dry lips.

"Don't you dare say another word until you feel better."

With a mock salute, Lex mouthed the words 'I love you'.

Another nurse came in later to see about her famous patient. She checked the monitors and smiled to herself before she left the room. The two had fallen asleep huddled together like tired puppies, Harlie tucked under Lex's arm, her head resting on his chest.

The myriad of test results the following morning showed that, miraculously, Lex hadn't suffered any permanent damage from the heroin overdose or the concussion. It was obvious to the physicians that he was no heroin addict. Whoever assaulted him had also been the one to inject him with the drugs. Lex showed no signs of withdrawal the past three days, which proved he wasn't a junkie.

Before Lex left the hospital, Detective Tim Garth stopped by to question him about the assault. Lex wasn't able to shed much light on the case, since his memory ended the moment he got conked on the head. He knew the janitor had to be the one who attacked him, but he didn't see the man's face and was only able to give a vague description. The suspect was of medium height and build, with short brown hair sticking out from under his baseball cap.

"Do you have any enemies you can think of, Mr. Callatori? Anybody who'd be happy if you turned up dead?"

"I piss off lots of people." Lex's sarcastic laugh let Harlie know he felt better. "I could give you a long list of the ones who'd call me an asshole, but I can't think of anybody who'd knock me out and shoot me full of heroin."

Harlie interrupted to tell the detective about the package she'd received, with the dolls hung by the neck, the strange card, and the thorn-covered rose. She explained why they thought Jack was responsible, briefly going over his violent history and ending with the recent fight he had with Lex.

"I still think Jack sent the Barbie dolls, but I just don't feel like he's responsible for this. Jack isn't the type to sneak up on somebody. He'd rather see their face while he does his dirty work."

Detective Garth paused his scribbling to flip back through his small black notepad, searching for some bit of pertinent information. "Ms. Steele, the flower you found in the package. What kind did you say it was?"

"A black rose."

Neither Harlie nor Lex had any knowledge of the matching black rose found in the car until Detective Garth dropped the bombshell. The short man Lex described was obviously not Jack, who towered inches above the musician and had blonde hair. Could he have paid someone to fly out to California to murder his ex-wife's new boyfriend?

Detective Garth advised them to double up on security. He took down the numbers where the couple could be reached as the case unfolded, and hoped to have new developments to share with them in the near future. Garth made his exit as a nurse came in with release papers for Lex to sign.

"Damn it." With his personal effects dumped on the tray in front of him, Lex noticed his yin-yang necklace was missing. The one that matched the inscribed pendant he gave Harlie. "I bet some dipshit on the night shift took it for a souvenir. More dues to pay the celebrity piper, I guess."

They spent the rest of the day in Lex's suite, with two muscle bound bodyguards posted outside the door. Harlie made him rest while he could. The Nefarious Tour would continue the following evening, since Dr. Cravitz had given the green light for Lex to perform. A good thing, since Harlie knew he would've gone on anyway.

She dreaded the flight back to Kentucky the following day more than she cared to admit. Besides her deep dislike for airplanes and the bad taste left in her mouth from the memory of her vomiting episode, she hated to leave Lex. His health was fine now, but the realization that someone wanted him dead made her sick to her stomach, and led to their first real argument.

"No, I mean it. Zeke's going on that plane tomorrow and he's damn well gonna stay with you until the tour is over." Lex's voice raised an octave as irritation set in. "That's what we'd planned in the first place. You agreed to it, remember?"

"But that was *before* somebody tried to kill you." Harlie huffed and shook her head. "I'm not going to sit around shooting the shit with your bodyguard while he should be by your side, keeping your safe. The sheriff can have a car pass by ever few hours to-"

"Zeke's staying with you and that's all there is to it!" Lex threw his hands up in the air in frustration and stepped toward her.

Harlie simultaneously flinched and raised her arm protectively in front of her face. Instincts brought on by years of abuse took over before logic could tell her she'd overreacted.

She opened her eyes and saw Lex take a step backward. He reached out to her, but then clasped both hands behind his neck.

"I'm sorry, baby." His olive skin went pale.

"You were so mad, and when you raised your hands . . ." Harlie bit her lip, trying not to break into tears.

"I swear I'll never hurt you, and I shouldn't have yelled." He opened his arms and she fell into them.

"Sorry I acted like an idiot." Harlie rested her head against his chest, the embrace helping put things into perspective. His arms were her sanctuary, her safe place. Damn Jack and her ugly past for making her forget that, even for a second.

"Don't you dare apologize." Lex leaned back and cradled her face in his palms. "If I have to bite my own tongue off to keep from yelling at you ever again, I will. I love you."

"Love you too." Harlie smiled up at him.

"Okay, but we still have to settle the matter at hand. Zeke needs to stay with you, cuz I'd never forgive myself if you got hurt."

"Zeke's a fun person to have around, but his job is to protect *you*." Harlie looked into Lex's eyes, willing him to understand. "You almost died, Lex."

"What if he decides to go after you next time? Or Zoey?" Lex kept his voice soft, and she knew his clenched jaw was due to the maniac ripping their life apart, not her. He took a deep breath and relaxed with the exhale. "You know how many guys we've got on

FireStorm's security team?"

"No, but I bet Zeke's the best." Harlie grinned, since there was no way he could argue that point.

"Well yeah, but that's why he's going to watch over Zoey and you. Stan's doubled up the security detail for the whole band and has two dudes that are supposed to hover over me until we catch the shithead responsible, since I'm special like that." He teased her with a kiss. "Okay?"

"Fine." It was the best thing for Zoey, after all. "Since you're so special. Weren't you about to show me what you meant by that?"

Harlie declined the flight attendant's offer of alcohol the next day. She took a couple of antihistamines instead, hoping they would make her sleep through most of the trip. They only managed to make her drowsy, so Harlie's thoughts were on Lex the entire time. She wouldn't have let him out of her sight if not for the pressing matters that forced her to return home.

She had to meet with her lawyer to discuss changes in the custody agreement, something she had to settle before their move to New York. She also wanted to see if she could stop Jack's visitation until someone was arrested for the attempt on Lex's life. Though she doubted he was responsible for this last crime, she didn't want to take any chances. If Jack did turn out to be behind it, she didn't want him anywhere near Zoey.

Not used to being away from her little girl more than a few hours at a time, Harlie ached to hold Zoey in her arms again. The thought of someone trying to hurt her one day was unbearable. By the time the plane landed in Kentucky, she was thankful Lex insisted Zeke stay at her house. Unconcerned for her own safety, Harlie felt a whole lot better knowing Zeke would protect her daughter with his life, if it ever came down to it.

Chapter Fourteen

Harlie's days trickled slowly into one another while Lex was away on tour. Zoey and Zeke kept her company, but she ached to see him again. She slept in one of his T-shirts, imagining his arms wrapped around her as she breathed in the scent of his cologne trapped in the cotton fabric.

FireStorm's hectic schedule allowed him to visit only twice before the tour ended. On his first visit, they took Zoey to the park and to Spumoni's for pizza. They had plenty of time to themselves after Lex sang Zoey to sleep at bedtime. On his next stay, Randi invited the little girl to sleep over at her house, something Zoey always loved since Aunt Randi played dress up with her and let her stay up as late as she wanted. Harlie agreed, but insisted Zeke go along to watch over them. The police hadn't arrested anyone yet for the assault on Lex and she wasn't going to take any unnecessary risks with her daughter.

Sheriff Maxwell Roberts paid Harlie a visit the day after she got back from California. They discussed the case over steaming mugs of coffee at the kitchen table.

"Well, Jack's still as big an asshole as ever but we've crossed him off the suspect list." He stirred another spoonful of sugar into his cup. "We tracked down the delivery boy who brought you that box full of dolls and dead flowers, then we traced the package back to Wyoming. A florist there received the parcel with typed instructions to add the black rose before they shipped it out. Nobody saw who left it at the flower shop. Personally, I just don't believe Jackson Steele has the mental aptitude necessary to think of all those details. Knocking Lex out and pumping him full of drugs really isn't his style. What do you think?"

"I think you're right, Max." Harlie nodded, glad the sheriff was doing a thorough job but a little disappointed her ex was off the hook. "Jack would've gone with something more painful, like sticking a lit Roman candle up Lex's ass. Plus, he'd never hire some little pipsqueak to crack Lex up side the head. He'd want to do that in person and take the credit for it himself."

"His alibi checks out, unfortunately. He was out of town when Lex was attacked." Max's tone made it clear he'd have liked nothing better than to send Jack up the river. "About the time Lex got whacked in the head, Jack was giving room service nine kinds of hell about sending up the wrong wine and overcooking his steak.

The big jackass."

The custody hearing went much better than she'd expected. Since Jack's court appearance for his attempted assault on her was scheduled for the following week, he agreed—most likely on the advice of his attorney—to comply with Harlie's wishes.

"I believe these arrangements are in Zoey's best interest. I don't like the idea of her being so far away or the company she'll be keeping, but New York could be a good experience for her." Jack's sanctimonious expression made her want to puke. The judge didn't seem to notice the sarcasm in his voice when he glanced at Harlie at the end of his spiel. "I'm sure her *mother* will move back here soon enough."

Harlie wondered if the bailiff would shoot her if she strangled Jack with the hundred-dollar tie hanging around his neck.

With Jack no longer a suspect in the attack on Lex or for sending the threatening package to Harlie, the judge wouldn't suspend his custody rights. His visitation changed from alternate weekends to five consecutive days during the last week of each month, effective immediately.

After the proceedings, Harlie went to the ladies' room down the hall. Jack blocked her path when she came out. He never could resist the chance to mouth off.

"What's with all this bullshit you and your ugly ass boyfriend tried to pin on me?" He kept his voice low as he glared down at her, his face so close to hers she smelled the bacon and coffee on his breath. "First of all, I've never even been to California. I was in Ohio for a business meeting when Dickhead got jumped, which I proved when that stupid sheriff came around asking me questions. And about me sending you some goddamn dolls, you know I'm too much of a man for that sissy shit."

"Go straight to hell and leave me alone," Harlie said through gritted teeth as she tried to walk past him.

Jack grabbed her by the arm, his fingers bruising her flesh when he spun her back around to face him.

Harlie opened her mouth to call for help, but closed it. Yelling wouldn't be necessary now. The man gripping the base of Jack's neck seemed to have things under control.

"Don't look like a man to me." Zeke's other hand squeezed Jack's wrist to release his hold on Harlie. His expression while on duty was normally stoic, unreadable, but now anger burned behind Zeke's eyes and the firm set of his goatee-framed mouth. "More like a big punk who picks on girls."

"Who the fuck are you?" Jack gawked at the man who towered above him, and panic flickered across his face before he could hide it. His six-foot frame looked like a tinker toy dangling in front of Zeke's massive physique.

"None of your business." Zeke tightened his grip, his deep voice steady and vehement. "My boss told me to break your neck if you came anywhere near Harlie. Good thing for you that we're in the courthouse right now or you wouldn't be breathing. Keep your distance, 'cuz I won't be this civil next time."

"I don't give a shit what that son of a bitch told-"

Zeke shook him by the scruff of the neck until he shut up.

"Don't let me hear you disrespect Mr. Callatori or Ms. Steele again. I don't appreciate it. Now, it's time for you to leave." Zeke punctuated the sentence by shoving Jack, who stumbled down the hall in the direction of the restrooms.

With no possibility of saving face, Jack hurried past the little boys' room despite the odd twitchy walk that suggested he needed to take a whiz. He left the building without a backwards glance.

In court the following week for attempting to assault Harlie on her porch, Jack's lawyer got him off with a stiff fine and the promise of a month in the county jail if he violated the restraining order again. With Zeke seated beside Harlie, Jack didn't even look in her direction.

The move to New York would be a major adjustment. Harlie visited with her family as much as she could, to cram in quality moments in hopes of making the transition easier for herself and Zoey. During their last week in town, Randi took them to an animated movie Zoey'd been begging to see. Zeke went along and treated everyone to ice cream at Baskin Robins afterwards.

One afternoon when she felt particularly lonesome, Harlie logged on to Facebook. Barbed*Ivy happened to be online and the two opened up the chat window. Of course the first thing Barb mentioned was the damned news story about Lex's heroin overdose. Then she warned her to dump him before he destroyed her life. Harlie explained that had Lex almost died after the assault and the police were trying to find out who was responsible.

Barbed*Ivy: Haven't U learned UR lesson on bad relationships from that jerk U used 2 be married 2? Does a rock with the words "Dump Him" written on it have 2 fall out of the sky and hit U on the head before U get the hint?

Harlie Dawn Steele: Come on, Barb, this isn't Lex's fault. He sent his own personal bodyguard to stay with me and Zoey while he's on the road, despite the fact some maniac is out there trying to kill him.

Barbed*Ivy: Good 2 know U have someone there 2 protect U, but I'm not impressed with Lex. I think U were better off before the musical Boy Wonder came around screwing things up for U, IMHO.

Harlie Dawn Steele: I can't imagine my life without Lex in it. I wish you could understand how happy he makes me. I'm so worried about him now.

Barbed*Ivy: R U still moving to NYC with him?

Harlie Dawn Steele: Yes, as soon as the tour's over. Not one word out of you about me only knowing him for 2 months, either! :) Hey, since you used to live in New York, maybe you could recommend some fun places to take Zoey and a few good restaurants. I'm a hick from the sticks so I'm clueless about the Big City, remember! LOL

Harlie had everything she planned to take packed up and ready to go a week before moving day. She took Zeke's advice—offered during one of their two-man poker games—and shipped most of it ahead early, to make sure her stuff arrived before she did.

She dreaded the teary-eyed ordeal of saying good-bye to her family and Randi at the airport. She would miss them, but she reminded herself she'd have plenty of time to see them each month when she, Zoey, and Lex came back to spend a week in her house in Kentucky. Harlie looked forward to starting her new life with Lex in New York, and hoped to leave their troubles behind them on the tarmac.

Chapter Fifteen

After a few days in the Big Apple, Harlie started to feel at home. Lex, unrecognized on the crowded sidewalks in his baseball cap and sunglasses, showed her and Zoey around. It amazed Harlie that everything was within walking distance of their building. Stores, restaurants, theaters; you name it and there it was. Lex's bodyguards tailed them whenever they were in public areas, but Harlie was getting used to that too.

"How's the big city treating my best friend?" Randi asked when she called Harlie a few days after the move. "Bet it's more fun than this rural hole in the map, huh?"

"It's different, that's for sure. Zoey's having a ball. You should've seen her on the airplane, looking out the window through the clouds, jabbering nonstop. I was glad she was too busy to notice her mom wasn't so thrilled with flying. I squeezed Lex's hand so hard, I'm surprised he can still hold a guitar."

"Oh, you skipped the hooch this time, huh? Zeke told me all about your first flight, you telling him jokes that'd make a biker blush."

"Hmmm, sounds like you've been spending a lot of time with Zeke here lately. Kind of makes me wonder-"

Randi interrupted, ignoring Harlie's implication. "Enough about Zeke. Did you and Lex join the Mile High Club?"

"That would've been kind of hard, with Zoey sitting right there. You're still the only one of us with membership."

"Too bad for you. So, tell me about New York. What's it like?"

"Well, I've ran into a few stereotypical New Yorkers who either ignored me or hollered for me to get out of their damn way. Most of the people I've talked to were nice enough, though. The traffic doesn't seem to travel over fifteen miles an hour and you never see open parking spaces. Guess that's why so many people take taxis instead of driving themselves."

"Does everybody dress all glitzy, like in *Sex and the City*, or like a bunch of weirdos?"

"You watch too much TV," Harlie teased. "Most of the clothes are like you'd find anywhere else. These people love to wear black, but I see plenty of ladies walking around in designer stuff. As for weirdness, there's nothing worse than you'd see at the mall in Evansville. Did I tell you about the homeless people?"

"No."

"Oh, it's the saddest thing. They really do sleep in alleys and on park benches." Harlie's heart nearly broke in two the first time she'd passed a transient man on the sidewalk. She wanted to give him money but wasn't sure what to do. When she pulled a twenty out of her purse, the bodyguard told her it wasn't such a good idea.

"What about the stores and boutiques? Have you been to Rodeo Drive yet?"

"Um, I think that's in California, you shopaholic." Harlie laughed, certain she'd spend most of Randi's first visit cruising every store in the city. "I haven't had a chance to shop yet. You want to know something cool, though? You can get take-out and groceries delivered to the door here, day or night. I thought we were living large last year when Spumoni's started delivering on weekends."

"Leave it to you to scope out food instead of fashion." With Godsmack seeping through the receiver, Harlie pictured Randi lounging in her living room, bobbing her head to the beat. "How do you like the apartment? Seems like I saw a few rooms on *MTV Cribs* a year or so ago."

"I wasn't really sure what to expect, but I love it. I always thought apartments were small, but this place is bigger than my whole house." Room by room, she described how Lex furnished his home with stuff he'd collected from all over the world, an eclectic assortment of things both beautiful and unique. "His personality is everywhere I look. He told me I could redecorate if I wanted to, but I like everything the way it is. Well, except the bedrooms. Zoey's picked out the cutest wallpaper for her room and she's excited about helping me put it up."

"You said bedrooms, plural. Oh my God. Does he have mirrors on the ceilings? Whips and chains hanging from the headboard, maybe?"

"No, that would be your dream room." It was nice to joke around with Randi again. The telephone conversation seemed to shorten the distance between New York and Kentucky. "I'm going to redecorate it, though. And no, you pervert, it looks like a normal bedroom."

Knowing other women had slept there in the past really didn't bother her. She just wanted to reflect their new relationship in the decor of the room where they spent some of their most intimate moments.

"I'm happy for you. It sounds like everything is perfect on the new home front."

"Well, almost everything. Lex has a housekeeper named Luisa. I *do* like her. She's sweet and friendly, Zoey loves her, and she has the most charming Italian accent."

"Oh, you lucky bitch! Not only do you have a gorgeous new rock star boyfriend with a penthouse, you get a Sicilian Mary Poppins too. Girl, you hit the jack-pot."

"Thing is, I feel like a big fat slob. Having a house-keeper come in to cook and clean isn't an easy thing for me to adjust to." Harlie knew Randi was the only per-son who'd understand. She'd tease her about it, but she would understand where Harlie was coming from. "You know my mom, she didn't raise me to sit around like the Queen of Sheba and let other people wait on me."

Luisa came in every Monday through Saturday from ten a.m. until two in the afternoon. She'd clean the apartment and cook the evening meal, which she left in the refrigerator with reheating instructions for Lex written on a Post-it note. She also did the laundry and fixed lunch if anybody was home to eat it. She and Zoey hit it off from the start, so Harlie wasn't surprised when Luisa offered to babysit whenever she needed to go out.

Lex jammed with his band in the afternoons, which left Harlie and Zoey with the apartment to themselves. Three days a week, Harlie spent a few hours bookkeep-ing for her father. Pete faxed her all the information she needed, then she'd balance the books and email everything back to him, including the exact figures to deposit in the bank. She played games with Zoey or read to her until naptime, which still left quite a bit of free time on her hands. Since she was used to cleaning up in the afternoons back in Kentucky, she decided to do the same thing at the penthouse. She washed the laundry in the hamper, straightened up, and whipped up some extra food in the kitchen, hoping to make Luisa's job easier and herself feel less like a lazy ass.

At the end of her first week in New York, everything was going great. Harlie felt comfortable in her new home and even started taking daily walks around the block to get a real feel for the city, barely noticing the shadow of protection steps behind her. Zoey loved her new room, redecorated with fairy tale wallpaper and frilly pink curtains.

With Zoey left in Luisa's care, she and Lex went out one night for a romantic dinner. During the entrée, Harlie called to see how things were going.

"Everything is a fine. We're having fun," Luisa said, her accent calming to Harlie's ears. It sounded like it too, with Zoey singing in the background and Mugsy barking along. "A repairman came to fix a problem with the pipes. He say something about the apartment below us have a leak. But everything checked out okay. A nice man, he gave Zoey a package of Gummi Bears before he left."

"That's one of her favorites. Sounds like you have everything under control." As the waiter refilled Harlie's wine glass, she said into her cell, "We'll be home in an hour or so. Thanks again, Luisa. I don't know what I'd do without you."

In their bedroom later that evening, Lex finished drinking a large glass of ice water and placed it on the nightstand. Candles cast a warm glow over the room and perfumed the air with the seductive scent of sandalwood. Overcome by wanton urges, Harlie took a mouthful of the crushed ice, then surprised Lex by jerking down his pajama pants and taking his manhood into the icy warmth of her mouth. Lex groaned when he reached his bursting point.

"Your turn, baby." He flashed a wicked grin as he maneuvered her onto her back. With the rest of the ice crystals from the glass in his mouth, he parted her knees. She was pantyless beneath her nightgown. She twitched at the foreign sensation of ice in her most private cavity. Lex's frosty tongue made her go wild with abandon. She pulled his hair and shuddered in release.

Harlie drifted to sleep wrapped in Lex's arms, his love flowing through her as she felt his heartbeat against her back. She couldn't imagine herself being any happier than this.

When Luisa showed up early one morning to discuss her job, Harlie was shocked.

"I'm sorry, but I must quit." Tears filled the old woman's eyes and her Italian accent became much heavier than usual in her distress. "I come in every day, and she's already done my work. She wash *a* the clothes, she clean *a* the whole apartment, she even cook enough food to feed army for a week. Good homemade food. A ton of brick not have to fall on poor old Luisa, oh no. Harlie's a good woman for you. She want to set up housekeeping but thinks I'm in the way. It breaks *a* my heart, but you don't need me anymore, Lex."

Harlie felt like a total bitch. She opened and closed her mouth a few times, searching in vain for the right words to tell this sweet woman how very sorry she was for giving her the wrong impression.

"No, Luisa. You know I think of you as family, not just an employee. You're not in the way." Lex took his housekeeper's hand and led her to a comfortable chair where he knelt beside her. "Harlie told me the other day how much she likes you. Do you know that you're one of the few people she's ever left Zoey with? That was her main concern when she moved out here where she didn't know anybody but me. And I know Zoey loves you, 'cuz I heard her telling her grandparents all about you on the phone."

"You mean it?" Luisa dried her tears on her lacey white apron. "Then why you do all my work?" She directed her question to Harlie. "You think I no do it so good?"

Harlie could swear she felt a huge 'Bitch' sign flashing over her own head.

"I am *so* sorry about this mix-up. I never meant to

hurt your feelings. And Lex is right about me trusting you with Zoey. I just felt like a lazy bum having you pick up after us so when I had spare time in the evenings, I tried to make myself useful and hoped to take the load off you a little. You always work so hard and do such a great job, I could hardly find anything to do." She'd been talking so fast, she had to pause a second to catch her breath. "I've never had a housekeeper before so I don't know the etiquette I'm supposed to use. Can you please forgive me?"

"Oh, yes, I forgive you! But do you forgive me? I'm a silly old woman." Luisa sniffled as a sheepish grin appeared on her face. Harlie and Lex assured her there was nothing to forgive. "You so nice, trying to help me, but you no have to worry yourself. I love my job."

"I have an idea. Why don't we compromise on this?" Harlie suggested. "Let me do all the laundry and the straightening up around here, and I'll clean up all the big messes Zoey gets in to. I promise to leave all the real chores to your expert hands, like the dusting, polishing, and vacuuming. Okay?"

Luisa nodded but didn't look convinced about the new arrangements.

"I'd like it if we could cook together. It'd be fun and I'd love to learn your delicious lasagna recipe, and figure out what the heck zabaglione is because Lex raves about yours. Plus Zoey just loves you to pieces, so I'm relying on you for all my babysitting needs, if you're up for it. Does that work for you?"

Luisa stood up and grabbed Harlie, patting her on the back as she sealed their agreement with a hug. Relieved, Harlie smiled at Lex over the older woman's shoulder.

Harlie and Luisa debunked the old myth about too many cooks spoiling the stew. Any gourmet chef would give their eyeteeth to make the culinary masterpieces that flowed from the kitchen shared by the Italian and the Southerner.

"I'll have to hire a personal trainer if you two keep feeding me like this," Lex said, filling his stomach one day at lunch.

Harlie loved watching him eat the dishes she and Luisa made together: fried chicken with pasta smothered in marinara sauce; Luisa's famous lasagna with Harlie's fresh garlic bread; the huge brunches of bacon, eggs, biscuits, grits, and gravy; and the wide array of dessert that streamed from the mixing bowl.

"I'm gonna have to buy bigger pants, but you never gain an ounce eating like this." Lex pulled Harlie into his lap and kissed her. "Not that it'd bother me if you did, 'cuz I love every inch of you."

Chapter Sixteen

One Saturday afternoon, Harlie curled up on the sofa to watch her favorite movie. She had the place to herself, with Lex in the studio a few floors below and Luisa and Zoey at a children's art festival for the day, followed closely by two of Lex's security people. It'd been weeks since they received any threats from whoever attacked Lex, but they weren't taking any chances.

A bodyguard had shadowed Harlie that morning when she walked to the Redbox kiosk on the corner. She liked to stroll down the busy sidewalk, passing interesting people in the crowd. A man in an Armani suit and Nikes speed walked past her, barking orders into his Blackberry. A girl with spiked purple hair, ripped fishnets, and black lipstick carried a poodle with chartreuse fur; both wore matching studded collars around their necks. A drunk who reeked of gin slurred a lewd proposition at Harlie, until the bodyguard slammed his ass into the brick storefront.

Harlie took a sip of RC and sat up a little straighter when her favorite part of *Thelma & Louise* came on. How many times had she and Randi watched this flick? She'd lost count. The scene with the big rig explosion was the best part, but, just when the trucker said "bitches from hell", the doorbell rang.

"Damn." Harlie stopped the DVD player and flicked off the television. In Kentucky, most people had the good manners to call ahead instead of just showing up unannounced on someone's doorstep. Slightly annoyed, she answered the door.

"Hell-o." The man leaning against the doorframe slid his green-tinted round-framed sunglasses down the slope of his nose. He groped Harlie with his eyes, then shifted his gaze to her face. "Would Lex happen to be home, luv?" he asked, a melodious lilt in his English accent.

"Uh . . . No, he's out rehearsing right now . . . down in the studio . . . with the guys." Harlie struggled to sound coherent. This guy was one of the most famous musicians of all time. In spite of his age, his long dark blonde hair was as thick as ever, his physique flawed only by the beginnings of a paunchy gut. She was growing accustomed to meeting celebrities, but it was quite a jolt to realize this particular one was standing there having a conversation with her.

"Allow me to introduce myself then." He made himself comfortable on the sofa while his host stood with her mouth gaping open. "I'm Sir Rance Williamson, knighted by Her Royal Highness. Actually, I'm better known for being the lead singer of Stonehenge, a little rock group you may have heard of." With a wink and a pause, he gave his words time to dazzle her. "And you must be Haylee, the new love interest I've heard so much about lately."

"Yes." Harlie nodded, surprised he had any prior knowledge of her meager existence. Realizing she must look like a simpering idiot, she quit nodding and tried to rearrange her face into a more dignified expression. "But my name is Harlie." She extended her hand to him. "It's very nice to meet you."

This was simply a man like any other, not much different from the rock star she slept with every night, strange as that still seemed. There was no reason she should be intimidated. As he shook her hand, her father's voice echoed through her head: *He puts his pants on one leg at a time, just like everybody else.*

"Oh, I'm sorry, *Harlie.* I've never been very good with names. And the pleasure is all mine. It looks as though my old friend's taste has definitely improved." He patted the cushion to his right. "Let us get better acquainted, shall we? Tell me how Lex managed to land a beauty such as yourself."

It never crossed her mind that she'd just accepted an invitation to sit down in her own home. She thought

Rance was being polite. They exchanged stories of how they'd each met Lex before Rance told her, in raunchy detail, about some of the more colorful escapades of his long singing career. His charming English accent added to his flair for storytelling, and her laughter elicited even more outlandish tales. Then the conversation took an unexpected turn.

Sir Rance scooted closer to her. He peered over his green lenses to better gaze into her eyes. "Come spend the weekend with me, luv. I'm sure we could find some way to keep each other amused."

Harlie leaned as far away from him as possible, until the back of her ribcage pressed against the sofa arm. She was used to the empty flirtation that fell so easily from other musicians' lips. Stix showered her with harmless flattery each time their paths crossed, whether Lex was in the room or not, which proved he had nothing to hide. She replayed Rance's offer in her head a couple of times to make certain she'd heard him correctly, then she laughed out loud. His proposition was so absurd that it had to be a joke, some twisted form of British humor.

But Rance was not amused. Dejection passed over his cool features before he regained the stoic expression of an impatient school teacher.

"I'm afraid it might piss Lex off if we ran away together like that." Not wanting to hurt his feelings but unsure of the proper way to handle the situation, Harlie tried to play his comment off as the joke she'd taken it for. "I know y'all are friends, but you can't be expected to share everything." Her nervous laughter punctuated the sentence.

"I'm sure Lex would get over it. Eventually. He usually does," Rance said, his tone somber despite the devilish glint in his hazel eyes. "You know, Lex and I have a sort of unofficial rivalry between us. He finds pretty girls, then I come along and take them off his hands. I have this maneuver I do with my tongue which the ladies are simply wild about." To demonstrate, he stuck his tongue out and licked the air suggestively. Harlie thought he looked like a demented bullfrog digging into a fly sundae. "If you would be so kind as to give me the opportunity, I'm sure I could make your toes curl .... I'm curious to hear what sort of sounds you make in the throes of ecstasy."

Okay, she thought, he's definitely crossing the line now. Suddenly uncomfortable seated near Sir Rance, she practically leapt from her seat and walked to the bar on the other side of the room.

"You musicians, always joking around. How *do* you keep from being taken the wrong way?" A blush seared across her cheeks. "I'm sure Lex will be happy to see you. Would you like a drink before you go down to the studio?" She hoped he would take the hint. "Name your poison."

"Yes, that would be nice. I think my thirst could be satiated with, oh, let me see." He rubbed his chin, mocking deep thought. "I'd like a comfortable screw up against the wall, if it wouldn't be too much trouble." His eyes twinkled as he watched for her reaction.

Harlie smirked. "You know, that just so happens to be my best friend's favorite cocktail. Every time we go out, Randi gets a thrill from the strange looks she gets when she orders that. It's a cross between a Harvey Wallbanger and a screwdriver. One mixed drink, coming right up." She grabbed the vodka and hoped to send Rance on his merry way, glass in hand, as soon as possible. Bent over to retrieve the orange juice from the mini-fridge, she felt an unfamiliar hand grope her ass.

An emotion somewhere between anger and impatience washed over Harlie when she spun around to confront Rance. "I don't mean to be rude, but I fail to see the humor in all of this. Go sit back down, way over there," she pointed to the sofa on the far side of the room, "and I'll finish your drink so you can be on your way. You did come here to visit with Lex, after all, and I'd hate to hold you up."

"Don't be so frigid, luv," he said, disregarding her attempt to brush him off. "Come on. Loosen up and give us a kiss. You know you want to." He raised his hand and reached for her breast.

Harlie knocked his hand away and jerked her foot

off the ground, attempting to smash her knee into his over-stimulated groin. Rance shifted his weight and took the blow in his thigh rather than her intended target. Apparently amused, he laughed. "Well, aren't you the little spitfire. Now, I'm ready for that kiss."

"Of course you are," Harlie cooed. "Pucker up."

Rance closed his eyes in anticipation, and reached to unfasten his pants.

A loud crash brought two bodyguards bursting into the room. They exchanged puzzled glances at the scene they found. Harlie stood to the side rubbing the knuckles on her right hand. Sir Rance Williamson lay sprawled over a coffee table, blood pouring between his fingers from his injured nose.

"Are you all right, Ms. Steele?"

"That bloody bitch just broke my fucking nose!" Rance roared, indignant, a tear of pain sliding down his red face. "What the hell would be wrong with her when I'm the one lying here, writhing in pain! Help me up, you blasted twits."

No one moved an inch until Harlie spoke.

"Everything's fine. Mr. Williamson was just on his way out when, for some unknown reason, he fell over that piece of furniture. Could y'all do me a favor and show him down to the studio? He came here to see Lex and I wouldn't want to keep him waiting another minute."

"You will address me as Sir Williamson, you ill-bred hillbilly bitch."

Security aided him to his feet and led him toward the open door.

"How stupid of me. *Sir* Rance." A mischievous grin twitched on her lips. "Y'all come back and see us now, ya hear."

One of the bodyguards returned with a message from Lex. He wanted Harlie to join them in the studio.

Waiting for the elevator doors to open, Harlie felt convulsive butterflies attack her stomach. Was Rance going to own up to what he'd done and apologize for his actions? Could she face criminal charges for punching the nose of someone with 'Sir' in front of his name? She hoped Lex wasn't upset with her for hitting his friend; after some thought on the matter, she figured he'd have done the same thing if he'd seen how Rance acted.

"Here he comes," Zeke said. Everyone in the band grabbed an instrument and pretended to have no idea what was going on. One guard called from outside the apartment as the other escorted Sir Williamson down to the studio. Zeke barely had enough time to explain what happened before their visitor made his entrance, wiping his nose with a bloody handkerchief.

"Hey, man, what happened to you?" On a stool beside his mic stand, Lex feigned concern while he fought the urge to strangle Williamson.

"Your psychotic girlfriend just attacked me, that's what happened. For absolutely no reason, whatsoever." Rance portrayed himself as the innocent victim, claiming he'd chatted with Harlie for a while before she went crazy and punched him in the nose.

Lex pretended to know nothing of the situation and tried to act shocked as he listened. Only the constant flexing of his right hand gave away his true feelings. He wanted to stomp the British bastard's ass himself, and he hoped he fucking bled to death from the busted nose Harlie had given him. That he had the audacity to come here telling lies about her was just too damn much to take. Lex wanted to run up to the penthouse and make sure the love of his life wasn't too upset, but first he had to handle this, man to man.

"Perhaps it was because I mentioned some of your past relationships," Rance continued with melodramatic flair. "Maybe she wanted me. Hell if I know what her bloody problem was. You should send her packing before she kills someone and you end up with a nasty lawsuit on your hands."

"You think so? I should kick her out, you say. Maybe she could stay at your place until she finds somewhere to live." Mad did not begin to describe Lex. He was livid, and felt his lip curl into a snarl as he rose to his feet, unable to listen to any more bullshit spew from Rance's mouth. "You make me sick, you arrogant son of a bitch. Harlie's off limits. I'd better never catch you anywhere near her again. Understand?"

"Don't worry. Keep that little piece of ass all to yourself. The wench is too violent for my liking, though I imagine she's quite the hellcat between the sheets." Rance winked at the guys, but looked puzzled when everyone started backing away.

Dylan hurried to return his Les Paul to the safety of its guitar case while Ray leaned against a stack of Marshall amps, watching Lex and Rance as if waiting for something to happen. Stix twirled his drumsticks through his fingers, smirking.

"Don't talk about her like that, you winking motherfucker! You want a piece of me?" Lex slung his leather jacket to the ground and bounded toward Rance. "Bring it on."

Zeke reluctantly caught his fist seconds before it slammed into Rance's eye. It took a lot of effort and some help from Dylan to hold Lex back.

Sir Rance Williamson made a hasty retreat, with a sputtered comment about fearing for his safety around these hostile Americans.

Exaggerated cheers welcomed Harlie to the studio a few minutes later. Ray lifted her hand high into the air, and mocked the monotone of a boxing announcer. "In this corner, we have the reigning champion, Red Hot

Harlie Steele. Congrats on your recent victory over Sir Rance the Rancid." Harlie laughed while Dylan squeezed her other arm, feigning amazement at the musculature of her biceps.

Stix inspected her bruising knuckles. "I hope you didn't hurt yourself smashing this dainty little fist into Rance's sharp nose."

Lex stepped in and wrapped Harlie in his arms. "You all right, baby?" He'd stood back watching the others fawn over her, calming himself down as he took a visual inventory of Harlie to make sure she was all right.

Harlie whispered something in Lex's ear that made him sweep her off her feet in a smooth Rhett Butler type move. Amid catcalls and wolf whistles, he strutted toward the elevator carrying Harlie, his blushing Scarlett.

Back in their bedroom, they took advantage of their privacy. Harlie covered Lex's face with kisses. When she reached his mouth, she couldn't resist sucking the full lips she found so sexy, taking them one at a time into her mouth, tasting their salty sweetness. His arousal pressed against his jeans and into her thigh. She unbuttoned the leather vest he wore in place of a shirt. Her hands explored his body as she rained kisses down his neck, over his chest, and on to linger at his navel.

Lex groaned when Harlie took him into the warmth of her mouth. She slid her lips slowly up and down his long shaft, flicking her tongue across the head of his penis. Her head twisted from side to side as she continued her bobbing pattern, and Lex could take no more. He pulled her up to face him as he undressed her. A playful smack landed on her curvy behind when she was naked beside him. Hands roamed, tongues caressed, and hips instinctively arched toward delicious sensations. Her breath came quick and erratic.

Lex quickened his gait, penetrating deeper with each thrust. "It would kill me if anyone else touched you like this." His voice was a husky whisper beside her ear. "I love you so much."

Her body writhed in ecstasy. She begged him not to stop, not now, not ever. They shuddered in unison, and moaned as they came to a feverish climax together.

Chapter Seventeen

Harlie felt like Cinderella on her way to the ball, her own Prince Charming seated beside her in the sleek black limousine. She smoothed her low-cut ebony cocktail dress, trying to prevent wrinkles in the sequined fabric. The paparazzi would be swarming at the premiere, so she wanted to look her best tonight.

"You look so handsome." Harlie stopped herself from kissing him, afraid of smudging lipstick on Lex's soon-to-be-photographed face. Instead, she ran her fingers through the dark hair that brushed the shoulders of his custom tailored deep purple suit. He wore a collarless white silk shirt underneath the jacket, which let him forego the agony of a necktie. A neatly folded black and white handkerchief embroidered with music notes peeked out of his breast pocket. Very few men could pull off such an ensemble, but Lex looked spectacular.

The couple emerged from their limo and walked the

red carpet, engulfed by photographers in a race to blind them with flashbulbs. Lex stepped into his flashy stage persona, nodding nonchalantly to the crowd while Harlie, smiling shyly, clung to his arm. Security flanked them to keep the overzealous paparazzi and cheering spectators at bay.

The atmosphere inside the theater intimidated Harlie even more than the screaming crowd she'd just waded through. Looking around, she found herself in the midst of wall-to-wall celebrities. Jewel-dripping movie stars mingled with musicians, producers, directors, and even professional athletes. Reporters speckled the room, cameramen in tow, to interview the Beautiful People.

To Harlie's relief, they didn't have to wait long for the screening to start. Since FireStorm recorded a large portion of the soundtrack, ushers seated them behind the actors and beside Stix, decked out in a Canali suit. Dylan and Ray were too busy at a party downtown to bother with this event, plus they'd joked about how Lex always stole the spotlight.

If the audience's reaction was any indication, this action-comedy film was destined to be a box office hit. The hero, portrayed by Colin Farrell, captivated the crowd with a daring stunt, catapulting his motorcycle through a blaze of fire while his beautiful co-star, Jennifer Lopez, hung on to him for dear life.

Foghat's classic "Slow Ride" played during the action scene. Heat rose in Harlie's cheeks. She was thankful the dark theater hid her crimson face from people seated near them. She exchanged wicked glances with Lex, her thoughts on one particular night they spent listening to this song. They'd kept pace with the beat of the music, from seductively slow to a fast and furious frenzy, back and forth each time the tempo changed. She shifted in her seat to stop the spasms between her crossed legs during the line about the rhythm being right, exactly the point where she'd reached one of the hardest orgasms of her life.

Lex watched her squirm, then leaned over to whisper in her ear. "We can listen to that again in the limo on the way home." He sang along with the track, his warm breath in her ear sending a lusty chill through her body. She giggled and begged him to stop it.

The lights came up while the audience cheered. Credits floated across the screen as everyone flowed back into the lobby for champagne, schmoozing, and inevitable encounters with the paparazzi.

During the past few months, Harlie noticed that celebrities seemed to have certain rules of etiquette amongst themselves. They rarely appeared in awe of each other, were usually courteous, and acted as if they were the best of friends with each other even when meeting in public for the first time, as was the case here.

Colin Farrell had sauntered over to shake hands with Lex and Stix and complimented them on Fire-Storm's work on the soundtrack. Draven Fox, a rock star with a kickass cameo in the movie, joined them, a drink in one hand and a pair of double-Ds on his arm. Both men were drop dead gorgeous, but in her eyes, they paled in comparison to her Lex.

She wished Randi was there, since she was gaga over Colin and Draven, and wondered which one her BFF would've drooled over more. Harlie was deciding on the best way to ask those two to take a picture with her, so she could text it to Randi along with the words 'Eat your heart out', but then something else drew her attention.

Jennifer Lopez strolled by wearing a beaded gown. Gossamer bronze fabric melded with the starlet's skin, a breathtaking vision with tiny faux butterflies and intricate beading. Harlie tried to get a glimpse of the shoes she wore with the gorgeous dress, and dismissed the voice behind her that said "Mr. Callatori" as belonging to just another reporter.

When she heard "You have the right to remain silent" followed by "What the fuck", she realized there was a problem.

Not eager to appear on tabloid covers in a legal dispute with the New York Police Department, everyone backed away from the sudden burst of flashbulbs exploding around the rock legend. A uniformed officer recited the Miranda Rights as he slammed Lex into the confection counter and handcuffed his wrists behind his back. This wasn't his first time on the wrong end of a cop, so Lex didn't say a word. The pissed off expression on his face showed exactly how he felt about the matter.

Harlie had absolutely no idea what to do. She stood there with her mouth hanging open, staring at the commotion going on three feet in front of her.

Stix stepped up to the detective who appeared to be in charge. "What's this all about? What, if anything, are you charging Lex with?"

"Domestic abuse."

Harlie, now more confused than ever, played the words back in her mind a few times to make sure she hadn't misunderstood. She stepped forward and cleared her throat.

"Excuse me, officer, but I live with Mr. Callatori. I think I'd know if there was any domestic abuse going on. There has to be some kind of mistake here. If you would please uncuff him, I'm sure we can straighten everything out."

"Are you—" the detective pulled out a weathered notepad and skimmed a beefy finger over a page of scribbles, "—Harlie Garrett Steele?"

Relieved, she nodded. "Yes."

"No mistake, ma'am. Says here that Callatori beat

the crap out of you last week. You should be thankful somebody reported the incident. It'll give you a chance to get on with your life and away from this loser. Why you let yourself get knocked around by this guy is beyond me." He glared at her as if she were an idiot. "If you could come down to the station and fill out some paperwork, it'd make things a lot easier."

"Why aren't you listening to me?" This accusation outraged and insulted Harlie. "You haven't acknowledged a word I've said. I am *not* pressing charges because he didn't do anything wrong."

Where was the law a few years ago when Jack used her for a punching bag? She could have used some help back then. Or when Lex had his head bashed in by some maniac the police still hadn't caught. Now this Barney Fife wannabe was accusing her of being a sadomasochistic bimbo who liked being slapped around. Lex would never lay a violent hand on her.

"You don't have to. Once a charge like this is brought to our attention, the perpetrator has to answer for it," the policeman stated, his voice a patronizing sneer. "It's policy. He's going downtown for this, whether you like it or not."

Harlie wanted to slap his condescending face, but refused to give the paparazzi the satisfaction of photographing her in an adjoining cell.

"Fine!" With one hand on her hip, eyes blaring, Harlie pointed her finger at the detective. "I will contact Lex's lawyer and we'll meet you at the station. And," she added as a clever afterthought, "I want your supervisor present while we get this mess straightened out. Surely he doesn't approve of the way you treat the innocent citizens of this city."

Lex gave her a wink and whispered his lawyer's name as he walked past her, en route to the squad car out front. Harlie figured Barney Fife must have wanted to see his own insipid face on the ten o'clock news, since he'd left the blue lights flashing at the entrance the whole time. He could have led Lex out the backdoor instead of parading him through a barrage of spectators, hands cuffed behind him as camera crews fell over each other shooting footage.

Lex looked straight into the cameras, his voice calm but sarcastic as he spoke. "Guess they thought this was a donut shop. I haven't done anything wrong. This is all a big mistake and I hope you guys follow us downtown to cover the real story, which is gonna be me suing these assholes for false arrest. Later." An officer shoved him into the backseat of the police car.

The congregation of outraged fans cheered his comments. They chanted "FireStorm" over and over as the cruiser pulled away with the icon sealed inside.

Chapter Eighteen

Seated next to Lex in the small interrogation room, Harlie hoped the attorney would hurry up. She'd called the law firm FireStorm kept on retainer, explained what happened, and practically begged for help.

Lex bobbed his head to a tune only he could hear, his hands drumming out the beat on the scarred wooden conference table as Harlie tried to make sense of the situation. The charges were obviously bogus, but why had someone told the authorities such a barefaced lie? It just didn't make any sense. She knew the press would blow this story way out of proportion, especially after accusing Lex of being a junkie during the Los Angeles incident.

She hoped to be done here in time to call her folks and let them know what was going on before it hit the news. The officer seated across from Harlie frowned at her when, staring impatiently at the door, she sighed in frustration.

Stanley Klein eventually showed up. He greeted Lex with a nod and opened his stylish leather briefcase before he addressed the police.

"I assume you have probable cause for dragging my client down here, so let's get this underway. What seems to be the situation?"

"Simpson, go tell the chief we're ready to start." The arresting officer shot an irritated glare at Mr. Klein as Lex introduced his lawyer to Harlie. "Finally."

"I was told you requested my presence, Ms. Steele," Chief McDougal said as he entered the room a few minutes later, sat down, and scooted his chair up to the table. Then he turned to the detective. "Let's get this taken care of so I can go eat my dinner. Didn't have time for lunch so I'm starving. What do we have, Carter?"

"It seems pretty cut and dried to me, Chief," said Detective Carter, known up to this point as Barney Fife in Harlie's mind. "The guy dressed like a pimp there is Lex Callatori, singer for the rock band called-"

"Uh," Lex interrupted, "this suit happens to be a Donatella Versace original, you son of a bitch." Harlie knew Lex couldn't stand having his wardrobe insulted, especially by this peon in his cheap wrinkled suit. "You must stay too busy writing traffic tickets to keep up with fashion trends."

Klein shot Lex an amused albeit warning look, urging him to tone it down a bit.

"Pardon me all to hell." Lex smirked at Carter, his hands in the air stick 'em up style. "Please, finish your ridiculous story. I want to see if I turn out to be a serial killer."

"We've been informed that he's in the habit of beating up his girlfriend, Ms. Steele here, who doesn't want to press charges." Detective Carter struggled to restrain the contempt oozing from his chunky body. "They're both denying the whole thing."

"Come on! Hearsay won't stand up in court," Klein interjected. "You can't arrest a man based on some bit of unsubstantiated gossip you pick up in the street. There isn't even a scratch on her, for Christ's sake!"

"Oh, we have proof, all right. Let's start with this." Detective Carter placed an old tape recorder in the center of the table. The smirk that spread across his jowls made him look like Bozo the Clown's evil twin. "We received this tape early this morning, a letter stating who the voices on it belong to, a brief explanation of the incident, and some other pretty convincing evidence."

"I don't suppose this Good Samaritan signed the letter in question." Klein crossed his arms. "You have any idea who sent this crap?"

"With this kind of proof, it doesn't matter who sent it," Carter snapped. "Care to listen?" Not waiting for a reply, he pressed the play button and adjusted the volume dial so no one would miss a syllable of what they were about to hear.

Everyone fell silent as the tape began to play. Luisa's unmistakable voice came through the speaker. "Come on, Zoey. I see you, hiding under you mama's bed!" A few seconds later, Harlie smiled as the house-keeper's laughter blended with her daughter's giggles. "Okay, if you done hiding and seeking, let's go make brownies." The recorder clicked itself off after the sound of a door closing.

"Well, that was incriminating," Klein declared. "I guess you'll have the DHS revoke the old lady's green card for unlicensed baking."

Carter narrowed his eyes at the lawyer. "You might not be such a comedian after you hear this next part." He hit the play button again, then leaned back looking smug and confident.

"Come back here, you little bitch!" All eyes shifted to Lex when everyone recognized the singer's voice. "Oh!" a feminine voice squealed from the recorder. Harlie exchanged confused glances with Lex.

Scuffling sounded over muffled music in the back-ground. "I'll never let you get away from me." Sounds of movement followed, then a loud smack.

"Lex, don't . . . stop . . ." The female voice seemed to gasp for air, in a frenzy of some kind.

Harlie's eyes widened, her pulse beating a cadence in her ears. "Turn that off, right now!"

The smudged two-way mirror on the wall reflected her complexion, which turned snowy white before mottled splotches of red tinged her cheeks. She grabbed Lex's arm, her eyes pleading under her raised brows for his help. The music in the background was unmistakably "Slow Ride."

"Hey, that's enough." Lex reached for the stop button when he realized what he was hearing. "Is this how you get your rocks off, you pervert?"

Carter grabbed his wrist. "You make me sick, you woman-beating little punk! We're going to hear this whole tape, then you can try to explain your way out of it."

"Fuck you!" Lex snarled, jerking his arm free.

"Quiet, both of you!" Chief McDougal frowned, his stomach growling as he leaned forward in his chair. "Something is off here."

"Please, oh please, sir, will you turn that damn thing off?" Harlie begged McDougal. She lapsed into a coughing fit to drown out the moaning and heavy breathing that poured from the recorder. She gave up and buried her face in Lex's chest, wishing the grimy tile floor would open up and swallow them both.

The chief looked a bit flustered himself when he jabbed the stop button to silence the machine. If looks could kill, Detective Carter would have been six feet under the precinct at that very moment, slain by the eight hostile eyeballs shooting daggers in his direction.

Stanley Klein gawked in his client's direction. Lex, with his arm around Harlie, grinned back at him like the cat who just swallowed a red-crowned canary. Klein turned to the Chief of Police.

"I believe a public apology is in order, since your men dragged my client out of a public place for this humiliating fiasco. Plus, you need to investigate how someone hid a recorder in the Callatori home and arrest whoever is responsible for breaking and entering and invasion of privacy. Were you even aware that these two are victims of a stalker who knocked Lex over the head a few weeks ago?" He received blank stares from McDougal and Carter. "I guess not. Well, I suggest you hand over your so-called evidence before a reporter gets a hold of it and makes the situation even more embarrassing than it's already proven to be."

"But Chief, what about the pic-"

McDougal cut him off. He leaned toward Carter, his voice low, trying to keep the people on the other side of the table from hearing him. "Just take a good look at her. No bruises and her hair's different. Somebody could've fixed those with Photoshop, if it's even her. I'm surprised you managed to get a warrant."

"He has priors for assault, so he's got a propensity for violence-"

"Give it a rest."

Chief McDougal apologized for listening to the most

intimate details of their love life, and Harlie managed to raise her head and nod in his direction. Then she glared at Carter until he shifted his focus to his scuffed shoes. McDougal removed the cassette from the recorder and told Carter they were about to have a very long talk.

"Uh, Chief. We have a problem." Carter squirmed in his chair as he explained. "You see, Callatori mouthed off to some reporters that they should come down here for the rest of the story. He was acting all big and bad, saying he was going to sue the department . . . . Anyway, one of the news guys got a copy of the tape."

"How the hell did that happen, I wonder!" Chief McDougal boomed.

"All right, I gave it to him. He called me an asshole in front of everybody and I wanted to pay him back for it. I thought he deserved to be exposed for beating her up. I had no idea it would turn out like this." Carter rubbed the back of his neck as the color drained from his face. "I'm really sorry, Chief."

A vein pulsated on McDougal's forehead and his stomach growled again. "Excuse us, please. I need to discuss something with Carter, in my office. I'll be back in a minute."

Calmer when he returned, McDougal agreed to make a public apology if Lex didn't file a complaint against the department.

"I'm going to launch an investigation to find out who's responsible for this mess. The recording sounded like it was either made with a voice activated device hidden somewhere in the bedroom or taped while someone listened through a bug. I'll personally supervise a search of your penthouse in the morning, if that's a convenient time for you."

On her way out, Harlie saw Detective Carter cleaning out his desk and heard him tell his partner the Chief gave him a two-week unpaid vacation. She wondered if he'd be able to sit down with McDougal's boot lodged up his ass.

Chapter Nineteen

The butterflies in Harlie's stomach did loop-de-loops while she waited next to Lex. Her weight shifted from one foot to the other and she wrung her hands. Was there enough time for one more trip to the ladies' room?

"Calm down, baby. This could be fun." Lex wrapped a leather-clad arm around her shoulders. "You know the old saying about picturing the audience in their underwear? Well, fuck that. Just look at me sitting beside you up there. Pretend I'm butt naked, with all my glory sticking up for the world to see. Then try to imagine all the salacious stuff I'm gonna do to you after we finish up here. But girl, try not to blush like that or they might ask what you're thinking about."

Just when she relaxed enough to grin at him, a young man walked up and propelled them forward by their elbows.

"We'll be starting in just a moment so you need to

take your seats. Please watch your step, though, because the stage lights will stay off until Mimi makes the
introduction, so the audience won't see you until then.
Right through there . . . Mr. Callatori, you sit in the
chair to your right."

Harlie hoped to get through the next hour without
puking all over the set. She'd never been on television
before, but today she was about to make one hellacious
debut. *E! News* had used her picture last month with a
statement she gave them, but that was nothing compared to this. Here she was, fixing to explain to all of
America why she and her rock star boyfriend had been
taped having sex—the really loud, toe curling, raunchy
kind—and how the audio came to be aired on the news
all over the world. At least Lex would get the juiciest
questions, since he was the one everyone tuned in to
see. She'd wanted to just do a phone interview, but no,
FireStorm's manager insisted she be here, live in the
flesh, to discredit all the bogus abuse charges.

The stage manager, wearing headphones and a cap
with *The Scoop* logo printed across it, signaled to Ms.
Lancaster. "You're on in three, two, one . . ."

The audience cheered as theme music filled the television studio. Four monitors hanging from the ceiling—two positioned for the audience members, the
remaining two for the guests' vantage point—zeroed in
on the toothy blonde talk show host.

"Hello and welcome to *The Scoop*! Today we're

joined by rock 'n' roll bad boy Lex Callatori," she paused as spotlights revealed her guests, "lead singer for FireStorm, as if anybody didn't know that already. Is there anyone here, by the way, who didn't recognize him?"

Cameras panned the crowd, showing that all present were well aware of his celebrity status.

"Seated next to him," Mimi Lancaster continued, "is the girlfriend we've heard so much about lately, Miss Harlie Steele."

Harlie's headshot crammed the monitors, which caused the buzzing audience to clap and whistle. She caught a glimpse of her own hot pink face before forcing her eyes off the screen.

"They're here today to straighten out the rumors once and for all. There's been a real media blitz surrounding them for the past couple of weeks. In case any of the viewers at home have been stuck in a cave in Siberia, which is really where they'd have had to be to miss all the innuendo, we have some clips that should bring everyone up to speed on this juicy subject."

Jake rolled a clip of the "Nefarious" video that had made Zoey freak out at the pizza place, the one where Lex's dark brown eyes morphed into those of a wildcat. An anchorman's voice announced, "Callatori was admitted to a California hospital after being found in a convenience store parking lot, unconscious in his car, apparently suffering from a heroin overdose . . ."

Mimi Lancaster read the headlines and photo captions that floated across the screen. "FireStorm Bad
Boy at it Again", "Callatori bucked from the Heroin
Horse in 7-Eleven parking lot", "Who is this mystery
redhead who set Bad Boy Lex Callatori's heart on fire?"
Harlie's head was superimposed onto a boxer's body,
gloved fist raised triumphantly over her head; beside it
was a shot of Sir Rance Williamson, his front teeth car-
toonishly blacked out, the caption reading "FireStorm
strumpet knocks Stonehenge for a loop."

Next came footage of Detective Carter leading Lex
to the squad car outside the premiere. A reporter's
voice described the scene, "FireStorm front man Lex
Callatori was taken into police custody this evening on
charges of domestic violence allegedly committed
against his live-in companion, Harlie Steele. Among
other incriminating evidence, NYPD has audio of the
crooner verbally abusing his girlfriend, then striking
her as she pleads for him to stop. The singer was recently treated at an Anaheim, California hospital for a
heroin addiction . . . ." The visual synopsis ended with a
clip of Chief McDougal apologizing on behalf of the
police department for the wrongful arrest, clearing Lex
of all charges and wishing him well.

Murmured speculation rippled through the audience. With a smile that threatened to crease her bo-
toxed face, Mimi asked, "What do you have to say for

yourself, Lex? The press seems to think you've been a very bad boy." Snickers swirled through the air.

"Hey, I've been called worse than that." A nefarious smile settled on his trademark lips. "But seriously now, we're here to clear this stuff up. If everybody will just bear with us for a few minutes, we can explain everything."

"Why don't you start with the domestic violence issue," Mimi suggested. "A few weeks ago, the two of you were at the premiere for *Smackdown*, the new movie featuring Colin Farrell and Jennifer Lopez, when police physically dragged you from the premises. Is that right?"

"Yep, in front of about three hundred fans. We'd just sat through the screening—and it's a great movie, if any of you guys haven't seen it yet. Anyway, everybody was hanging out in the lobby, everything was cool, then out of nowhere, this son of a-"

The guy in headphones caught his attention by waving a 'No Profanity' sign, prompting Lex to choose a more G-rated word. In the Green Room, they'd been briefed about watching their language, since it was hard to bleep out expletives on live television.

". . . gun slammed me against the popcorn counter and starts reading me my rights. I was arrested in front of my lady, a crowd of my peers saw me get handcuffed, and then I was led through the front door past every two-bit tabloid shark in the country. The worst part was what they charged me with. I love Harlie with all my heart and soul." His gaze aimed toward Harlie, sincere love smoldered in his eyes. "I would never think of hurting her." Lex looked directly into the camera. "I will protect her with my life if anyone tries to harm one red hair on her head."

"Harlie, I think everybody wants to hear from you on this one. It's hard to tell whether you're nervous about being on the show or if you're afraid of something else," Mimi insinuated, then sugarcoated her voice with a more sympathetic tone. "Has Lex ever hit you? Or hurt you in any way?"

Every eye in the studio turned to her. Harlie swallowed the huge lump in her throat and willed herself to calm down. Knowing she had a tendency to talk way too fast under pressure, she focused on speaking as slowly and coherently as possible.

"No, that's absolutely ridiculous. He's never laid a hand on me. I mean, not a violent one, anyway." As soon as the words left her mouth, she realized how they sounded. Lex shot her a naughty, sidelong glance. An impish grin spread over her face.

"I have some pictures I'd like you take a look at." Mimi's eyes sparkled in anticipation as she glanced at the gossip mongers seated around the studio. "After we announced the subject of today's show, someone sent us these." Two pictures filled the huge screen that had been wheeled onstage and placed about two yards to Harlie's left. "That is you, is it not?"

Gasps echoed through the audience.

Every speck of color drained from Harlie's face, until she knew she must be as white as the ghosts that had came back to haunt her. She'd never seen these pictures before, but she knew instantly where they'd come from. Her mind flashed back to the hospital on the day she'd left Jack. Dressed in a flimsy gown that tied up the back, salty tears had stung her abrasions as the nurse snapped pictures to document the brutal attack. Nickel-sized bruises dotted her arms and shoulders, showing the exact path Jack's fingers had taken as they dug into her tender flesh. A black welt formed on the swollen skin underneath her left eye and dried blood from her mouth and nose marred her face in a crusty smear.

"Oh my God," she whispered. Tears rained down her cheeks as she wept for the girl in the photos, the girl she'd once been in that living nightmare. Then, mortified, she realized thousands of people had just learned the secret shame she'd allowed herself to suffer.

Defeated boxers emerged from the ring looking less mangled. The images showed Harlie to be gaunt although she'd given birth only days before, her silhouette resembling that of a broken doll. But there was defiance on her visage. Her strong spirit had let her escape that war zone of a marriage with her life and sanity still intact.

The Scoop's camera crew also caught Lex's expression. It seemed to take him a few seconds to comprehend that Harlie was the battered woman on the screen in front of him. His mouth dropped open as realization twisted his face in anguish.

Lex wiped his eyes on his jacket sleeve, then turned to Harlie, now shaken and pale. He pried her hand from the chair arm she gripped as if to keep herself from being sucked into the photographs. He kissed her cheek and whispered in her ear, seeming to forget the people watching them.

"It's okay, baby. *That*," he pointed at the screen, "is all ancient history. I admire the hell out of you for getting out of that mess. All by yourself you stood up to that bastard, saved your own life and maybe even Zoey's. You should be proud of your own strength. Remember, that picture was taken the day *you* beat *him*."

Theme music played as *The Scoop* took its first station break, the cameras zooming in on Harlie's head on Lex's shoulder. When they were off the air, Lex turned his vehement glare on the host.

"What the hell was that all about?" he yelled. "Her ex-husband did that to her three years ago. Do you realize the pain you're causing her? Do you even care? I told my publicist we should've done the Oprah network, but no, he insisted we do your show instead. Well, fuck this! Come on baby, we're outta here."

Mimi Lancaster ran across the stage and jumped in front of the couple to block their way. "I'm *so* sorry, please don't leave. This is a live broadcast on Sweeps week, for Christ's sake! The last thing I need is to come off looking like a heartless bitch. When we got a hold of these pictures, our sources really thought you did that to her. We wanted to confront you with hard evidence that hadn't been aired before, something we thought you couldn't deny. If you'll stay and finish the show, you'll have the whole next segment to straighten it out. Okay?"

"Sources, my ass. You brought us here to rub salt in our wounds."

Harlie interrupted their nose-to-nose disagreement. "Wait Lex, it *would* be a good idea to finish this. If we leave now, it's just going to look like we have something to hide and that's why we came here in the first place. This is our chance to set the record straight. Besides, what other bombshell could they possibly drop on us now?" While Harlie would be thrilled to put this day behind her, she knew they needed to get these issues resolved, as originally planned. She made a mental note never to watch this bitch's show again. "What do you think?"

They took their seats after Lex bowed to the voice of

reason. Mimi Lancaster began the next segment with an apology and a brief explanation of the real story behind the graphic snapshots.

Harlie acknowledged the host's apology. "Since that part of my life is behind me, I don't want to discuss it anymore. I'd much rather clear up all the rumors about Lex. He's the best thing that's ever came into my life. Well, he and my little girl, Zoey," she clarified, "and I want to go on the record as saying he treats me like a queen, nothing at all like those slanderous articles you've all read." She paused and the cameraman zoomed in until her face took over the monitor, her passionate eyes burning straight into the hearts of those she now addressed. "I need to add that nobody ever deserves to be treated like that, whether it's the physical abuse or the head games that are every bit as bad. So, if any of your viewers are in that situation right now, I'd like to urge them to get out immediately. Before it's too late. I mean, take a good long look at that picture and you tell me, what are the chances I'd still be alive if I'd stayed with that monster? Get out while you can."

Embraced by warm applause, Harlie spotted a dozen women in the audience wiping tears from their eyes, clapping their hands so hard she thought their palms would turn black and blue.

The drug issue came next on the agenda. Mimi faced Lex with compulsory concern. "Exactly how did you come to be found unconscious in a parking lot with a pocket full of heroin?"

"I brought documents from the Los Angeles Police Department and a medical report signed by the Chief of Staff. They say, in so many words, that I was set up," Lex explained. "There were goose eggs on my head where somebody clubbed me. The tests they ran proved I wasn't addicted to anything, least of all heroin. I've never shot up in my life. The report explains that the angle the needle went into my arm would've been impossible for me to do by myself. Some guy knocked me out, drove me to that 7-Eleven, then shot me up with dope, probably hoping it would kill me."

Ms. Lancaster showed the documentation he cited to the audience. She also gave the results of a drug test Lex had agreed to take that very morning. It confirmed him to be clean, sober, and drug free.

"Was anyone arrested for doing this to you?" Mimi arranged her features into an apprehensive expression.

"Not yet," Lex replied, "but they're working on it. The stalker who sent Harlie that stuff in the mail to scare her was most likely the one who's behind those pictures you shared with the audience. The bastard snuck past my security staff dressed like a repairman, got into our apartment, and planted bugs all over the place. That's where the X-rated audio came from. This guy tapes us, in a very . . . *intimate* situation in our own bedroom, then sent it to the cops to get me arrested."

"So now we come to the part everyone has been waiting for. The sex tape! You all know what I'm talking about, right?" Mimi directed the question to those seated closest to where she stood.

Snickers spread through the studio audience, with snide comments uttered just loud enough for the microphone to pick up. From her euphoric expression, Harlie guessed Mimi was daydreaming about the ratings for her show climbing up the chart with each outburst.

"How embarrassing! So that was actually meant to incriminate you? I wonder why the explicit parts weren't edited out? You'd think the culprit would want to make it sound as bad as possible before he turned it over to the authorities. By the way, this recording has been aired on virtually every news program in this and several other countries."

"I think if the police have a psychological profile drawn up on this stalker," Lex said, "they'll be looking for an impotent little sicko, probably so ugly he couldn't get laid in a whorehouse, since he's too ashamed of himself to show us his face. The cops already think he's sexually obsessed with one of us, and he seems to be pissed off about something. If he had any balls at all, he'd face me one on one, *mano a mano*, to settle this. And he wouldn't be harassing Harlie. What kind of sissy picks on women?"

Supportive applause answered his rhetorical question.

"Actually, the detective who arrested Lex listened to the whole thing before he got the warrant. There was a letter and some other stuff that helped convince him it was on the level," Harlie said after her long silence. Since her emotional outburst in the previous segment and the support voiced by the audience, she felt more at ease. "Chief McDougal thinks it was intended to sound like he beat me up, then raped me. But it was pretty clear to everybody else that we were enjoying ourselves." Blushing seemed to be fast becoming Harlie's trademark.

"We have portions of that recording to show everyone what she's talking about, as if we haven't already heard it before," Mimi Lancaster said, looking overjoyed. "We had to cut out a couple of the X-rated parts, obviously, but here it goes. Play it, Jake."

FireStorm's publicist had warned them about this. Still holding Lex's hand, Harlie fixed her gaze on the ruby setting in his silver ring, willing herself not to show the deep embarrassment when she, along with the rest of the free world, would listen to herself in the throes of orgasmic bliss. Oh God, how she hoped her folks would miss this part of the show. Harlie silently prayed for one small lightning bolt to strike the television in Pete Garrett's den. She pictured her loving parents sitting there, munching on their popcorn as black smoke billowed mercifully from their set.

Lex and Harlie knew exactly what was coming since this audio had been the media frenzy's focal point for the past few weeks. Lex's raspy voice sounded first, "Come back here, you sexy little bitch . . .You'll never get away from me . . ." A smack resonated as his hand made contact with Harlie's bare ass, followed by the sound of scuffling. The foreplay led to deep breathing from both of them, and finally, hysterical moaning as Harlie reached what sounded like the climax of a lifetime.

When the tape ended, Harlie slowly looked up, her face now a darker shade of red than her hair. Sporting a smile rivaling that of *Alice in Wonderland*'s Cheshire cat, Lex winked into the camera.

The studio erupted bawdy cheers, whoops, and wolf whistles. Mimi Lancaster fanned herself to mock the steaminess she'd just witnessed. She spoke after the uproar died down. "Well, well, well. I think that speaks for itself. This seems like a good time to get some comments and questions from the audience."

Hands shot up, all vying for a chance at the mic.

"I have a question for Harlie," an attractive brunette said, a rhinestone stud twinkling on the side of her nose. "Could you tell me the name of the perfume you wore that night?" When Mimi asked why she wanted to know that, she replied, "Because if it turns a guy on like that, I'm going to order a case of it!" Guffaws erupted all around them.

Mimi turned the microphone to a man wearing a Tommy Hilfiger sweatshirt and cargo pants. Throughout the taping, he'd been cracking people up with his comments. "I think I'm gonna be a big FireStorm fan after this, Mimi. Harlie, you're one gutsy chick. I just have to say one more thing. Lex, you the man!" By the tone of his voice, it was obvious he was referring to the rock star's sexual prowess.

Lex nodded his head in egotistical agreement. "Look at her and you can understand where my libido gets its inspiration." He gestured toward Harlie with a flourish of his hands. "Damn, ain't my baby fine!"

While everyone agreed that, yes, she was one fine piece of work, Harlie shot back, letting her blithe personality show through as she tried to focus the attention back on Lex, "Is this not the sexiest man y'all have ever seen? With his handsome face, that hair, and oh, those lips." She appeared to surprise everyone with her moxie, relaxed and spunky now in contrast to all the blushing she'd been doing for the past half hour. "Stand up and turn around for me, sweetheart. I want y'all to take a look at the butt I've drooled over since I watched his videos as a teenager."

Nearly every female present squealed in delight when Lex obliged by shaking his derriere at them.

"And he has the biggest heart, among other things. I'm the luckiest woman in the world."

Mimi chimed in, "We'll have to take our eyes off Lex's nice backside for a station break. Sorry, everybody. We'll be right back after these words from our sponsor."

Chapter Twenty

After a short station break, the cameras rolled again.

"For those of you just joining us, Lex Callatori and his new love interest, Harlie Steele, are here talking with us today." Mimi Lancaster turned to address the couple on the stage. "I believe the only thing we have left to clear up is the part about," she said, then paused to laugh. "Now get this everybody. The story goes that sweet, tiny little Harlie punched out Sir Rance Williamson! He's the lead singer for Stonehenge, by the way. What's the deal with that?"

"It's like I said in my statement to *E! News*," Harlie answered. "Rance showed up at the penthouse when I was alone one afternoon. We'd never met before, but I knew he and Lex were friends so I let him in. We talked for a while, then he sort of started to, um, insinuate things that just weren't appropriate. I suggested that he go down to the studio where the band was rehearsing."

"What did he say then?"

"That's when he got fresh. He started groping at me so I tried to knee him to make him stop. I just couldn't believe he was acting like that."

"Did it work?" Mimi prodded. "What happened next?"

"He still wouldn't back off, and he had the gall to ask me to kiss him. I'd had about all I was going to take. Lex wasn't there, the man was grabbing me, and I didn't want to have to call security in to make a scene. It was ridiculous." Harlie shook her head. "Finally, I had to jab him to get him to leave me alone. He lost his balance, fell over the table, then the bodyguards ran in and showed him out."

The crowd clapped, giving her their stamp of approval.

"Yeah, that's when he showed up at our studio." Lex leaned back in his chair and crossed his ankle over his knee. "Gave me this cock-and-bull story about how Harlie was all jealous and crazy. When he said she'd been all hot for him, I'd have given him a black eye to match the bloody nose Harlie gave him if Zeke hadn't held me back."

"How do you feel about Sir Williamson now?" A suspicious gleam danced in Mimi's eyes.

"We haven't spoken to him since it happened," Lex answered. "It's not like I hate him, I just don't want him around Harlie."

"We don't have any hard feelings," Harlie added. "At first, we were really upset about the whole thing, but now we can see the humor in it. Sort of. He's used to having things his way, so maybe he just can't help himself. Who knows?"

"I must say, that's very big of you." Mimi's anxious gaze searched an area just off stage right as if she were waiting for something. Suddenly, Jake performed a twirly pointing maneuver that made him look like he was swatting at a swarm of invisible hornets.

Mimi resumed the discussion. "You wouldn't believe how happy I am to hear that. We have someone waiting in the wings who wants to say something to you. Please welcome Sir Rance Williamson!"

After more signaling from Jake, a chair appeared on the set. Meanwhile, cheers encouraged Sir Rance to walk onstage. He bombarded the audience with thrown kisses and bowed in Mimi's direction, then turned to face the surprised couple.

"I'm so sorry, luv!" Sincerity rang through his British accent. "I came to bury the hatchet for my transgression during our last meeting. Will you do me the honor of accepting my humble apology?"

Harlie stood up and shook hands with the knighted luminary, took a step back when he attempted to hug her, and smiled in spite of herself. "Apology accepted. Just behave yourself from now on."

"I promise," Sir Rance agreed. "And thanks so much for not pounding my head today."

The audience clapped and roared at his response. This man emanated a presence that made him impossible to hate.

He aimed his next act of contrition toward Lex. "I'm sorry, old friend! I stepped over the line this time, even for me. I'll be strictly hands off the goods from now on, if you'll give me the opportunity to prove myself. Shall we give it a go or what? Friends?"

Lex appeared to give the situation some serious consideration before he answered. "If you bother her anymore or talk about her like that again, I'll kick your fuckin' limey ass!" A crew member ripped the 'No Profanity' sign he'd been waving in half, threw it on the ground, and proceeded to stomp all over it. "But yeah, I'll accept your apology."

Heading toward the final station break, the camera focused on Sir Rance pulling Lex from his seat for a reconciliatory hug as the audience applauded. Rance made his exit before the show resumed.

"I believe we have one more surprise scheduled for today. Right Lex?" Mimi asked, winking.

Zeke appeared from the wings carrying a massive bouquet and met Lex at the edge of the stage. Harlie's first thought was that Zeke planned to make a public bid for Randi's affections, since she knew they both had mutual crushes on each other. She cocked her head in surprise when Lex walked back to her.

"Baby, I just want you to know how much I love you, and that I'm sorry about all the crap you've had to put up with since we met. You're not in my heart, you *are* my heart." He handed her the most beautiful bunch of flowers she'd ever seen, red roses mixed with lilacs and sprigs of baby's breath. Their heavenly scent added a magical touch to the euphoria she already felt. She didn't think things could get any better.

Lex went down on one bent knee in front of her, looking to Harlie like her very own knight in black leather armor. He asked, his voice raspy with raw emotion, "Will you marry me?"

This being the last thing Harlie expected, she couldn't find words to express the thoughts that spiraled through her mind. She feared her heart was on the verge of bursting with joy.

Some members of the audience cried as everyone gave the kissing couple a standing ovation.

Harlie glanced over at the host. Mimi had probably shit her pants realizing this episode would most likely win her a Daytime Emmy.

"I'm as stunned by the proposal as the rest of you. I was told that Lex wanted to give his girlfriend flowers for putting up with all the media hype, but I had no idea the modern day counterpart to John Lennon and Yoko Ono planned to get engaged on my show." She had to yell to be heard over the ensuing pandemonium. "Congratulations! I'm going to set you guys up tonight in the Michelangelo Hotel, all expenses on me, including a romantic dinner for two and all the champagne you can drink! I wish you every happiness in the world!"

Signing off as she did after every episode, she faced the camera for her final close-up of the day. "This is Mimi Lancaster, and that's it for now. Join us again Monday for *The Scoop!*"

Chapter Twenty-one

Lex and Harlie stepped out of the elevator in front of their penthouse still wrapped in the rosy afterglow of their romantic night at the Michelangelo. Dozens of perfumed candles had lit their suite, with its silky sheets and enormous tub for two. Mimi had sent over steak and lobster with chocolate covered strawberries for dessert. One simply couldn't have the strawberries without French champagne, hence the three bottles of Cristal on ice.

"If I carry you over the threshold, will you let me practice for the honeymoon?" Lex inserted his key into the lock, flirting over his shoulder. "Or did you get too much of me last night?"

"You know I could never get enough of you." Harlie shot him a seductive grin. "Aren't you in a hurry to go tape that radio interview? I thought that's why we had to haul our butts out of bed so early." They'd frolicked all over the suite until the first rays of dawn painted the walls golden pink, so neither had been eager to leave the king-sized bed when the alarm jarred them awake at six o'clock that morning.

Lex went to shower and change while Harlie headed for the kitchen to fire up the espresso machine, since both of them needed a stiff shot of caffeine to stay awake. The scent of coffee beans wafting through the air turned her thoughts to Zoey. She missed her little shadow who loved to help operate the sputtering contraption.

Zoey had spent the night with Luisa, her new best friend. She picked up some of her native language too, which caused Harlie to choke with laughter one morning at the breakfast table. Behind his untouched plate, Lex looked up from his newspaper when Zoey tapped him on the arm. With her little elfin face scrunched into a frown, she chided, "Wex, you be too *a* skeeny." Mimicking the gesture Luisa used to coax her into finishing her vegetables—touching the fingertips of her right hand to her thumb, then flexing her wrist back and forth —she ordered him to eat, using the Italian mantra, "*Mangia, mangia!*" Lex hid his amusement behind his napkin and dug into his waffles to humor her, though it was hours before he could look at Zoey with a straight face.

Harlie was arranging some of Luisa's delicious homemade biscotti on a serving tray to go along with the cappuccino when she heard something that made her blood run cold. Lex's scream sent her running to the bedroom.

He sat on the bed, his back to the door.

"What's the matter? Did you hurt yourself?" She moved to the other side of the bed and gasped. Her hands flew up to cover her mouth when she saw what made him cry out.

"I can't believe that son of a bitch did this." Lex rocked back and forth, his listless dog cradled in his arms. "Goddamn it!" Anguish contorted his face as tears glistened over his cheekbones.

Beside him, Harlie placed her hand on Lex's back to offer what little comfort she could. She knew Mugsy was much more to him than just a pet, that he loved him like a child.

"Is he . . . gone?" She couldn't force the word 'dead' from her mouth. Mugsy's head lolled to the side and his eyes stayed closed, though she didn't see any visible injuries.

Lex moved his hand to the bulldog's chest. Hope sprang into his eyes. "I think he's still breathing." Harlie could barely see the small ribcage contract and expand under his fingertips. "Come on, Mugsy, old buddy . . . . We need to get him to a vet, quick."

"What happened?" Harlie asked.

"This was around his neck when I found him," Lex said, his jaw muscle flexing as his pain turned to rage.

"That stalking bastard tried to choke him to death with it."

Goosebumps sprang up all over Harlie's arms when she saw the heavy chain with the yin-yang pendant in his open palm, the same necklace that disappeared two months earlier during his hospital stay.

Lex carefully stood up holding the injured dog and headed for the door. Harlie grabbed his arm.

"At least Mugsy made his mark on the guy." She pointed to the quilt at the foot of their bed. "This has to be his blood. Look, it goes from the spot Mugsy was lying to the edge of the bed, and there's some over there on the carpet too. He must have taken a pretty good sized plug out the son of a bitch."

"What's that? On the pillow?" Lex asked, motioning in that direction with his head.

Harlie picked up the folded note, its words typed in the same font as the card in the shoebox. A shiver dripped down her spine as she read the message out loud. "The dream is almost over. Go home or else."

Harlie, still uneasy about steering a car down the bustling New York streets, was glad Zeke was there to drive them. During the ride to the veterinary clinic, she phoned Chief McDougal to report the incident. He promised to dispatch men to investigate the break-in immediately. Then she called Luisa, told her two of Lex's security staff were on the way to her apartment, and asked her to keep Zoey away from the penthouse until after the police checked it out. Zeke called Fire-Storm's publicist to postpone Lex's interview, which was due to start taping in less than an hour. With a faint whimper, Mugsy came to as the car pulled into the parking lot.

The veterinarian said Mugsy was going to be fine, though his throat would hurt for the next couple of days and he'd have to eat soft food until it healed. Dr. Hoskins said it was a miracle the bulldog's windpipe hadn't been crushed. It was lucky he'd lost consciousness when he had, since the intruder must have thought he was dead.

When they arrived back at the penthouse, Chief McDougal's men were waiting for them. Detectives Kirk and Lantree combed the premises for any evidence the perpetrator might have left behind, though they didn't seem to have much luck.

A statement from the security guard on duty the previous evening explained how the stalker got inside. Jim Smit had seen the man dressed as a repairman on a previous occasion, thought he was on the level, and let him in. Nondescript in appearance, the slight man wore a baseball cap pulled down so the bill obscured most of his face. Smit hadn't noticed any company insignia on his uniform.

Lex fired him on the spot. Smitty was a likable guy and all, but there was no way he could tolerate that kind of lax judgment, especially not under these circumstances.

Detective Kirk, a middle-aged congenial type with a Brooklyn accent, asked Lex and Harlie to walk through each room and point out anything that might have been disturbed. Their findings were strange, as if the intruder made himself at home before attempting to kill the dog. A two-liter of Pepsi sat on the dining room table beside an empty crystal goblet and a plate holding the remnants of leftover lasagna. Detective Lantree suggested that Harlie throw out any unsealed food, just in case the stalker had decided to spice it up with poison. The intruder cut the strings on a Greek bouzouki and, like a wild beast marking his territory, pissed on a couple of guitars in Lex's music room.

When they opened Zoey's door, Harlie let out something between a groan and a yelp, the muffled garble made in a nightmare when the mouth tries to scream but doesn't quite succeed.

Positioned on the child's pink comforter were the remains of Sassy Susie, Zoey's favorite doll. She'd spent many happy hours feeding it bottles and dressing it up for tea parties. Now it lay broken, the severed head resting beside the miniature body. The meaning couldn't be any clearer. If things didn't change, Zoey would be the next target.

The shock was too much for Harlie. She hadn't had time to eat anything since the previous night, which was the only reason she didn't puke on the spot. The stress of dealing with Mugsy had been bad enough, but this menacing site in her daughter's room was more than her mind could handle. The room swirled into darkness around her as her legs buckled.

Lex caught her before she hit the ground.

Still shaking a few minutes later, she opened her eyes to find herself in Lex's arms in the living room.

Until the stalker was caught, a police officer would be posted outside the penthouse around the clock, in addition to the staff of bodyguards already stationed there. Nobody from the Callatori household would go anywhere without this double security coming along as an escort. No one was above suspicion.

Detective Kirk promised to call them the minute they had any leads. The FBI might be able to match the fingerprints from the goblet with some already on file, though it was a long shot. The blood sample from the carpet could be used later to match the suspect's DNA, when and if they had a suspect to apprehend.

Luisa brought Zoey home after the detectives left. The first thing out of her mouth was, "Me home, Mugsy!" She waited a couple of seconds, placed a hand on her tiny hip, and asked her mother, "Where Mugsy at?"

Luisa crossed herself, then rushed from the room mumbling in Italian.

Every day but this one, Mugsy wagged his stubby tail and trotted to the door whenever Zoey walked through it. The bond between toddler and pooch had grown stronger since she and Harlie moved in. The dog even slept in her room most nights, so it was no wonder his absence alarmed her.

Harlie explained that Mugsy was hurt but would be fine in a few days. This was nothing like the speech she had prepared in her head to give her daughter today, when she'd planned to spend the afternoon celebrating the engagement. That would have to wait until a more opportune time. Holding her hand, Harlie led her to Mugsy's bed where Zoey doctored him with baby talk and gentle kisses between his eyes.

Later that afternoon while they munched on chocolate chip cookies, Harlie thought the time was right. "Zoey, how would you like for Lex to be your stepdaddy?"

"Yay! Wex be my 'nother daddy!" After a moment of thought, confusion registered on her face. "What 'bout my old daddy? What we do wiff him?"

Harlie smiled at her daughter's question, then kissed her on the nose. "He's still your daddy, honey, and you'll still have your visits with him. You're such a lucky little girl, with your old daddy to see each month, and now Lex to be your full time stepdad. Pretty cool, huh?"

Zoey cheered in agreement, then asked for another

cookie.

Harlie stayed behind when Lex went to make up the interview he'd missed that morning, going on live that night to compensate. Left to her thoughts, she tormented herself with worry over the safety of the two people she most loved in all the world, Zoey and Lex. Why was this happening to them? Why now, when they were so happy? What had she done and to whom? She paced around the living room, racking her brain for answers.

Harlie rubbed a hand over her churning stomach. She did not want to throw up again. Luisa had practically force fed her a bowl full of minestrone, a dish that at any other time Harlie would have gobbled down and raved about. She needed to keep at least some of that in her belly.

"Get a grip on yourself, Harlie. You've got to calm down," she said, knowing she must look like an idiot wandering around the room talking to herself. Since she needed something to divert her attention away from her troubles for a while, she decided to check out the old chatroom. Even if Barbed*Ivy wasn't there, she'd find someone to talk to.

Logged on as CyberBitch, Harlie found Barb chatting away. She decided not to bring up the break in or Mugsy. Barb would just insist it was an omen that she should leave while the getting was good.

~ CyberBitch has entered the room. Welcome ~

Barbed*Ivy: Well if it isn't our very own TV star showing up 2 honor us with her presence! How's it going, Bitch?

CyberBitch: I've had better days. I guess U saw us on *The Scoop*, huh? What did U think about it? Did the camera catch my good side? LOL

Barbed*Ivy: U looked beautiful but that boyfriend of URs still looks like a crack house reject. But hey, I know UR sensitive about that and I don't want 2 piss U off.

CyberBitch: Thanks for your sensitivity! LOL I guess I won't hold my breath waiting for U to congratulate me on my engagement.

Barbed*Ivy: I just want U 2 B happy and think U can do way better than that monkey-faced music man. U should've let me fix U up with my cousin. But I'm still going 2 B UR friend and stick by U, no matter what. So CONGRATULA-TIONS! Happy now? I just want U 2 B happy. :)

CyberBitch: G thanks. I'm sooo moved. Not! LOL But THNX for the congrats.

Barbed*Ivy: LOL Why did U say U'd had better days? Something wrong? I figured U would be on top of the world after yesterday. Didn't Mimi say she was going 2 put U up at the Hilton?

CyberBitch: No, it was the Michelangelo. Oh, Barb, the suite was beautiful and we had the most romantic night! But I didn't get much rest (wonder why! LOL) and I've been busy with this

and that lately, so I guess I'm just a little sleep deprived. I'd sure like to get away for a mini-vacation pretty soon, just me and Lex, maybe out in the country for the day, somewhere the paparazzi can't bother us. U know of any place like that?
Barbed*Ivy: As a matter of fact, I know just the place.

When the radio program came on that evening, Harlie could picture the host buried in audio equipment, his face hidden behind trademark sunglasses. His endearing lisp flowed through the microphone and into the ears of his late night listeners.

The show kicked off with heavy breathing from the infamous tape. Shock jock Paulie Starke and Lex were old friends so they spent much of their airtime reminiscing about their wilder days. Later on, the interview turned to the stalker. Since the police advised them not to go public with the last break in, the comments were mainly a recap of the details aired on *The Scoop*.

Much to Harlie's horror, the program ended with Paulie begging Lex to send him some naked pictures of her.

"Hey, show some respect," Lex said, giving his friend a good-natured reprimand. "That's my future wife you're talking about. She is pretty hot, but she's all mine."

The radio station wasn't that far, so Lex should make it home within the hour. Exhausted from worry and lack of sleep, she curled up on the couch to wait for him, positioning herself between the door and Zoey's room just in case anyone happened to get past the guards.

Lex came home with a large bag from the Toy Emporium in hand. He'd been lucky enough to get the last blue-eyed Sassy Susie doll in the store and hoped to replace the mutilated one before Zoey missed it. Before he'd made it to the register, a fairy doll with auburn ringlets, emerald green eyes, and a heart shaped mouth caught his attention. Dressed in a shimmering gown with buttery-soft wings in the back, that doll would have to keep Sassy Susie company until he could surprise Zoey with her in the morning.

He found Harlie sound asleep, snuggled against the sofa cushions. She looked peaceful, except for the closed butterfly knife clutched at her chest. Looking at her now, his heart swelled with love and happiness. He'd known for weeks that he wanted to marry Harlie, but had been waiting for the perfect moment to ask her. Yesterday on the talk show, he'd only planned to give her the bouquet and tell her how special she was to him. The emotions between them were so intense, and the way she looked up at him with those big blue eyes, he'd known the time was right. He went down on his knee without a second thought.

Lex took the knife out of Harlie's hand before he woke her with a kiss and carried her to bed.

Chapter Twenty-two

A beat-up Buick, painted the color of a turd when it tumbled off the assembly line in the early nineties, made its way down the winding country road. Harlie took in the rustic scenery as they cruised along, and relaxed for the first time in weeks. She and Lex needed this day of fun in the open sunshine, just the two of them, somewhere they wouldn't be spotted or harassed by anyone.

Lex wasn't likely to be recognized in the old relic he borrowed from one of his roadies. People expected to see him step out of a stretch limo when he wasn't speeding through town in one of his own red sports cars. He rented the occasional bland sedan while on tour, but under no normal circumstances would he drive a piece of shit like this. The stereo's CD player didn't work and the dinged up body could stand a trip through the car wash, but at least everything under the hood worked fine. Nobody would ever guess this turdmobile carried a celebrity.

The past few days had gone pretty well. Mugsy recovered from his injury, thanks in large part to Zoey's love and attention. The toddler spent hours each day narrating fairy tales to the pooch, pointing out the corresponding pictures in her storybooks as she went along. Zoey insisted on being the one to fill his bowl with canned food, and with Luisa's help, used bits of Swiss cheese to coax the finicky dog into swallowing his smelly green medicine.

Luisa had snapped some photos of the playmates one afternoon, one of which Harlie had taped to the dashboard. Seated at Zoey's miniature table, Mugsy suffered the indignity of wearing a princess costume with a pink bow taped between his wide set eyes. The replacement Sassy Susie rested in the chair to his left, and the fairy doll sat spraddle-legged on the table's edge. Zoey had doled out cups of imaginary tea from her little china set all afternoon, pausing every once in a while to brush cookie crumbs from Mugsy's chin and to remind him time and again that sticking out his tongue was bad manners.

Harlie savored a deep breath of August air, so much fresher than the foggy gray stuff her lungs inhaled in the city. She watched Lex's hair blow in the breeze and felt like Bonnie and Clyde sneaking away to a secluded hideout. The policeman stationed at the penthouse threw a fit when told he couldn't come along. Lex had explained that they were going to the country where no one would see them, and yes, they planned to go alone. The officer only agreed to stay behind after Lex slipped him a couple Franklins and gave him a phony destination address.

The clear sky above was the exact cornflower blue shade of Zoey's eyes. Harlie missed her something awful. It'd been the hardest decision of her life, but two days ago she sent her daughter, accompanied by a small entourage, to stay with her parents until the stalker was captured. Nothing, not even separation anxiety, was worth risking the life of her beloved little girl. She knew Zoey and Mugsy were safe in Kentucky under Zeke's watchful eye. Although Luisa couldn't give a clear description of the man who'd planted the listening devices, she had seen him. She'd been sent along not only because she was terrified to be alone in the penthouse, but also to recognize his face if he showed up in their vicinity.

Harlie had spoken to her mother before leaving with Lex that morning. Roxanne, with Zoey and Mugsy playing at her feet, said everything was fine on their end. Her granddaughter settled in nicely, Luisa had the spare bed, and Zeke was comfortable on a cot in the den. "Everyone's enjoying themselves and I'm happy to have some female company around here, though I do wish Luisa wouldn't try to help so much with the housework. Don't worry about a thing. You and Lex have a nice time, dear, just be careful." Roxanne's maternal tone gave Harlie a sense of normalcy. "I'll talk to you tonight."

The situation kept everyone pretty rattled, with Harlie worried about Zoey's safety and Pete and Roxanne wound tight as a drum over the maniac terrorizing their daughter and Lex. To ease everyone's nerves, they'd decided to play a sort of phone tag while all of this was going on. Each morning, someone from the Garrett household called Harlie's cell phone—a lifeline that never left her side now—to make sure the couple hadn't been murdered in their sleep. Harlie or Lex rang Pete's house every evening around Zoey's bedtime to make sure nothing out of the ordinary had happened. So far, their plan had helped give them all a little peace of mind.

"It was cool of your friend to let us use this place," Lex said, breaking the tranquil silence. "So you just know her through the 'net, huh? Never seen her or talked on the phone?"

"That's right." Harlie knew the situation must sound strange. "Actually, I count her as one of my closest friends, next to Randi, of course. It'd be nice to meet her one day, but the anonymity of the whole thing is kind of nice. That's the beauty of the internet. People get to know you for who you are and what you post, and don't care so much about how you look or if your clothes are still in style. It's funny, if you think about it. It took modern technology millions of dollars to make this space age tool, and every day people all over the world use it to get to know each other on a basic level that seems almost unattainable in the real world anymore. Well, for that and those addictive damn Facebook games. Amazing, huh?"

"I never got into computers that much," Lex admitted. "I check the FireStorm website the publicist set up, and I can play a mean game of stud poker on the thing, but that's about as far as my interest goes."

A growl from Lex's stomach turned the conversation to food. "I hope you packed enough stuff in that picnic basket. I'm already starving, and," he paused to shoot her a lascivious glance from the corner of his eye, "you're gonna need to keep your strength up, baby. Fresh air makes me horny, don't you know."

The couple stopped flirting when a deafening crunch split the air. A pickup smashed into them from out of nowhere. Their car spun like a top across the pavement.

The macabre twirl ended when two of the Buick's tires rose into the air a split second before the vehicle slammed into an oak tree. The steel underbelly now faced the road, the passenger side crushed against the ground on a downward slope. Both sat stunned, their tranquil morning ripped away.

Suspended by his seat belt, Lex spoke first. "Harlie, you all right . . . . Baby, are you hurt?"

"I'm fine. I think. How 'bout you?" She reached out to brush the hair from his face and make sure he wasn't bleeding.

A snake-like hiss sputtered from the far end of the hood, probably a busted radiator. A three-inch-deep dent protruded into the cab and extended across the length of the roof, perfectly outlining the tree they slammed into.

"Are you guys okay in there?" A man wearing a red cap and denim jacket gazed at them through the cracked windshield. "Need some help?"

"Yeah, we're fine," Lex answered, dangling from his seat like a rag doll. "Are you the one who hit us?" There was no malice in his voice as he asked the logical question.

"Naw, another truck was hightailing it out of here when I pulled up. Probably drunk or somethin'." Judging by the way he practically yelled through the glass in his nasally twang, Harlie figured he must have thought they were deaf. His wild-eyed expression startled her at first, but she guessed the accident had him pretty keyed up. "Tell ya what. I'll back my truck around here and you can climb up onto the tailgate. I'm afraid the car would tip over if you two just try to crawl out." Not waiting for a reply, he yelled "Be right back" and disappeared as quickly as he'd shown up.

Harlie heard a motor rev, the crunch of loose gravel, and then saw the man peering down at them from above.

"You might want to hand me your stuff, so you don't have to worry about it later," the man suggested, then took the picnic basket and Harlie's purse, which they passed up to him through the driver's side window. "Take a hold of my hand before you undo that seatbelt. Wouldn't want to fall on your pretty daughter, there."

"Uh . . . She's my fiancée," Lex said, poking his head up through the window. "Thanks." Harlie was glad the comment hadn't seemed to offend Lex. People didn't usually mention their fifteen-year age difference.

A thump sounded in the truck when Lex climbed out, footsteps echoed from the truck bed, and then the smiling face appeared once again. "Let's get you out of there, young lady."

Harlie couldn't put her finger on it, but something didn't seem right. She'd expected Lex to assist her, but figured it really didn't make any difference so long as she got out. Her nerves were just jittery from the collision and she was being silly. Before she extended her hand to the helpful stranger, she checked to make sure her butterfly knife hadn't fell out of her back pocket.

Pulled from the wreckage and into the sunshine, she saw nothing in the back of the truck except a large blue cloth and assumed Lex had stepped behind a tree to take a leak. She lost her footing and tripped, falling onto the lumpy mass of coarse fabric.

"Sorry about that, Harlie. Don't know why I'm so clumsy today," the man said as he fell over her, victim of some unseen circumstance.

A sharp pain pricked her thigh. She grabbed a fistful of the bulky material and tried to pull herself up. The tarp fell back to reveal something hidden underneath.

"Lex!" she screamed, staring at his motionless body.

Her tongue tingled on the bottom of her mouth as a green-tinged blackness settled over her.

Chapter Twenty-Three

A solitary man sat at the table in the center of the tidy cabin. He needed to keep his mind sharp and alert, now that things were finally coming together, so Arthur Bowen poured himself a cup of strong black coffee.

He wiped up a drop that slid down his mug before it soiled the coaster, reflecting on how well his plan had played out during the past few hours. Everything he'd worked so hard for these past six months was paying off. All he'd planned for, toiled for, broken the laws of man and morality for, had transformed his dream into reality. *They could have made it easy on themselves, if only they'd heeded my warnings,* he thought, *but they chose to force my hand.*

He'd waited in his pickup since dawn, knowing their plans but not their time schedule. From his vantage point, he watched the bend in the road a quarter of a mile away, invisible within the thick shrubbery he'd backed into. He started his engine the second the brown Buick crept into view. Thanks to the security cameras in the parking garage, he knew exactly what to look for. Information was so easy to come by these days. Arthur had hacked into the apartment building's computer system in a matter of seconds, a simple task for someone skilled at retrieving hospital records, legal documents, unlisted phone numbers, and the like.

Even startled, Harlie looked beautiful. He'd gotten his first close in-the-flesh glimpse of her when he rammed into their car. Knowing he'd outwitted *him*, Bowen relished the adrenaline rush that followed. Callatori proved his level of incompetence when he lost control of the vehicle, spinning four donuts before the Buick crashed into the tree. *And he was so eager to accept my help*, Arthur remembered, *poking that boney arm of his through the window, expecting me to pull him to safety. Oh, how I loved zapping him with the stun gun the second he had his footing.* The music man had fallen over with a loud thump, twitching sporadically from the electricity that coursed through him, a delight to Arthur's eyes. To insure his victim would stay under for at least an hour, Bowen administered the syringe he'd prepared days in advance. Then he kicked Callatori's mangy body to the corner of the truck bed and covered him with a blue tarp.

At last, the brass ring is within my grasp! Oh, how soft was the hand she'd reached out to him as he pulled her up from the steel frame that entombed her. Her perfume filled his nostrils with a soft floral scent, the perfect complement to her delicate femininity. But Harlie broke the web of magic spinning around them when she fell over onto *him*, screaming when the canvas shifted to reveal her *lover*—the very word formed in his thoughts caused pain to shoot through his jealous brain, even now. He'd injected her with a second syringe, then kissed her cheek before he tucked her under the blue canvas.

He'd originally intended to drag the Buick into the little nook where he spent the morning waiting, but since he stood little chance of budging that wrecked hunk of metal, he had to switch to his clever backup plan. He had the two passengers hand up all their personal effects before he helped them out of the car. Before leaving the scene, he removed the license plate and stuck a yellow tag on the steel undercarriage that now faced the road rather than the ground. Anyone who passed by would think some drunken teenager careened into the tree the previous night, the tag falsely alerting them that the tow company was on its way.

On his drive through the deep woods toward the cabin, the pickup never passed another human being. Besides seasonal hunters, only the occasional Sunday driver taking in the scenery used this remote country road, no one else. It angered Bowen that Callatori thought so little of Harlie's safety that he'd endangered her life by giving his bodyguards the day off, just so he could have her all to himself. *Stupid for him, but fortunate for me.*

He sipped the last of his coffee, dabbed the corners of his mouth, then neatly refolded his napkin along its creases. In his usual fastidious manner, he scanned the cabin—which consisted of one multifunctional room and a small lavatory—for anything out of order. He found nothing to straighten.

It wouldn't be long now until his house guests opened their eyes. All the weightlifting he'd done over the past few months paid off when he'd dragged that longhaired asshole into the cabin. Harlie, on the other hand, felt as light as a kitten in his arms. Arthur gave her the most comfortable seat in the place before he tied her hands behind her back as loose as common sense would allow. He heaved Callatori into a rickety ladder-back relic with no cushion and watched his digits turn red from the tension of the ropes that bound his wrists and ankles.

I do so hope she'll call me Artie. No one ever had before, but he longed to hear the endearment fall from Harlie's sweet lips. His parents had never addressed him by anything short of his given name, since they thought Arthur sounded dignified and refined. Some of the mean children from elementary school, apparently jealous of his IQ and high marks, had given him the cruel nickname of 'Art the Fart'. Having been born with his left leg hanging a full two inches shorter that his right caused him to walk with a limp which, his classmates rudely pointed out, made him look as if he passed gas with each step he took. The special shoes his mother ordered did little to rectify the situation.

Bowen estimated it would take approximately a week to win Harlie's affections. She might mourn the lost love of her music man for a day or two, but once she realized the depth of Arthur's love for her, she'd certainly listen to her heart and be his. No price would be too great to pay for the love of this woman.

What had she ever seen in Callatori in the first place, he wondered, shifting his gaze back and forth between them, from his sleeping beauty to that repulsive beast. Arthur intended to maim him beyond all usefulness. He had no qualms about killing him, if need be, just like that mongrel house pet.

He waited patiently, knowing they should come to any minute. Soon he would taste the delectable fruits of his labor.

Chapter Twenty-four

The minute he noticed Harlie begin to stir from her induced sleep, as he mentally referred to her current state of unconsciousness, Arthur ran to the bathroom to comb his hair. With all the effort and preparation he'd put into this meeting, he didn't want to make a bad first impression. He smiled at himself in the mirror, confident she'd find him attractive. At thirty-eight, his sandy brown hair had only recently started to recede, untarnished by a single strand of gray. His mother, on her last visit, said he epitomized the perfect gentleman, and that the few fine lines around his eyes and mouth made him look even more distinguished. His new muscles made him believe he looked taller, a comforting thought since his small frame had always made him feel a bit inadequate. Satisfied with his image, he hurried back to his guests.

Harlie's head hurt so bad she could barely open her eyes. When she did pry her lids apart, the light streaming through the window made her squeeze them shut again. She had no idea where she was or how she'd come to be there. Why couldn't she move her arms? Then, slowly, her memory returned. She recalled being helped out of the wrecked Buick . . . seeing a mass of blue . . . and Lex's unconscious body.

Panic forced her eyes to fly open. A man sitting at the table directly in front of her came into focus. The red cap was gone now, but she recognized him from the accident. She didn't like the way he was looking at her. Like a starving man drooling over the last piece of chocolate cake.

She scanned her surroundings. To her far right, a single bed stood on the wooden floor. To her left, she saw Lex tied to a chair. His head slumped forward so that his chin rested against his chest, his long dark hair obscuring his face from view.

"Lex," she whispered, the word sounding more like a plea than anything else. She tried to reach out to him—he was only a few feet away—but the ropes would not grant the movement. "Oh my God." The restraints bit into her wrists as she struggled to free her arms. Her throbbing skull made it impossible to get a handle on things.

She squinted toward the man responsible for this situation. The light from the window behind him burned into her retinas. She shook her head and asked the obvious question, "Why?"

"Hello." His eyes gleamed and a crazed smile swept over his face. "I hope you aren't too uncomfortable. Sorry we were forced to get acquainted under less than ideal circumstances, but I'm so happy to finally meet you in person."

Harlie stared at him in a blank stupor. If he expected her to say it was a pleasure to meet him and could he please serve tea and cookies now, he was in for a disappointment. She noticed his speech pattern was much different now than it had been at the scene of the accident. Earlier, he spoke with a loud, twangy, unsophisticated inflection; now she heard the trace of a northern accent. It was obvious he carefully planned each syllable before he open his mouth to speak, as if attempting to sound better educated.

She had no idea how to respond. She didn't want to give him the impression she enjoyed sitting in his house all tied up like a human shoelace. On the other hand, she didn't want to say the wrong thing and get herself and Lex chopped into little pieces, frozen, thawed, and served for dinner at this raving lunatic's next barbeque.

"I'm Arthur Bowen. I don't expect you to know who

I am, of course, but I've been interested in you for a very long time. I hope you don't mind my saying so, but you're even lovelier in person. You look so warm." Bowen must have noticed the beads of perspiration Harlie felt sliding down the perimeter of her face. He jumped up and hurried to the thermostat. "Let me turn on some cool air for you. There, that's much better already, isn't it? Just let me know if you catch a chill and I'll turn it back off. Are you feeling all right?"

Well, he certainly had to be the most polite kidnapper in history, Harlie thought. This man, for whatever reason, seemed to be trying to impress her. Logic told her she needed to stop the pounding in her head before she could figure out what to do, and, since her host seemed to be in such a hospitable mood, she decided to risk asking a favor.

"Uh, could I please have an aspirin? I have a terrible headache."

"Oh, you have the voice of an angel," Arthur sighed, clasping his hands together in front of his chest. "I never knew you had such a beautiful Southern accent until I heard you on that talk show. And you certainly may have something for your headache." He rushed to the refrigerator with a glass, then filled it with ice cubes and water from a plastic jug.

"Open up." Beaming, he shook the medicine from a small bottle and held the tablets up to her dry mouth. Harlie saw 'Tylenol' stamped on them, relieved the letters didn't spell 'cyanide'. He carefully tilted the cool water to her lips, then patted her chin with a napkin.

"Thank you." This didn't make the slightest bit of sense to her. She thought it best to keep her part of the conversation to a minimum until her head felt better and she could think straight. She was worried that Lex hadn't come to yet.

Harlie knew she was in the presence of the stalker, the monster who'd tormented them for months, put Lex in the hospital, and threatened her daughter's life. An enigma plagued her mind as she began to feel sick at her stomach. Why was this cold-blooded monster busting his ass to get on her good side? What could he possibly hope to achieve by holding them captive like this?

She knew she'd never laid eyes on this man before today. After replaying Bowen's words in her mind, she decided to question him, hoping for a clue about whatever had sparked his infatuation with her or, better yet, a way out of this mess. "It was sweet of you to say that a while ago, that I look better in person. Do you know me from the tabloids?"

"No. I was aware of you long before your liaison with *him* got you into those rags," he scoffed. "I did read all those articles, but I realize they're comprised of lies and fabrications. I'm sure you'll be glad to be out of the limelight, since the press should lose all interest in you after this absurd relationship breaks up."

Harlie was trying to decipher the meaning behind her captor's words when Lex groaned. He violently jerked his head back, wild-eyed, as if breaking the water's surface after almost drowning. His frantic eyes sought her out, seeming to take a visual inventory to ensure she was in one piece and unharmed. Then his glare shifted to the party responsible.

He looked Bowen up and down, then grunted his disapproval. "So your sissy ass got tired of playing with dolls, huh. Untie me and we can settle this like men." The challenge twisted his face into a sneer.

"The matter is already settled. You should've taken my warnings seriously and it would never have come to this. If you really loved Harlie, you would have left her alone." Bowen's demeanor transformed into one of loathing, his face a mask of hatred. "Instead, you decided to endanger not only her life, but her daughter's as well. Would it have satisfied you to attend their funeral, had I been deranged enough to murder them like your stupid mutt? That should've convinced you I was serious, that you should send her back home where she belongs. If this situation hadn't played you into my hands, I planned to shoot you rather than let you destroy her life. You should have made it easy on us all and died in California."

Straining every muscle in his body, Lex lurched forward, fighting his bonds but unable to gain his freedom. "Who the hell are you, anyway?" he spat, bringing himself back under control. "You'd take these ropes off me and fight me like a man if you had any balls."

Harlie watched the two men glare at each other, struck by the irony of their appearances. Had anyone peeped in through the window, they probably would've jumped to the conclusion that Lex, with his long hair and T-shirt, was the bad guy. Arthur looked like a paragon of virtue in comparison, with his short cropped hair and creased pants.

Arthur's maniacal laughter rang through the cabin. "Let me reiterate the situation for you." He grabbed Lex's silver cross earrings and ripped them out, slitting the lobes. Harlie screamed when she realized what he'd done. "It's already over. As for who the hell I am, my name is Arthur Bowen, your worst nightmare."

"Can't you at least untie her, or do girls scare the shit out of you too." Lex sneered, not showing any reaction to the pain in his bloody ears.

"Too bad she has to stay like that until you're out of the way," Arthur said, shaking his head. "She has to be shown that I am the better man, the only logical match for her. You'll be good for nothing but sitting in a wheelchair, drooling oatmeal for the rest of your life when I'm done with-"

The cell phone ringing in Harlie's purse interrupted the threat. "Who is it?" he asked, his voice calm but

urgent. "I know you're expecting someone specific or
this wouldn't have been left on today . . . It's your parents, isn't it?" Bowen fished the phone from her hand-
bag.

"Yes." She saw no point in lying, afraid of what
might happen if he suspected her of deceit. Plus, he'd
probably already read the caller's name by now.

Arthur scooted Harlie's chair over until her elbow
touched Lex's arm, then told her what to do.

"You're going to answer it and act as if nothing out
of the ordinary is going on. Tell your folks you're having such a wonderful time you decided to stay until tomorrow. I'm going to be listening, and if you slip up
even the least bit, give them the slightest clue something is amiss . . ." Bowen grabbed a Bowie knife Harlie
hadn't noticed hanging from his belt and positioned it
against Lex's throat. The silver blade glistened at the
tender spot where his neck connected to his jawbone. "I
will slit his worthless throat on the spot. No second
chances before you watch him bleed to death. Slowly.
Do you understand?"

"Yes." Defeated, a tear slid down her cheek as she
gazed at Lex, whose eyes avoided hers by glaring toward the ceiling. "I'll do whatever you want, just
please, *please* don't hurt him."

Arthur pressed the button to answer the phone just
after the fourth ring, hit speaker, then quickly position
it between himself and Harlie. He seemed to take

pleasure in the closeness, but never moved the knife he grasped in his other hand.

"Hope I'm not interrupting anything." Just as Harlie suspected, Roxanne's voice came through the receiver. "I needed to ask if it's okay for Zoey to spend the night with Randi. Zeke said it's fine with him, and he'd be happy to go along and sleep on her couch. The girls want to camp out in front of the television in her living room. Zoey's been begging all day to watch *Attack of the Killer Tomatoes*. Is that alright, dear?" Roxanne had a tendency to be long winded.

"That's fine, Mom." Harlie hoped she wouldn't mention the dog that was supposed to be dead. "I'm sure they'll have fun."

Bowen seemed to know an awful lot about her, even guessing her parents would call. She racked her brain for some small detail her mom might catch on to. It was imperative to drop subtle hints Arthur wouldn't notice.

"Are you and Lex having a nice time out in the country?"

"We sure are. Actually, we've decided to stay here all night. I'll call you tomorrow afternoon to let you know how everything goes." A quick wit had never been one of her sweet mother's attributes, so she doubted she'd catch on. They had the phone schedule worked out so her parents called every morning, and she called them every evening around eight o'clock.

Why, oh why, couldn't her dad have been the one to call?

"If you see Louis anytime soon"—she never, never, ever called her brother by that name—"be sure and tell him I'm still waiting for the gift he's supposed to be mailing me. I can't wait to see what my present is. He called twice last week to tell me about it, so I'm irritated I don't have it yet." Harlie spoke in a very upbeat conversational tone, hoping against all odds her mother would talk to Louie very soon. Her brother hated talking on the phone and never called Harlie unless there was an emergency. He'd know she was in trouble if he heard about the fictitious gift, since he always referred to the butterfly knife he'd given her as 'the present'. She hoped her mom would be worried about the package supposedly lost in the post office and remember to give Louie the message.

"Wasn't that sweet of your brother? Oh no, I have to go, dear. Zoey's on the potty chair and I need to clean her up before she spills pee all over the carpet."

"Okay, Mama." Harlie hadn't called Roxanne that since she was about twelve years old. "I'll talk to y'all tomorrow afternoon. Tell Randi thanks. Love you. Bye."

Hopelessness squeezed her heart when her mother disconnected.

"That was very wise of you." Arthur turned the phone off and scooted Harlie's chair a few feet away from Lex. Apparently, he hadn't detected anything out of the ordinary in the conversation. "I knew you were a lady of high intelligence."

Watching him resheath the knife, Harlie exhaled breath she didn't realize she'd been holding.

"You deserve a reward for cooperating with me. Why don't we have an early supper?" Arthur opened the picnic basket and began arranging the contents on the table in front of him. "Everything looks so delicious. Did you make it yourself?"

"Yes." Harlie forced a pleasant tone through her lips to avoid provoking him. "I like to cook."

"I know you do," Arthur doted. He unload the fried chicken, biscuits, potato salad, deviled eggs, and a large jug of lemonade. Under the napkins and paper plates lay packages of graham crackers, marshmallows, and Hershey bars for making s'mores over a fire, something Harlie learned back in her Girl Scout days. He opened a Tupperware container full of cold spaghetti and turned up his nose.

"Only a wop like Callatori would eat this crap." He opened the door and threw the pasta, container and all, into the yard.

The racial slur caught Harlie's attention. She had some information about her own family tree she hoped might disenchant him. "If you don't like people with ethnic backgrounds, I'm afraid you won't like me much, either. My grandpa was Irish, born and raised in County Cork."

"How nice! I didn't know that, but I imagine that must be where you inherited your red hair. The Irish are such lovely people, nothing like that dago trash from Italy." Arthur scowled in Lex's direction.

Harlie's pulse raced when she saw Lex's flaring nostrils and flexing jaw muscles, terrified he was about to lose his temper big time.

"Y'all look hungry," she blurted, trying to steer things in a safer direction. "I'm sure we'll all feel better after we eat." Food was the farthest thing from her mind.

Lex took Harlie's cue and appeared calmer after he took a deep breath. "She's right. We should eat, then we can straighten everything out. My people will wire you all the money you want, if you let us go."

"I couldn't care less if you drop dead from hunger and I have no interest in your money. I'll eat your portion and thank you to keep your disgusting rubbery lips shut long enough for Harlie and I to enjoy our meal." Bowen looked at Lex as if he were shit stuck to the bottom of his shoe. "I'll be replacing you, after all, and this is a good place to start. Both of you better get used to the fact that you'll be out of her life after today. Her heart and affections will belong to me."

He popped a deviled egg into Harlie's mouth. She had no option but to chew.

"She made that food for me, you fuckhead," Lex snorted, losing his composure when he saw the way Bowen was leering at Harlie. "Are you stupid enough to believe you could have a woman like her? She loves me, not you. Hell, Harlie wouldn't piss on the best part of you, man, much less fall in love with you." He burst out laughing.

Harlie saw a vein on Arthur's temple pulsate. She wished his head would explode.

"And what's with that limp? Let me guess. You dropped one of my CDs on your foot and now you want to steal my woman." Lex laughed even harder. "Ain't gonna happen."

The laughter struck a nerve in Bowen. "I've never been one to tolerate that sort of insult and I'm certainly not going to take it from you, of all people."

He pulled a container of pepper spray from his pocket and squirted Lex, his perceived tormenter, making a point of saturating his eyes and gaping mouth. Harlie screamed for him to stop, but Bowen rolled his eyes and sprayed him again. It went to work burning Lex's soft tissue as the foam filled the room with a smell like melted plastic.

A haughty smile on his face, Arthur strutted back to the table and began to eat his meal.

Lex thrashed in his seat, gasping and coughing uncontrollably. Involuntary tears streaked the slick orange goo dripping from his face. His hands strained against the ropes that bound him, helpless to wipe the substance from his eyes. Powerless to help him, Harlie could do nothing but watch in horror as he lurched in pain.

Arthur savored a bite of fried chicken. "This is delicious! The best I've ever eaten." He looked at Harlie, shaking his head from side to side as he chewed. "I'll never see what fascinated you about him, my sweet. Look how pathetic he is, crying like a schoolgirl. And the way he tosses that stringy mane of hair around like some convulsive transvestite. What *were* you thinking when you agreed to marry him? Isn't it obvious why I couldn't let you throw your life away on *that*? You deserve so much more. Not to worry, though. I intend to be the best husband a lady could wish for."

He spooned potato salad into his mouth and raved about the texture while Lex writhed in agony.

With a lot of struggle and intensive neck work, Lex finally managed to wipe his face on the shoulder of his T-shirt. Even his scalp felt like it was on fire where the pepper spray soaked through his hair. Still in considerable pain, at least he'd quit gagging and wheezing and his nose had almost stopped running. The tearing helped wash some of the goddamn substance from his burning eyeballs.

Lex watched Bowen eat the food Harlie packed for what was supposed to be a romantic getaway. He pictured how the son of a bitch would look with a chicken leg shoved up his ass. It would take every ounce of self-control he had, but for Harlie's sake, he resolved to keep his smartass comments to himself until he came up with an escape plan. He could imagine the perverse plans Bowen had in mind for Harlie, but he wasn't about to let the bastard lay one sick finger on her. *Over my dead body, and Bowen's.*

Chapter Twenty-five

The room was quiet while Arthur finished his dinner, poking food into Harlie's mouth despite her protests. She stared at her antagonist and forced herself to swallow a huge piece of chicken. How did he know so much about her? Did he have a connection to someone she was close to?

There was no real possibility that Jackson Steele would have paid this man to abduct and torture them. He would have been happy to do it himself, if he could have gotten away with it. No, Jack wasn't involved.

Could Arthur Bowen be a customer of her father's? She dismissed the idea when she remembered the old pickup truck he rammed into them. Pete did bodywork on Harley Davidsons and classic cars, not ragged out jaloppies.

Maybe Arthur had dated Randi, been jilted, and decided to take revenge on her best friend. Insanity aside, Bowen was reasonably handsome, someone Randi might have gone out with. But Harlie knew about all the guys she'd dated since high school and Arthur wasn't one of them. Randi would have mentioned the limp and his obsessive-compulsive behavior.

"I have a surprise for dessert!" Bowen announced as if presenting circus tickets to a five-year-old. "Much better than those Hershey bars you packed. I knew these were your favorite." He reached into the cupboard over the sink, the hinges creaking from rust and lack of use, and removed a box of candy bars.

Harlie's lips twisted into a wry expression at the sight of the Standard Candy Company of Tennessee's logo. "Where in the world did you find Goo-Goo Clusters?" She'd put Luisa on the lookout for her favorite candy, a gooey marshmallow confection topped with caramel, peanuts, and chocolate. Harlie hadn't tasted one since her move to NYC.

"There's nothing you could ever crave, or need, or want, that I would not walk to the ends of the earth to bring you, Harlie." Arthur looked like a lovesick puppy with neurological problems.

"Have I talked to you in a chatroom?" Harlie asked apprehensively. That had to be it. She didn't have many friends, though she'd chatted with hundreds of people over the last four years on the internet. Last month she'd asked her cyberpals if they knew how she could get Goo-Goo Clusters delivered. "What did you go by? Are you Studmuffin?"

"No, but you're on the right track, CyberBitch, my love." Arthur smiled at the woman with whom he intended to spend the rest of his life. "Statistically, when love develops over time out of a strong bond of friendship, that love will endure a lifetime."

At least now Harlie knew where he picked up most of his information. Bowen must have been lurking when Barbed*Ivy gave her directions to the cabin. There was no other way he could've found out, since they hadn't told anyone exactly where they were going or which route they planned to take. Not the police, not FireStorm's security staff, not even her own parents. If by some miracle her mother caught on to the clues she'd dropped, there was no possible way anyone would find them. She realized it was going to be up to her and Lex to save themselves.

"Can't you tell me what your username is?"

"I'd rather you figure it out for yourself," he said, removing the long-sleeved chambray button-down he wore over a spotless white T-shirt. He lifted one of the candy bars from the box and opened the wrapper along its seam. Harlie noticed a partially-healed dog bite on his wrist, happy to see Mugsy left a permanent mark.

The scar gave her a flicker of hope. This lunatic was not infallible, after all.

She wondered exactly where they were. They'd been on the way to Barb's cabin when he crashed into them.

Had he taken them somewhere else or were they sitting in her friend's property this very moment?

"Here you go. You get the first bite." As Bowen held the candy bar to her unyielding mouth, she noticed the tattoo wrapped around his biceps. Nicely ink, with heart-shaped leaves entwined around razor sharp thorns. Sensing something familiar about the configuration, Harlie had the same feeling she got watching *Jeopardy*, knowing the answer but unable to pull it to the surface of her thoughts.

"Please take a bite. You don't want to hurt my feelings after all the trouble I went through, do you?" Arthur asked through an exaggerated pout.

Well, you fucking psycho, I don't want to piss you off, now do I? Harlie reluctantly parted her lips. After what he'd done to Lex, there was no telling what he was capable of. She bit off a small hunk of the candy bar and studied the tattoo as she chewed, hoping to find the answer to the mystery hidden among the inked vines.

Arthur noticed her gazing at his arm. He seemed eager for her reaction.

She gasped, and nearly strangled when she sucked a peanut down her throat. Arthur patted her back until the coughing subsided. Try as she might to focus on anything else in the room, her eyes homed in on the tattoo. Those weren't thorns, she realized. It was barbed wire. And those delicate leaves could only be ivy.

A horror she'd never known sent chills down the back of her neck. Feelings of betrayal and confusion swept over her. A million thoughts ran through her head, countless conversations replaying themselves in her spinning mind as the gravity of the situation sank in.

"Damn it," Arthur shouted. A slimy mass of egg yolk, chicken, and chocolate chunks oozed down his pants and dripped to the floor.

When Harlie threw up on him a second time, he slapped her, unable to rein in his temper when the bile spattered over his shoes.

"Is this how you repay my kindness? By puking all over me!" None too gently, he wiped a speck of vomit off her chin, then swabbed the puddle off the floor before attempting to clean himself up.

"I'm gonna kill you, motherfucker!" Lex strained against his ropes, irate at witnessing Bowen strike Harlie.

"Oh shut up," Bowen hissed, then jabbed his fist into Lex's nose. He stalked to the bathroom to change clothes, leaving Lex to bleed all over his shirt.

"Harlie, baby, you all right?" Lex kept his voice low so Bowen wouldn't hear him. "Do you think he poisoned you?"

"No, I'm fine." She blamed herself for letting her

queasy stomach worsen the situation. "It's just my nerves making me sick."

"I'll kill that son of a bitch as soon as I get loose. He's not gonna get away with this shit, I promise you that."

Afraid Bowen might hear her, she decided not to divulge what she'd just figured out about his identity. Harlie reached for the knife in her back pocket, but her hands were tied on the outside of the back of her chair. She wouldn't be able to reach through the opening between the cushion and seat with her hands bound together. Trying another strategy, she concentrated on shifting the knots from side to side, hoping to loosen them enough to free her wrists.

"Are you going to be okay?" Harlie asked, watching drops of blood splatter from Lex's nose onto his shirt. He didn't have a chance to answer.

"Why are you even speaking to him?!" Bowen trudged back into the room, his footsteps echoing loudly off the wooden floorboards. "He and his worthless life are no longer of any consequence to you. Don't you understand? You belong to me now."

"Mr. Bowen, I'm afraid I need to be honest with you." Harlie looked directly into his eyes, her voice civil but firm. The knots had shifted toward her left wrist, the tension eased on her right until she could almost slip her hand through. Wishing she didn't have the thumb that stood between her and freedom, she continued, and hoped to force this madman into a reality check. "I'm flattered that you're infatuated with me to the point of going to all this trouble," she lied through her teeth. "I'm touched, but I'm in love with Lex. Nothing you could ever do is going to change that. You seem to know me so well, and if you care about me as much as you say, why not let me be happy for the first time in my life?"

"You stupid bitch!" This closed-fisted blow sent bloody spit flying from Harlie's mouth. "Looks like your ex-husband knew the best way to control you. If that's how you want to play, then so be it." He didn't seem to hear Lex shouting for him to stop.

Harlie sat dazed as Bowen glared down at her.

"Give me that goddamn piece of trash!" he yelled as he ripped the yin-yang necklace from Harlie's neck. He threw it into the yard the same way he'd disposed of the cold pasta. The windows rattled when he slammed the door shut afterwards. "And try not to get any blood on the chair cushion."

"Don't touch her again. Take these ropes off of me and fight me like a man!" Lex's eyes darted back to Harlie, worry creasing his brow as he studied the unnatural expression plastered on her face since Bowen hit her. "Come on *Artie,* you afraid of me?"

"Don't you dare call me Artie! Only Harlie is allowed to address me that way. Where's that goddamn ham-

mer?" His voice reached a maniacal crescendo as he riffled through the cabinets and drawers. "To hell with it,
I'll make do with the doorstop." He seized a rock the
size of a loaf of bread. Lugging the heavy weight, he
walked behind Lex's chair.

"Let me see," Bowen pondered in a childish sing-
song voice. "Which hand do you use to play your stupid
guitar? Hmmmm. Don't imagine a musician can write
many songs if his hands are fucked up. Come to think
of it, I believe a person has to use both for that instrument, one to fret the chords and the other to strum the
strings. Guess I'll have to smash both."

He placed himself at a right angle behind the rickety
chair and swung the rock three times. Using the motion with which one swings a baseball bat, he slammed
the rock into the musician's tied hands. A sickening
crunch sounded as the tiny carpal bones snapped.

Lex's jaw muscles worked overtime to prevent him
from screaming. He obviously didn't want to give Bow-
en the satisfaction of knowing the amount of pain he'd
caused.

The mind can be very humane sometimes. It switch-
es off the pain receptors and lets a person slip deep into
themselves in times of great duress. Harlie hadn't felt
any pain when Bowen rammed his fist against her
mouth. Not even a tingle. Her eyes just glazed over until she no longer saw the maniac who stood in front of
her. She was barely cognizant of what Bowen was do-

ing to Lex. Like a war veteran having flashbacks, the violence she'd suffered in the past replayed in her mind: her ex kicking her pregnant stomach; the sight of her own face, a lumpy black and blue in the mirror; the smell of urine as she almost drowned with her head held in the toilet; the beating she took the day she left Jack.

She unconsciously struggled to free her hands, her breath uneven. Now the movie in her mind showed the hellish images caused by Bowen. Barbie dolls hung in effigy, Lex lying unconscious in the hospital bed, Mugsy near death, the threat on Zoey's life, Lex covered in pepper spray as blood dripped from his ears. Then her own words rang through her head, the mantra that gave her strength during some of the worst days of her life: *I'll never be anyone's victim again.*

She didn't feel the slightest bit of discomfort when she jerked her right hand free, scraping a layer of flesh off in the process. The part of her mind controlling Harlie's actions focused on things far more important than pain. Her wrists kept behind her back, she eased the butterfly knife from her pocket, released the latch with her thumb, and waited.

Bowen had thrown down the gauntlet. Now Harlie was prepared to pick it up and sodomize him with it.

"That is enough," Harlie said, her voice a harsh monotone. She didn't give a shit what Bowen did to

her, but she'd be damned if she sat by and let him torture the man who meant everything to her. The last bit
of rationality—maybe even a piece of her sanity—had
drained from her with the last arc of the rock crashing
into Lex's hands. She swallowed a mouthful of her own
blood before she could speak again. "It's me you want,
so come and get me. Beating the hell out of him is
soooo not the way to a woman's heart."

"Oh, but I'm not finished with him yet." Arthur
kicked Lex in the shin for the hell of it. "I intend to
come and get you, as you phrased it, right after I take
away your songbird's voice. Can't say I ever cared for it
in the first place. A cup of Drano should do the job
quite nicely. Just enough to destroy the vocal chords
and leave him with severe brain damage. But, he'll
live." He turned to beam at Harlie and explained his
point of view. "Unless you want to spend the rest of
your life changing his diapers, that should put an end
to your relationship."

He pulled a jug of drain cleaner from under the sink,
sat it on the floor at his feet, and riffled through a
drawer for a hose to shove down Lex's throat.

"Okay. Suppose he's off living out his days in a rest
home. That doesn't guarantee that I'd fall in love with
you. If you know me so well, you'll remember the one
thing I can never forgive is a liar . . . or someone who
pretends to be something they're not." The voice coming from her lips was unrecognizable as her own. Each

syllable dripped venom.

Worry spread across Arthur's face at her declaration.

Harlie fingered the metal handle concealed behind her, wishing she'd let her brother talk her into a gun. "Didn't you pay attention during all those times we spent chatting the hours away? And this cabin isn't quite as homey as you told me it was. The tattoo gave you away, but you don't look at all like I'd pictured you."

She met his stunned expression with a look of pure hatred, then drawled out the name until it sounded like a thing more loathsome than death itself. "Barbed Ivy."

"You're mad now, but you'll get over it if you know what's good for you," Bowen said, ignoring the way she glared at him. "Did I mention that I've been inside your father's shop? It would be easy to put a bullet right between his eyes, and your mother's. Such a kind woman. She offered me homemade fudge and coffee when I visited, since she believed I was running for some political office. Sure would hate for anything to happen to such nice people."

Harlie never batted an eye. "If you killed every living soul I've ever met, even if you cut off my arms and legs and glued my hair to the goddamn bedpost, you could never make me love you." With a flip of her wrist behind the chair, the knife butterflied open in a fraction of a second. "Let me spell it out for you, *Art.* Take all the love I feel for Lex, turn it around and multiply it a million times. That extreme emotion would almost match the depth of hatred I feel for you."

Her heart pounded against her ribs as she fought a losing battle with her own self-restraint. "How do I hate thee, let me count the ways. I hate you to the depth, and breadth, and height my soul can reach," she parodied, her eyes burning a hole through her captor.

At first it appeared as if her words had pierced Bowen's heart, but then he shook it off and turned back to the drawer.

"You will either agree to marry me and be the affectionate wife I deserve, or I'll grab Zoey when you least expect it. You can't expect to keep that Neanderthal bodyguard around after Lex turns into a vegetable. . . . Ah, here's the funnel!" He held up the device he planned to use to force Drano down Lex's throat.

Bent over to lift the jug from the floor, he finished his threat. "What kind of mother would you be to let your baby girl get herself molested? Or have her Kewpie doll body turn up dead in a ditch somewhere? No, you'll do what is expected of you or pay the price."

Bowen's biggest oversight proved to be his failure to secure Harlie's feet and ankles.

When her window of opportunity showed itself, Harlie's spirit took over her body, propelling her forward with a burst of primal strength. Arthur Bowen had bent over for the Drano—with his back to her.

She would have no memory of the events that un-folded after that.

Chapter Twenty-six

Lex had never witnessed anything like it. A guttural battle cry spewed from Harlie's mouth, raising the hair on his arms and neck as she leaped through the air like a wildcat.

She tackled Bowen from behind and knocked him onto his face. Caught off guard, he flailed an instant before she stabbed him. On its downward arc, the stainless steel blade glistened in the sunlight streaming through the curtains before it embedded between his shoulder blades. Harlie sank it to the hilt, and seemed to enjoy the bloodcurdling scream it caused. Then she grabbed his hair in her bloody hands and beat his head against the oak floorboards until he lay motionless. The sneer of satisfaction that spread over her face during her blood lust was an image forever engraved on Lex's memory.

Using her foot for leverage, she pulled the bloodied weapon out of Bowen's back. Without a word, she stood and wiped the blade clean on her jeans before she cut Lex's ankles and wrists free. Harlie closed her knife with a flick of her wrist and tucked it away in her pocket.

Devoid of any trace of emotion, she stared sightlessly at the wall, muttering, "Barb. I paid the price, all right." Lex couldn't tell whether she was replaying the scenario in her head or hiding in a safe mental refuge. After a moment, she buried her face in Lex's shoulder.

He held her for a long time. As he led her toward the door and the sanctuary on the other side, the unthinkable happened.

Driven by pure rage and adrenaline, Bowen flipped over on his side and grabbed Harlie's leg. She attempted to stomp his skull with her other foot, but lost her balance and fell.

He reached for the weapon sheathed at his side.

Lex kicked his fingers away and grabbed the Bowie knife, then struggled to grasp it as pain shot through his broken hands. Holding it between his fractured palms, he sank the long blade directly under Bowen's sternum. Lex visualized it puncturing an icy heart. He wished he could prolong Bowen's pain after the horror he'd put them through.

Harlie put her hands on the end of the hilt above Lex's, careful not to hurt his mangled hands. Together, they forced the dagger down until they felt it dig into the floor beneath Arthur, the dying man who tried so hard to destroy their lives.

Lex paraphrased Bowen's threat, and hoped Arthur could hear it as he took his final breath. "'Sometimes dreams do come true.' Mine is for you to die, mother-fucker."

"Rot in hell," Harlie said, her voice an eerie whisper before she fainted.

Lex called 911 on Harlie's cell phone. He had to use his left thumb to push the buttons.

He took Harlie in his arms and carried her down the country lane, wanting to put as much distance between her and this nightmare as possible. He trudged forward, his broken hands held out in front of his unconscious fiancée, until he met the police cars and ambulance on the gravel road.

Lex had glimpsed his reflection on the way out of the cabin and knew he looked a mess. Pepper spray residue matted his hair and blood covered his face and shirt. Harlie's tears glued auburn curls to her cheeks, and streaked the bloody smears around her busted lip as she came to.

She refused to let anyone other than Lex touch her. In the ambulance, she sat pallid and trembling beside him, clinging to his neck as if it were a lifeline. While one EMT tended to his injured hands, Lex convinced Harlie to let the other technician put the blood pressure cuff around her arm and shine a small light into her eyes.

Lex overheard Harlie's attendant tell his partner, ". . . BP low, rapid pulse, pupils dilated, breathing irregular, skin cold and clammy." They tucked a heavy wool blanket around Harlie in spite of the eighty-two degree weather. The EMT aimed a reassuring half grin in his direction. "It looks like she's in shock, but she's going to be fine."

The siren roared on their way to the hospital.

"Everything's okay, baby," Lex whispered in her ear. "We beat him together, girl. Just you and me. The rest of our lives will be a walk in the park after this. I love you, Harlie."

She snuggled against him, her eyes squeezed shut as if to block out all the ugliness she'd been through. Lex sang quietly into her ear until they arrived at the Emergency Room.

Chapter Twenty-Seven

The spacious New York penthouse overflowed with family and friends fresh off the plane from Kentucky. Zeke and Luisa both had keys to let everyone in, so the group was waiting to greet the couple when they came home from their overnight stay in the hospital.

The orthopedic specialist gave Lex some optimistic news. Most of the bones in his right hand were fractured, but only two fingers of his left had been broken. As far as the doctors could tell, there didn't appear to be any permanent damage to the nerves or tendons. After a few months of healing and physical therapy, he should regain full use of both hands. With a little luck, he'd be as talented with the guitar as he'd always been. For now, he had enough movement in his left hand to hold a fork, but that was about it.

Harlie had stood beside Lex while the specialist set his hands. She believed her injuries were nothing compared to his and ignored the nurses buzzing around her. The sight of his fingers, swollen and mangled, made her head spin, but she leaned against the gurney and refused to pass out again. Had those horrible things really happened to them? A nurse gave her a paper bag to breathe into when she hyperventilated.

Lex's eyes were okay, though still a little red from the pepper spray. It also left an oily residue in his hair that didn't come out, even after Harlie shampooed it twice. He was in a lot of pain and found it difficult to sleep, what with stitches in his torn earlobes, one hand in a cast and finger splints on the other.

After a nurse cleaned the dried blood smears off her face, Harlie held an ice pack to her busted lip. A doctor applied ointment to the abrasions caused from jerking her hands free of the ropes, then covered the raw area with gauze. The staff seemed more concerned over her anxiety level and mental state than anything else. A psychiatrist came in to speak with her and scheduled an appointment for her to see a psychologist a few weeks later. He suggested Harlie's abusive past probably triggered her reaction to Bowen's threats as well as the blackout, and believed both issues would haunt her until she talked them out and worked through them.

Still emotionally shaken when she arrived at the apartment the next morning, Harlie smiled when Zoey jumped into her arms. She couldn't hold back the sobs when her parents hugged her and she saw the tears in Roxanne's eyes.

"I knew something was bad wrong when Mom told me what you said, about the package I was supposed to be sending you." Louie gave his sister a quick peck on the cheek. "I called the cops as soon as I could get off the phone with her."

"Yes, Louie went ballistic, asking me if I picked up on anything strange when I talked to you," Roxanne interjected, blowing her nose on Pete's hankie. "You phrased things kind of funny, but I figured you might've been a little tipsy, you know, since you were supposed to be having a romantic getaway. I'm so sorry I didn't understand what you were trying to tell me. I might've been able to-"

"No, Mom," Harlie said, shaking her head. "You did exactly what I wanted when you talked to Louie. There's really nothing else anyone could have done."

"I'm just so glad you're both all right." Randi gave Harlie and Lex quick hugs. "Now that the psycho's dead, you can get back to living a regular life. Well, as normal as a celebrity can, I guess." Her contagious smile lightened the mood. "I feel like I'm moving up in the world myself, staying in a penthouse that's been featured on *MTV Cribs*. This place is awesome."

After a bit, Zoey trotted down the hall with Mugsy to play in her bedroom. Zeke and Luisa fell back into their usual roles while Pete, Roxanne, Louie, and Randi got in each other's way fussing over Lex and Harlie's every need.

The next afternoon, Mimi Lancaster started *The Scoop* with a special segment to update the recent events that made headlines around the globe. The paparazzi worked overtime to get new footage of the couple or a statement about the kidnapping and escape. Mimi had called to wish them a speedy recovery and begged them to come back on her show. Harlie sighed in relief when Lex refused; neither of them needed the added stress. Mimi would just have to settle for media clips this time.

Zeke and Randi took Zoey to the park, to conveniently keep her away from the television while the show aired. Harlie didn't want her to see it, especially since Zoey asked so many questions about how Lex hurt his hands and why Mommy's lip looked funny. The first fifteen minutes of Harlie's morning now went to camouflaging her bruises with makeup, a skill she never thought she'd have to use after her divorce.

When Mimi gave her opening spiel on *The Scoop*, Harlie fought the urge to run to her room and hide under the covers. She wasn't eager to relive those memories again.

Clips rolled in classic Lancaster style. Aerial footage shot from a helicopter above the cabin showed tiny people milling around on the ground below as blue and red lights flickered atop police cars and ambulances. A reporter announced, ". . . police and medics are on the scene. Moments ago, FireStorm front man Lex Callatori and his fiancée Harlie Steele escaped from the cabin where they'd been held captive by the man who stalked them both for months. The suspect is believed to be dead. Callatori and Steele are alive, currently being treated for injuries in the ambulance. We don't have many details yet, though we do know Harlie Steele's brother contacted the NYPD with his suspicions about the same time the 911 call came in . . ."

A close-up of Chief McDougal shot later that day filled the screen. "The body of the kidnapper has been confirmed to be Arthur Bowen, a self-employed salesman living in the New York area. His rap sheet shows priors for rape, harassment, battery, arson, and petty theft."

"Is it true that Miss Steele stabbed Bowen?" an off-camera interviewer asked.

"Miss Steele and Mr. Callatori are lucky to have made it out of the situation alive," McDougal answered. "Bowen was killed in self-defense, and I don't intend to shed any tears over the scumbag."

A headline reading 'Callatori and Fiancée Slay Kidnapper After Being Tortured' replaced the film of McDougal. Mimi summed up the article, "Bowen's obsession with Harlie led him to kidnap the couple after crashing into their car. Both were tied to chairs and beaten pretty badly. Lex was doused with pepper spray, had his earlobes ripped open, and both his hands were broken. Arthur Bowen died from stab wounds from a knife he'd used to terrorize his victims."

The segment ended with a clip of them leaving the hospital, FireStorm security acting as a buffer between them and the photographers. Mimi looked into the camera before the commercial break, her eyes glistening with crocodile tears. "Lex and Harlie, we wish you a speedy recovery and send you our love."

"Well, glad that's over." Harlie turned off the television. Pete and Roxanne exchanged concerned glances with Lex as Harlie, a fake smile plastered on her face, pretended to be unaffected by the show. "I'm going to see if Luisa needs any help in the kitchen."

That night, Harlie forced herself to log onto the chatroom one final time. She felt compelled to warn her friends—the people she'd chatted with for so many years and hoped didn't turn out to be as insane as Barbed*Ivy—to be careful on the internet after the ordeal she'd been through. Shivers raced down her spine when she saw her own cybername flash on the screen. Creeped out, she typed one quick message, wished them well, and then logged off permanently.

A string of horror shows haunted Harlie's sleep on a nightly basis. Waking up in a cold sweat from nightmares seemed to be part of her routine now.

Lex performed on a hazy stage. He flashed a lusty smile toward where she stood in the crowd, then spun around and jumped through the air like an acrobat. When he landed, he transformed into Arthur Bowen as he slid toward the front of the stage on his knees. He pranced around in a satanic strut, the barbed wire and ivy tattoo snaking its way up his neck toward his face. Bowen sang "Nefarious", the familiar words pouring from his throat infused with a perverse new meaning. 'Nefarious', chanted twice in unison by the other band members, accented the end of each line of the chorus. Lex reappeared center stage, hog-tied. Stix, Dylan, and Ray watched as if it were a normal part of the concert. Bowen kept singing as he walked toward Lex.

"Now's your last chance to run and hide."

Arthur raised the guitar like an axe over his head, then turned to look over his shoulder at Harlie. She suddenly found herself tied to an amp on the edge of the stage.

"In just a minute I'll be coming inside."

His eyes danced maniacally as the band chanted. The instrument started a downward arc toward Lex's head while Bowen sang, a demented expression on his now tattooed features.

"Done warned you once, I'm bad to the core."

Harlie's muted screams begged him to stop, to come

after her instead, but to no avail. The victim lying at the madman's feet changed in strobe-like succession from Lex to Zoey, Pete and Roxanne, Louie, Randi, Zeke, Luisa, and even to Mugsy. The sequence repeated itself over and over as the guitar descended in slow motion. The music continued.

"I'll do what I want and leave you screaming for more."

A crash echoed in her ears. The band chanted "nefarious" as the lights went out. Seconds later a spotlight illuminated Harlie, the sole survivor. Bowen's decapitated head rested on a tray of deviled eggs beside his body. A lifeless Stix sprawled over his busted drums. One mic stand speared through the hearts of both Dylan and Ray, pinning them to a hulking stack of amps. Across the stage floor in front of her, all her loved ones lay scattered—broken, bleeding, and dead. With her bloody hands held out in front of her, Harlie screamed until she woke herself up.

Harlie noticed Pete's raised eyebrow when he walked into the kitchen. Not yet five o'clock in the morning and she stood over a pot of boiling water, sterilizing her butterfly knife like it was a baby bottle.

"This isn't as ridiculous as it looks." She removed the weapon from the bubbling pot with a pair of tongs.

"I just need to get every last trace of Bowen's blood off this thing." She poured the scalding water down the drain and threw the pan in the garbage.

"Sit yourself down, honey." Pete guided his daughter toward a chair. "I'll whip us up some breakfast."

"Just coffee for me, Daddy." Harlie's appetite still wasn't back to normal yet, thanks to her nervous stomach. She did, however, nibble on the piece of toast he set in front of her.

"You want to talk about it?" Pete poured water into the coffee maker. "The way Lex tells it, you're the big hero."

"No, he's the hero. We wouldn't have been in trouble in the first place, if it wasn't for me being so stupid and trusting the wrong people." Harlie hadn't remembered anything at first, and wished it'd stayed that way. She wanted to lose the mental image of her bloody hands banging Bowen's head against the floor.

"That psycho would've come after you regardless of anything you did. Y'all were both lucky to get out of there in one piece." Pete hunted through the cabinets until he found two cups. "You did the only thing you could under the circumstances."

"I know," she said, not sounding at all like she meant it. A small grin twitched on her lips as she watched her father pour their coffee. He made a great cup of joe, even if it could walk across the table by itself.

Pete sat down beside her. "Why don't you tell me what's got you so bothered that you're up boiling that fancy pocket knife of yours at the crack of dawn."

"It sounds kind of stupid." This was the first she'd spoken of the incident since she came home. She needed to get some things off her chest and sitting there with her dad seemed like the perfect time. "In a way, I'm proud of myself for going off on him like that. I just snapped when he was fixing to pour Drano down Lex's throat. And he threatened y'all too. He said he'd shoot you and Mom, then grab Zoey. That he'd . . . ." She couldn't bring herself to verbalize the threats Bowen made to molest and murder her daughter.

"I know what that son of a bitch said. I've got plans to piss on his grave before I head back home," Pete said, lost in his own thoughts for a few seconds. He motioned for her to continue. "Go on. Tell me what's on your mind."

"He deserved what he got and I'm glad he's dead." Harlie stared into her cup while her finger traced the rim. "I just don't like knowing I killed somebody, especially somebody I thought was my friend. The creepy thing is that I spent so many hours talking to someone I believed was a harmless saleslady. She—well, I guess I mean he—was the only person I could talk to when all that crap was going on with Jack, right before the divorce." She sipped her coffee. "Then I remembered the

Christmas card I sent Barb. You know, the one with a picture of me and Zoey by the sleigh. I think that's what must have started the whole thing. I still don't understand why he fell for me."

"The world is full of sick bastards, Harlie. You did what you had to do. Simple as that. And I'm very proud of you." Pete took a biscotto from the jar on the counter and bit into it without dipping it in his coffee. His eyes widened in mock surprise. "This has to be the hardest damn cookie I ever saw in my life. I 'bout broke my teeth on it."

Harlie realized his comedy act was for her benefit and laughed her first real laugh since the ordeal. She'd always be her daddy's little girl.

Chapter Twenty-eight

Harlie waited, surprised she didn't feel a lot more nervous than she did, and wiped her sweaty hands on the seat of her pants. After Lex had talked her into that video shoot in which she'd gyrated like a charmed snake, this was a piece of cake.

"Ready? You're on in about two minutes," Zeke said, smiling down at her through his goatee.

"You know, I think I am. It gets a little easier each time." Harlie slipped her hand through the crook of Zeke's arm before they walked the short distance from backstage to where the main event was happening.

On the way, a curvaceous woman with purple hair gave her a high-five. "Knock 'em on their asses, Red."

"Thanks, Izzy. I'll give it a shot." Harlie appreciated the encouragement, especially from the female lead of the opening act. They'd been hanging out during the tour and though Harlie never knew what crazy hair color Izzy would show up with, she could always count on her new friend to drag her into some kind of outrageous chaos, anything from pranking the paparazzi to being yanked out of bed at two a.m. to give her opinion on the lyrics she was working on. Two nights ago, Harlie had watched the sun rise through the tour bus window as she tried to help her find a word that rhymed with vagina. She couldn't wait to hear the finished version of that song.

Zeke led her past sound equipment, made sure she didn't trip over a tangle of extension cords, and gave her the thumbs up sign.

"Uh-oh, here comes the Missus," Lex announced, Harlie's cue to walk onstage. The fans went crazy.

FireStorm's latest CD, *Red Hot*, sold over a million copies the day it hit store shelves. The album broke sales records, thanks in part to all the publicity surrounding it. The lyrics and sudden tempo change in the title cut put it in a class by itself. Harlie cried the first time Lex sang the intro to her, romantic words from his heart to hers. Accompanied by Dylan's acoustic guitar, the first lines were slow and melodic, reminiscent of an old-fashioned ballad.

"Oh, baby. I love you.
There's nothing in this whole wide world I wouldn't do for you.
My heart is yours, girl. Don't you see?
I'll keep you safe forever. You are the air I breathe."

The soft melody lasted a few more bars before a hardcore, fast paced, bluesy rock 'n' roll beat took over. Ray alternated between the fiddle and flute on this tune, while Stix tickled the high-hat. Sound bites of Harlie in various stages of orgasm peppered the song. What better way could there be to play off those raunchy clips that had made her famous? Recording the sound effects in their bedroom, taking many cuts to get just the right 'pitch', Lex had worked hard to capture Harlie at the peak of euphoria.

Things had changed so much since the cast came off Lex's hand four months ago. The psychologist healed scars Harlie hadn't even known existed, plus therapy helped put an end to her nightmares and the guilt that caused them. She was glad to have those issues resolved before her honeymoon.

Lex and Harlie held their wedding in the same Episcopal Church where the Garretts had been married a generation before, the surrounding trees painting the landscape with leaves of brown, gold, and red. Harlie donned a lacey cream gown, loose ringlets from her auburn up-do framed her face, and she carried a fragrant bouquet of daisies, lilacs, and red roses the florist had to special order. Lex looked like a prince dressed in a classic coat and tails that accentuated his chocolate brown eyes and Italian features.

Stix acted as best man while Randi served as Maid of

Honor, followed down the aisle by Louie and Tasha, Harlie's soon-to-be stepdaughter. Harlie caught Randi winking at Zeke a few times during the ceremony; the two had spent so much time together those last few months, it was little wonder they fell for each other. Zoey looked like a little angel sprinkling the aisle with rose petals, and Mugsy trotted beside her with a diamond ring swinging from the silk ribbon tied around his neck. Pete handed a sniffling Roxanne his handkerchief during the romantic ballad from Ray and Dylan. At the reception, Stix gave the toast amid a sea of raised champagne glasses: "Here's to my best friend and his red-hot spitfire of a wife, the sweetest lady I know. I wish you happiness and bliss the rest of your days. No one deserves it more."

On the Red Hot Tour with FireStorm, Harlie took the stage each time they played her song. She danced during the vocal breaks and pounded a tambourine against her hip beside her new husband as he sang, eyeing her up and down the entire time. The audience ate it up.

Thanks to their appearance on *The Scoop*, when Mimi had shown the world those horrible pictures of her, Harlie became a spokesperson for domestic violence. With a bit of pressure from the boys in the band, FireStorm's manager agreed to donate a portion of the profits from the *Red Hot* CD to the cause. The win-win arrangement generated even more sales.

Now Harlie had fans of her own, which she'd discovered one day when she opened her Facebook page and found over eight thousand friend requests. She shivered and deleted them all; no way in hell would she make personal connections to more possible psychos. Lex had his publicist set up and manage a website for her fans instead, which featured information on the safest ways to end an abusive relationship. She spotted anti-abuse T-shirts with her picture on the front mingled with concert tees throughout the crowded auditorium.

Onstage beside Lex, Harlie still went weak-kneed watching him sing. Their relationship had transformed her from an introverted divorcee into a happily married sex symbol—she still couldn't believe that part herself, but that's what the paparazzi called her—who encouraged women to escape domestic violence. Her hips swayed to the beat and she smiled, happy to have karma on her side. She lost herself in Lex's sultry voice.

"She's my auburn-haired beauty with eyes of blue.
Face of an angel, she'd give the devil his due.
She's a walking contradiction, sinfully sweet.
Daddy's little girl is my bitch in heat.
Girl, you walk in looking all red hot.
I've got to get some more of what you've got.
Look out, I'm coming now. Ready or not.

Why ya have to be so damn red hot?
Since my eyes met hers, I've never been the same.
Sugar and spice, she's the yin to my yang.
She moans in my arms all night long,
Screaming my name each time we get it on."

Lex repeated the chorus during Harlie's dance segment. The crowd responded with a standing ovation.

Pride radiated from Lex's infamous stage persona. He held her hand up above their heads and urged the hoard of fans, "Give it up for my baby!" Harlie felt herself blush as the crowd cheered and whistled.

They walked off stage with Lex's arm draped across her shoulder. Life just didn't get any better than this.

Acknowledgements

To everyone at TheNextBigWriter, especially Nathan B. Childs, Natalee Binda, Patti Yaeger Hauge, Jessica Chambers, Joy L. Campbell, Courtney Vail, Sybil Nelson, Bisi Adjapon, Sara Basrai, Jeanne Bannon, Cathy Jones, Amy Metz, Christina Jean Michaels, Denise Nolan, Adrianna Cordelle Sofer, Mallot, MissyV, and NMWriterMom. I appreciate your help, critiques, advice, and friendship.

The Louisville Romance Writers, a gifted and fun-loving group of authors who inspire me.

I want to thank my family and friends for their love and support, but my kids most of all. Amanda, Brittany, and Tyler, you're the first to know about my writing projects and your encouragement means the world to me.

About the Author

Photo courtesy of Brittany Hayes

Tina DC Hayes writes gritty romantic suspense and cozy mysteries. She lives in western Kentucky with her husband and three children. A few very pampered Boston terriers, German shepherds, one goofy Yorkie, and two parrots keep her busy, but guard against writer's block.